Do-Overs

by

Christine Jarmola

Do-Overs

By Christine Jarmola

©2014 by Christine Jarmola

Cover Design: Darku Jarmola

Published by Tubb's Publishing
ISBN-13-978-1502903945
ISBN-10-1502903946
Also available in eBook publication.

Printed by CreateSpace.

This book is dedicated to

my daughter,

Kaisa,

who I would never do over.

Oh, wait.

That's not what I meant.

I mean, I'd never change anything about her.

Where is that blasted eraser when I need it?

Acknowledgments

Although my name alone is on the cover of this book (how cool is that?) I could never have completed it without the help and support of so many people. I could write another entire book of thank yous, but here is the abridged version.

Starting at the beginning: Thank you to **Bill Bernhardt** and my fellow workshop participants—the first people to meet Lottie Lambert. Your enthusiasm for my nutty protagonist told me this was a book worth refining and publishing.

Thank you to all the **Bartlesville WordWeavers** who read bits and pieces throughout the first draft.

Thank you to **Mackenzie Case** for reading the first rough draft and pointing out that people with magic erasers need to react more drastically when they accidentally reverse time.

Thank you to **Deanna Boone** for helping to take all the "old ladyness" out of the book.

Thank you to **Kerry Cosby**, who said he wanted a rough draft for his wife read, but it was just a cover, I know. And he loved Lottie. Loved her so much he told me to lose the first chapter and give us the real Lottie from page one. Did it Kerry. Hope you like it.

Thank you to my indispensable critique partners, the GOTITS: **Marilyn Boone, Heather Davis** and **Jennifer McMurrain**. Our weekly critique and therapy sessions have kept the dream alive in each of us.

Thank you to my editors: **Beth Reburn** for the first round of edits and **Mari Farthing** for polishing it up.

Thank you to the **Atheneans** and all my OBU friends who made college such a great experience that in my "old age" those are the days I want to write about.

Thank you to my husband, **Darek**—my own Al Dansby—for paying the bills so that I can live my dreams.

Thank you to **DJ Darku J** who took time out of the music business to create such a fantastic cover.

Thank you to **Kasia Jarmola** (the original Lottie Lambert) for inspiring me to write this story. She will soon be setting out on her own college experiences. May she never step in dog poop but still learn to love an imperfect life.

Thank you to **God** who sets our paths in motion and then keeps guiding us back even when we think it's going the wrong way.

Most of all I want to thank **you—the Readers**! Without you there would be no reason to write. Hope you laugh, maybe cry a little, fall in love again with Lottie and Al and realize along the way that mistakes are often the serendipitous moments that make life special.

Contents

The Ending

The Beginning

The Ending

Some stories start at the beginning and then go forward. Some start at the end and are told in retrospect. From the utter chaos around me, the ambulances, the Lifeflight, the twisted wreckage of cars, I had kept the beginning that should have started at the ending from ever being.

The Beginning

-1-

Granny Panties & Other Unmentionables

"Granny panties!" came twin, screeching voices as I looked up to see a cardboard box of my clothes spilling out of my brother's arms and down the front steps of my new dorm at my new college on the first day of my new life. Out tumbled all my unmentionables, soon to be blown far and wide across the campus by the unrelenting Oklahoma wind. (There is a reason our state song says, "The wind comes sweeping down the plain.")

It was a simple disaster that could have been easily remedied by normal people, but not by my family. Oh no, my twin teenage sisters, Jennifer and Jessica, were shouting at rock star level decibels and whipping out their matching iPhones to take photos. My all-American jock brother, Jason, sat down on the steps of my new abode laughing like a demented jackal while my longsuffering mother ran frantically after some humongous drawers, which I had never seen before in my life. The entire student body was out and about on campus that move-in day and in less than ten minutes at my new school, my family had made a spectacle out of my new life.

Welcome to the world of Lottie Lambert.

At least things couldn't get any worse.

But they did.

Out of the corner of my eye I saw him. Passing one of the ivy-covered, redbrick buildings was the most amazing, gorgeous, sexy, hot guy I had ever witnessed in my life. Suddenly, my world went into slow motion as he walked down the sidewalk, his brown hair tousled ever so gently by the Oklahoma breeze as if he had been Photoshopped for the cover of a magazine. And needless to say—he was staring right at me.

Why oh why didn't the ground just open up and swallow me right then and there when my mom held up an enormous pair of pink and blue-flowered granny panties and shouted, "Don't worry Lottie, I'll get them all."

Yes, she made sure to say my name, lest by any miraculous chance someone didn't know the owner of the über sexy undies. I was at least grateful that she didn't throw in my last name for clarification.

Like a toddler playing peek-a-boo I covered my eyes hoping to make it all go away. But it didn't. No, it got worse. After a deep breath, I looked up to see Mr. Gorgeous reaching up to help my mother retrieve an especially gigantic purple pair from the lower branches of a tree. He smiled at my mom as he handed them to her and said something I couldn't hear, before walking off to catch up with his friends. I hadn't noticed the others at first as I was so mesmerized by his perfection. I wished I still hadn't noticed them at all, as they were laughing hysterically and pointing at me and my flying underwear.

3

I didn't know whether to cry or just die. Instead, as my mother came walking back to me with her arms full of the geriatric lingerie, I did what I always did. I, Lottie Lambert, the queen of the wrong word at the wrong time in the wrong place, said the wrong thing. And no, three wrongs never do make a right.

"Where did those hideous things come from? What idiot packed those?" I shouted at my mother under my breath—which by the way is hard to do, but every teenage girl who's ever had a mother has mastered it.

My mother's face spoke volumes. It was a high stress day and there I was ragging on her when she thought she was being helpful and saving the day. "Your father was trying to help out again and he ruined some of your clothes last week doing the laundry, so I thought I'd just replace them," she explained. "Thought perhaps you could use some Christian underwear for once, rather than those hideous tiny bikini contraptions you insist on wearing. Excuse me for trying to help." With that she scooped up the last of my new intimate apparel and headed up the grand staircase, past the white columns and through the door of my new dorm.

Great, not only did everyone at Oklahoma Methodist University now know that I had a vast variety of old lady undergarments, but I had also hurt my mom's feelings. Why did the simplest thing always have to turn into an incident? From then on, at all our family gatherings, this story would become family lore passed down to all future generations, told and retold, as *Lottie's Great Granny Panty Fiasco*.

"Sorry, Mom. I really mean it," I apologized as we entered Asbury Hall. Why did all my conversations seem to begin or end with me saying I was sorry? If I could back up and start this whole conversation over, I would save myself so much grief. But I knew, as all people do, that life doesn't give you second chances.

4

Fortunately, or maybe unfortunately, our conversation was interrupted as Aphrodite incarnate entered the dorm carrying one small Louis Vuitton tote while five hunky guys carried bags and boxes behind her. As she stood along side my mother and me looking at the roster posted for dorm assignments, the inevitable became evitable. It wasn't bad enough that I had spent my whole life being the boring, mousey-brown-haired, middle daughter sandwiched between an University of Oklahoma football star big brother and beautiful blonde twin sisters, now I was the laughingstock of Oklahoma Methodist University and the granny-pantied suitemate to the most glamorous girl on campus.

I should have simply stayed at my former school as my new fresh start already stank.

-2-

The Genesis of the BFFs

"Sorry I can't quit laughing, Lottie, but you have to admit it was funny," Olivia apologized again. "You did make a memorable move-in day for all of us."

There we were. My new suitemates including Olivia Corazon, the beauty of OKMU, with her thick black hair and her flawless tan skin, who made sure to tell the others of my grand debut on the steps of my new abode. My family was gone. My things were slightly unpacked and it was bonding time with three girls I hoped would become my new BFFs.

Asbury Dorm was divided into suites—one bathroom between two bedrooms. Shared by four women. How were we ever to be ready on time for anything sharing one bathroom? It was either designed to help us with the bonding process, or as a proving ground for the survival of the fittest.

"I'm just glad to know that you wear panties if we're going to be roommates," said Christina Hart, known as Stina to her friends and she counted everyone as her friend. Stina was one of those petite, pixy girls with short choppy chestnut hair and a cute little nose to match. It took almost thirty seconds together for me to want her as a friend for life.

"No more of the P word," interrupted Rachel Herz, the fourth member of our suite. Rachel was our token redhead, although it was the most luxurious shade of auburn I had ever seen. "That is over and done and I'm ready to learn more about Lottie." It was apparent that Rachel understood my embarrassment. I would come to learn over the next year of Rachel's kindness. She once told me that if there really were such a thing, she would be an empath, like on *Star Trek,* as she could always feel other people's pain.

"So why does someone change from the top state school to a tiny private college as a junior?" questioned Olivia in a demanding manner. "Were you flunking out or are you changing majors?"

"Did you get arrested?" Stina chimed in giggling.

Just what I didn't want to talk about. Did I confess or did I play it cool and not give out my whole life's story to people I had just met?

A month before I had been in a similar situation. Well not actually similar because nothing involving my extended family is ever like anything else. It had been my parents' twenty-fifth anniversary and my entire family had gathered to celebrate. I had put on my best celebratory game face but my heart wasn't in it. And to make my day even more trying, my Crazy Aunt Charlotte had focused in on me from the moment she arrived.

Aunt Charlotte was my great aunt, nobody knows how many times removed. However in our family she was commonly known as Crazy Aunt Charlotte when she wasn't around. When it came to colorful, unique, interesting and eccentric, Aunt Charlotte held the prize. My dad always said she was once married to a Gypsy and traveled in a caravan. My mother said no, she had been a flower child on a commune. All I ever knew was that she dressed in yards of flowing, gathered skirts and had tons of bangles and beads stuck on her anywhere they would stick. She was a character that I tried to avoid, yet was curiously drawn to, like knowing not to look at the dead and rotting deer carcass on the side of the highway but

7

looking anyway.

"Now, Lottie," said my peculiar aunt in her fortuneteller voice that day. "What's this I hear about your changing colleges? I thought you always wanted to go to the University of Oklahoma just like your brother. Although I remember at the time saying it would be better if you went your own way and didn't have to languish in your brother Jason's shadow all the time. But nobody listened to me. They never do."

Never one to worry about voicing her opinion—that was our Aunt Charlotte. Yes, as a junior in college I was switching schools. It wasn't because of grades, or majors, or scholarships. It was totally personal. And it definitely wasn't the kind of intimate information I wanted to discuss with some eccentric woman somewhere between the age of 70 and 1,000. But, we all knew that with Aunt Charlotte nothing was private. Maybe that comes from having lived in a commune?

Trying to change the subject I picked the first idea to come into my head. "Don't my parents look lovely? Isn't it just crazy to think they've been married twenty-five years." Did the word *crazy* come out of my mouth? I started to apologize just for the word association going on in my head, but Crazy Aunt Charlotte interrupted me.

"How many times do I have to ask? What's up with the school thing?" my aunt persisted. There was no simple way to derail that freight train but to give an answer. I knew it would happen in the end so I might as well get it over with at the beginning.

"Aunt Charlotte, have you ever just wanted to start over? Get rid of all your past mistakes? Have a clean slate?" I tried to figure out how much I would have to tell her before she would let the subject drop.

"Oh honey child, we all do. What was it you girls used to call it when playing? Um, do-overs, wasn't that it? Yes, I think we all need those sometimes. So how bad did he break your heart?"

I was flabbergasted. I hadn't said anything about a *he* or a *broken heart*. All I'd admitted to was a desire to start over. Yet, she had hit the nail right on the head. That was exactly it. He had broken my heart and my spirit. Was Crazy Aunt Charlotte really clairvoyant or did I just have the pain still written on my face?

"Pretty bad," was all I answered.

"Let's go outside where's it's a little quieter and talk," she said as she took me by the arm and led me through the crowded living room to the outside door. "You know I wasn't always older than Methuselah."

So Aunt Charlotte and I spent a half hour that afternoon sitting in lawn chairs out under an oak tree while I did most of the talking. I didn't realize how great it would feel to talk it all out with someone who had lived a lot of life and had been there and done that herself. I was beginning to think that maybe Aunt Charlotte wasn't as mental as the family legend said when the Double J's, Jennifer and Jessica, my twin sisters, came walking over to rescue me. As Aunt Charlotte saw them coming across the lawn a furtive look passed over her face and she began frantically rummaging through her humongous carpetbag purse.

"Sometimes in life you just need a do-over." Then she placed her old gnarled hand in mine whispering as if giving me the most coveted secret to life, "When that time comes, just erase it away and do it again." With that she dropped an old pink, four-inch eraser like I had used back in fourth grade in my hand.

I knew then and there that Aunt Charlotte really was completely, totally, absolutely, thoroughly crazy after all.

"Hell-Low?" Olivia said, laughing and snapping me out of my thoughts. "What kind of deep dark secrets are you hiding?"

9

Telling Crazy Aunt Charlotte about my disastrous love life had proven to be a mistake, one I didn't want to repeat on my first day with my hopefully new friends. Unable to think on my feet, I became flustered which unfortunately often appears curt and rude. Later, I would think of just the perfect response, but in the heat of the moment I felt put on the spot. "It's really complicated. My personal business. I don't want to talk about it." I stammered.

Obviously that was the wrong thing to say, as evidenced by the shocked look on Stina's sweet face and the defiance on Olivia's. I quickly deduced that people did not speak to Olivia Corazon in that manner very often.

"It's okay," Rachel quickly said. "We have ages to learn every intimate detail of each other's lives. Don't tell it all in the first chapter," she said with a laugh. Yes, Rachel seemed to always have the insight to defuse any awkward situation. Maybe, someday I'd learn to be more like her.

"We need to tell Lottie about ourselves," chimed in Stina regaining the relaxed mood from before. "We'll let Olivia start. She loves to talk about herself. Don't you, gorgeous?" They all three laughed.

"I get the gorgeous comments a lot. But I can't help it. I'm just the way God made me," said Olivia as she stuck out her very ample chest and gave a cover girl smile, while Stina and Rachel rolled their eyes. Obviously that was a conversation had many times before.

Stina giggled. "God was in a very good mood the day you were made, *chica*."

"Tell me about it. Here I am gargantuan woman living with *Mademoiselle Magnific*."

I'm not lying. It wasn't until that point that I noticed how large

Rachel really was. She had to be close to five nine and hadn't seen the lighter side of three hundred pounds in years. Yet, she had been so instantly kind and caring on meeting me that all I saw was her kind face, gorgeous red hair and sympathetic spirit.

"I'll tell you about Olivia," Rachel continued taking charge. "Let's see, she's a junior Communications major. Is that still it?" She looked to Olivia for affirmation, who nodded her head. "She's changed her major a few times."

"Seven," squealed Stina.

"Not true," Olivia countered back. "Only five. I just changed back and forth a few times, but there have only been five different majors."

"A question of semantics," Stina answered.

"Back to my very interrupted narrative," continued Rachel. "Olivia Corazon," she stressed the last name with her best *gringa* accent, "started out as a Spanish major, but after flunking Spanish 101, she changed to English."

"The first Hispanic to flunk Spanish 101," Stina couldn't help commenting.

"There were legitimate reasons," defended Olivia. "It was an eight o'clock class. And the prof wanted grammatically correct Spanish. No one in my family ever conjugated a verb or knew there were gender issues in the language. They just spoke it. Anyway, it really wasn't the major for me. I was doing it because I thought it would be easy - and then it wasn't." She laughed and continued. "Enough about my shortcomings. I'm now a Communications major and doing very well at it."

Feeling more comfortable, I volunteered my own roundabout arrival as an English major. "All my professors at OU kept pushing me to do the English Ed route, but I could never be a teacher. I have no idea what I'll do

11

with my degree," I lied. I knew exactly what I wanted to do. I just didn't feel comfortable enough to tell my true dream to people I'd met only a few hours before. It seemed too farfetched a fantasy to confide in anyone that wasn't a true confidant.

"I'm going to be a teacher," volunteered Stina. "Elementary Ed. It's what I've wanted to do since I started first grade and met Mrs. Askins. She was the perfect teacher and I've always wanted to be just like her."

"All hail, Mrs. Askins," Olivia said as Rachel gave a fake bow of worship. It was instantly obvious that they were very familiar with Stina's hero.

"Okay, so I do talk about her a lot. But she made a permanent impression on my formative years," Stina giggled.

I was beginning to notice that giggling was one of her major characteristics. And it was contagious. Stina was like a bottle of bubble soap that just couldn't be contained and soon had everyone around her joining in the fun.

"My mom was an Elementary Ed major too," I said. "She taught third grade for about five years and decided it wasn't the right job for her. Didn't like all the rules. Walking in straight lines, raising their hands to talk. My mom is a free spirit. She probably gets that from my crazy Aunt Charlotte. She's had lots of jobs. None ever for over five years. Whereas my dad has been a CPA for the same company for all his adult life." I was babbling on about a topic they probably didn't care a flip about. I do that too, when I'm nervous. Talk too much about the wrong things. Then the awkward silence always comes. But, not that time.

"Moms are like that," agreed Stina. "We still haven't heard from one in our group."

I turned to Rachel with a questioning look. But Olivia was the one to answer. "Isn't it obvious. Rachel's a Psych major. She's always reading our minds and solving our problems. Be careful, Lottie, or she'll use you as one of her mental guinea pigs."

Without a comment, Rachel crossed over to the mini-fridge and pulled out a huge butcher knife. I was a teensy bit worried that the Psych major was psychotic herself until she also grabbed a roll of frozen cookie dough. "It's time for us to partake in the sacraments of the suitemates," she said in her most solemn voice. It lasted for a nano-second and then the three were laughing again. Rachel began slicing off chunks of dough for a major snarf fest.

"Here." Rachel handed me a glob.

"We work out daily so we can pig-out nightly," they all chanted in unison.

-3-

Camo

The pig-out continued that night at our dorm's welcome back party. Asbury Hall was the oldest dorm at the university built by donations from little old Methodist women circles raising money through bake sales and stiff-arm donations. I had learned as a young child, from my father, that when Methodist women want a donation for a cause, you don't say no. Thankfully, the dorm had been majorly remodeled a few years before my arrival.

Our suite was in the basement. That sounds depressing, but it was actually only half in the basement, so we had windows at eye level inside and at ground level outside.

Originally I hadn't planned on living on campus. I was twenty. I was ready to live on my own. But my meddlesome and sometimes very wise mother felt I wouldn't make friends and was worried that I'd be depressed living alone off campus. She was right, but I would never tell her that. Instead I'd blown out a big frustrated breath and rolled my eyes—very maturely—and agreed to try student housing. At least for the first semester.

As a junior I thought I knew all about dorm life, so dreaded the obligatory welcome/orientation meetings. But this group was different. Every meeting was a reason to party. There were pizzas, nachos, ice cream and cookies and one tiny plate of fruit. I guess that was to ease the collective conscience that health food was available. I was going to have to start a very vigorous exercise program or my size fives weren't going to fit much longer.

As we scarfed calories, there was a human bingo game going on. Each girl had a bingo card but instead of numbers it had facts, like who was from out of state, or who was engaged. We had to go around the room and find different girls who fit the criteria and have them sign the square. First one to get a bingo won. Of course the prize was chocolate.

Most people hate being forced to mingle, but I appreciated it. I'm not exactly shy, but I can be awkward at meeting people. And almost always I'll say the wrong thing. So having a structured way practically forcing me to meet and greet my new dormmates helped me lose some of my anxiety.

Square one-*a blonde*. Oh that was easy, over two thirds of the room. Wonder if it had to be a natural blonde. That would narrow things down. I approached the closest blonde I saw.

"Hi, I'm Lottie. Would you sign my card here on *blonde*?"

I was rewarded with a thousand-watt smile. "Sure, but you might want me to sign on the *suitemates that names all start with the same letter*. That's us. The K's." She was joined by three more blondes. All four looked like they had been picked by central casting to match with each being about five foot three, one hundred five pounds, and perfect Hollywood white smiles. "I'm Kasha," she continued. "This is Kaylee, that's Kyra and that's Keesha. People say they have trouble telling us apart."

"But it's not that hard," chimed in the girl on her right—Kaylee or was it Keesha. No I think Kyra.

"We're all different," said another. They all chimed in talking at a rapid pace and finishing each other's thoughts.

"Kasha's left handed."

"Kaylee plays soccer."

"Kyra has four brothers and I'm an only child." File that for future reference. One was an only child, but I didn't know which one.

"I'm a vegetarian, but the others are carnivores."

"No plasmavores." They all laughed. I'd have to think on that one later.

"She has a boyfriend. He's on the basketball team."

"Keesha just likes soccer players."

"Well, why not? They look good in their shorts."

"That's right!!" They all said in unison. I would learn as the year progressed a lot of what they said was in unison.

Kasha, I think, signed my card. I looked down at the signature. No, it said Kyra. Having lived my whole life with twins I should have been better at seeing the differences, but they were like a carnival shell game. Every time I thought I knew which shell the ball was under it had moved to a different one.

"Here sign our cards." They said as one.

I looked over the list looking for a category that fit me. Oh there was one. *Sister of twins*. But I didn't want to sign that one. That was a classification I was trying to get out of. *New at OKMU*. That fit me to a tee. I signed all four cards and the wave of **K**-inetic energy went on its way.

Friends seemed plentiful in Asbury Hall. Sure there were the stereotypical groups. I could see six very stylish, very bored, very too-cool-to-be-there girls over in one corner making a diligent attempt to make sure everyone knew they did not find our sophomoric games amusing. The tall,

16

brunette alpha female of the group looked as if she could model on any swimsuit magazine cover. I didn't foresee us becoming bosom buddies.

In the opposite corner were two girls of the extreme opposite—Goths with their jet-black hair and multiple piercings. I never really understood Goths until I had to sit by a girl Goth in my eighth grade algebra class. Mid-way through the year, after I quit being terrified of her, we became quasi-friends. She confided in me that she came from a rough part of town and an uncaring family. Actually she phrased it much more colorfully, including words for excrement and the not so pleasant part of the afterlife. In her world it was important to look tough. If she looked weak she would be preyed upon by the more powerful. It was a real eye-opening experience for me. Most Goths are just like the rest of us, trying to find a way to survive. Not fitting in is their camouflage just like the snooty mean girls on the other side of the room hid behind the camouflage of designer jeans and $800 handbags.

In the middle of the chaos was the volleyball team. They shared our wing. I'd already had to maneuver through an impromptu practice in the hallway earlier in the day. They were the life of the party group. And of course in the middle of it all was Stina, loving life as always.

As I looked around the big basement meeting room of Asbury Hall, I was pleased. New potential friends were all around. This looked like the perfect place to regroup, put the past behind and restart. Unfortunately, this wasn't the first time I'd tried for a new start.

-4-

Beginning Again

Going from a huge conglomerate university to a small tranquil college was a major, but pleasant change. It took less than an hour to find all my classrooms and labs. They were within easy walking distance, so I'd never have to be late again from searching for a parking spot within a mile of my class. New faces were quickly becoming familiar. At OU arrangements had to be made to see friends; at OKMU every meal was a gathering of the entire campus as there was only one cafeteria.

I was amazed at how quickly I settled into my new niche in life. Rachel made sure to always save me a place at her table in the cafeteria. Stina, I quickly learned, was everybody's friend. At every meal she was entertaining a different table with her effervescent personality. To Stina there were no cliques, just different groups of bosom buddies.

Olivia, on the other hand, seemed to be choosier, almost to the point of being a snob. When in the dorm she was inclusive of me in her life, but once we left our suite, she became the beautiful ice queen. Not totally snubbing me, just not going out of her way to include me. It only took me a few days to catch on. Olivia didn't talk to girls when guys were around.

And she was always surrounded by guys. They were her adoring fans, doing her bidding. It was almost comical to watch as she ever so gently manipulated the opposite sex to do any task she deemed appropriate. I never saw her carry a book or a cafeteria tray. Doors magically opened as she neared. Seats were always available in the center of every group. The most mystical element was that she never asked, these things simply happened. She ruled and she knew it. Olivia had it all working for her.

Like I said, it only took me a few days to catch on, but I would have saved myself a lot of embarrassment if I would have sooner. It was my third meal in the cafeteria. Rachel was at a meeting with a professor and Stina was "Stina-ing" somewhere on campus. I had started to wait for Rachel, but I was a big girl and big girls could go eat on their own. That was the pep talk I had given myself as I mentally put on my big girl panties—not to be confused with my granny panties that had somehow mysteriously ended up in the dorm's charity donation box—and entered the cavernous room full of strangers. Then like a lighthouse on the windswept shore I saw Olivia. I had a friend. I wouldn't have to sit alone. And there was even an empty seat next to her. I purposefully walked to that island of refuge and smiled at the table of guys and Olivia. "Is this seat taken?" I asked as I proceeded to put my tray down.

"Actually it is," Olivia's replied with a pleasant smile. "Matt just isn't here yet."

And that was it. No sorry. No introductions. No let's make room for Lottie. I stood there like a moron waiting for Olivia, or someone, to come to my aid, but it didn't happen. The conversation turned to wondering where Matt was and I stood there without a plan B.

I looked around for an empty table. Everything was full except for the nether regions across the room. Standing there feeling like a fool, sure that every person was tuned in to my dilemma, I saw him again. The gorgeous guy who had witnessed the granny-panty exposition. Now he was watching the whole seating fiasco. Two spottings and two disasters. Our eyes caught briefly. Was there concern on his face? Pity? Or simply acknowledgement that I wasn't part of Olivia's popular crowd? Why couldn't I ever run into this guy when I was feeling confident and self-assured rather than always in some mortifying situation? I quickly turned and hurried across the room to a small table in the corner turning my back on the room as I sat. Trying not to choke on a mouthful of mystery meat, I opened my phone and pretended to read some non-existent text message so I wouldn't look as pathetic and lonely as I felt.

"Hi, Lottie. I almost couldn't find you. Hope you didn't have to wait too long. Professor Freud is very long winded."

It was Rachel. Grateful to see her kind face, I started to explain the Olivia debacle but stopped; afraid I'd burst into tears. Instead I asked the obvious.

"Do you really have a psychology professor named Freud?"

"That's not his real name," Rachel laughed. "It's really Dr. Freedman. But he's obsessed with Freud, same beard and glasses. He's such a Freud wannabe the nickname just stuck. Behind his back, of course. I'll just die if I ever see him smoking a cigar." She laughed really hard on that. I didn't get it. Must be one of those psychology major things. But, I laughed along because I didn't want Rachel to know I didn't get it.

"I really need to stop doing that, renaming people that is. It's kind of an OKMU unwritten tradition. Maybe every college does it. Don't know. Never went anywhere else. Do they do that at OU?"

"Not that I know of."

"Well, the important thing is to never mix the alter ego name up with the real one. Fortunately, I've never done that. Hate to be the fool who did."

"Yep, me too," I hastily agreed. "That would be the ultimate embarrassment and an automatic ticket to an F in any class."

"Speaking of names..." I said thinking there was one real name in particular I wanted to learn and any insights into his alter, inner or super ego would be just fine with me. Hopefully, Rachel could tell me it if I pointed out the gorgeous guy to her. I tried using a spoon as a mirror to look behind me, but all I saw was an upside-down distorted view of what might possibly be people or aliens from Pluto, the non-planet. Next, I tried unsuccessfully to discreetly turn around to see Him, but by the time I had drummed up enough courage to completely turn around and really look, He was gone. Perhaps that was for the best. It hadn't been the luckiest day of my life and I simply couldn't handle any more rejection.

-5-

Oh Crap!

School started much the same as any other year at Hogwarts. Oh, sorry wrong story. Anyway, my classes did start rather unspectacularly. My professors seemed nice enough. It was a pleasant change to be taught by people with actual doctorates rather than graduate students, but it was also more challenging. My fellow students were accommodating and friendly. However the same question arose with everyone I met—why had I switched schools? As always I gave vague answers about wanting some change in my life. But is change always for the good, or had I made these drastic decisions to simply end up right back at the same crossroads as before?

After all the obligatory dorm meetings, advisory meetings and final registration, I was off to my first class at my new school and my new beginning. Transferring to a church sponsored school required that I take a couple of Bible classes. I thought that would be so easy. Hey, I went to Sunday school as a child. I could quote a few Bible verses. "Jesus wept. John 11:35." I was quite the theologian.

When I received my syllabus for Old Testament, I rapidly found out this wasn't Vacation Bible School—no crafts, no Kool-Aid, no recess. He wanted us to read books—big honking books—and write papers—enormous, indexed, cross-referenced papers—and take exams, the massive essay types. Dr. Pharisee (Okay that wasn't his real name. But I had latched on to the OKMU nicknaming idea and it really did fit him better than Phillips) took his class seriously. A little too seriously. Like we had no other classes to prepare for in our lives. Like we had no lives.

I sat down in the back. It was obvious those were the coveted seats as the entire front two rows were vacant except for some over eager, overachiever, Hermione Granger types. The pathetic guy on my right looked like he had slept in his clothes, and not for just one day, but the whole week. He must not have gotten the memo that saggy pants were so 2008, because he was the typical suburban teenager gangsta wanna be. On my left was Susie Sorority. I'm all for clean cut and preppy, but she was the poster child for *bring back the eighties.*

There I sat, a junior in a sea of freshmen, getting preached at like I had never had a college class in my life. My attitude was slowly corroding. It was time to relax and remind myself this was a freshman class, thus, it would make sense for the Prof. to treat us like freshmen. Breath in. Breath out. Mistake. Something smelled awful. What could that horrible stench be?

I looked over at Miss Preppy. Yup, her petite, pert nose was upturned also. Like a gross, invisible, but would be green if seen, fog, the smell was working its way across the classroom. The professor preached on, but everyone could tell it was taking all his years of experience to not shout out, "Who stinks?"

Poor slept-in-his-clothes guy. I knew it had to be him. Didn't he know to shower once in awhile, even if momma wasn't there to tell him to? Pitiable guy, everyone's first impression of him would always be the loser that stunk up the Old Testament class. And he had the nerve to be looking at me like I stank. In fact everyone was starting to look my way. Actually it didn't really smell like B.O. More like dog poop.

Oh crap! It *was* me. I looked down at my shoe. Right there on the side of my new silver glitter Toms was a blob of brown, gooey, stinking dog S***! I grabbed my books and fled the room. Outside the door I jerked off the shoe and threw it into the first trashcan I saw. Limping, I fled the building for the sanctuary of my dorm. I've no idea why I kept the one shoe on. I don't know if I thought I'd find a half off sale on Toms that literally meant half as in one shoe, or if it just seemed to save a tiny portion of my dignity to wear at least the one shoe.

I went trudging back toward my dorm, when who should appear walking my way but the hunky him from the granny-panty-fiasco and the cafeteria-seat-rejection-scene. Was I only destined to meet him when I was in the middle of some humiliating situation? Well, not that time. I maneuvered to hide behind some hideously ugly statue of a benevolent donor to OKMU. It was a very close call, but he didn't see me. The last thing I wanted was to meet the man of my dreams while one-shoed and then feel obligated to confess why. And confess I would do. Because for some unknown reason whenever there was something in my head that my mind wanted no one to know my tongue would always rat me out and spill every detail.

The coast was clear. I had saved myself one tiny shred of pride on an otherwise total humiliation day. Sure the one shoe gig had worked for Cinderella but her glass slipper hadn't been covered in *caca*.

Change the one shoed-ness to barefooted; as I looked down to realize I had stepped in more excrement with my remaining shoe. New rule for my new life at OKMU, always look where stepping. Throwing my second shoe away in another nearby garbage can, I finished my barefoot walk to the dorm mentally juggling my days schedule to figure out when I could go see my advisor about dropping my Old Testament class. There was no way in Hell or Heaven that I was going back to that class as the dog-poop-shoe girl.

-6-

Oops, I Did It Again

Clean shoes, necessitated changing my entire outfit so I still matched. Which then required a slight tweaking of my hair to accentuate the wardrobe change. New purse and good to go. In the midst of it all, I had to stop and read five text messages from my mom talking about everything from did I have enough money in my checking account to was the cafeteria food okay. When I was younger I would have seen the texts as nagging or manipulative, but an older and wiser Lottie, I knew them for what they really were: little, tiny, repetitive reminders that she loved me. I knew that she knew nothing of the dog-poop-shoe incident, but my mom could always sense when I needed reminding that I am loved. An hour later and my confidence quasi-restored, I set off for the class I had looked forward to more than any other.

My Advanced Nineteenth Century Women's Novel class looked very promising. I loved everything about the women novelists this class was to cover, from Jane Austen to Mary Shelley to the Brontë sisters. They were my heroes. Their centuries old stories, simple and pure, still spoke to the hearts of my generation.

That was my secret ambition. To write simple but profound stories that made people think beyond the boundaries of their ordinary lives. It was such a lofty unreachable dream that there were only two people I had ever shared it with: my mother, who encouraged it, and my former professor, who ridiculed my work as sappy and sentimental. The worst was when he had used the C word on my writing—cliché. That was the day I knew beyond all doubt that if I ever taught English I would never crush someone's dream as lightly as if I were telling her she had a piece of broccoli stuck in her teeth. It was also the day I tucked my writing dreams away, doubting I would ever be good enough.

Instead, I studied other people's books. Read their thoughts. Lived their dreams, spending many days with Jane Austen, and I must confess a few too many nights with Mr. Darcy.

The class looked promising as I entered. No one seemed to recognize me as the dog-poop-shoe-girl. At the state university a small class still had fifty people in it, but here less than ten. All women, except for one token guy. I sat in the chair next to him.

"Butch," he said.

"Huh?" was my eloquent reply. Was he commenting on my appearance? I thought my replacement outfit looked simple yet stylish in an unpretentious way.

He laughed. "My name's Butch."

Life is always full of ironies. Had his parents hoped that by calling him a tough guy macho name he would follow suit? Hadn't worked. Butch was slim, small boned, very metro and I didn't even need to turn my gaydar on to know which way his screen door swung.

"Lottie," I finally said.

"Are you new here? I don't remember you from any other class."

I confessed that I was a transfer.

27

"You'll enjoy Dr. Jekyll."

"Oh, snap! Am I in the wrong class?" I jumped up gathering my books to leave before everyone realized I was the goof in the wrong room.

"No, you're fine, Lottie," Butch laughed. "That's just our affectionate nickname for Dr. Jamison."

"Oh, my friend told me the nickname traditions here," I said trying to be all in the know of the OKMU heritage. "But why Jekyll?"

"You'll understand after a few weeks with the menopausal woman and her mood swings. If you can learn to watch for the transformation signs you'll love her class. Just need to be prepared for the evil side to come out when least expected."

I was about to ask Butch what sign to look for when the professor started the class by calling the roll.

As long as I've been in school I've always dreaded that first roll call of any class. I'm naturally a little shy and hate having any attention thrown my way when in a large group. To top that off my actual name isn't Lottie. No I'm not in the witness protection program. I simply have a mother who tends to think outside the box, sometimes even outside the entire packing crate. My real name is Charlotte. Like Charlotte Brontë. Alas, I am not her namesake. I had thought most of my life that I was named after Crazy Aunt Charlotte and wondered what horrible thing I had done in the womb to deserve such retribution. When I was twelve I asked my mom why she had named me after the looniest person in the family. She had stared at me blankly.

"You were named after one of my all time heroes—Lottie Moon. A heroic woman missionary to China who gave her life trying to help the people there," she finally said. "Not a relative."

I was even more confused. "Why didn't you name me Lottie then?"

"Lottie is a nickname for Charlotte," she replied like it was common knowledge like the missionary herself, when neither was. It never made sense to me. If they wanted to call me Lottie, why not just put Lottie on the birth certificate? From kindergarten on I had to endure the yearly ritual of the roll call: the calling of Charlotte Lambert, the clarification that I go by Lottie and the confused look on my teacher's face.

However, my Nineteenth Century Women Novelist class was the exception. Dr. Jamison began class like all the educators of my past. I waited nervously for her to reach the L's so that I could as quickly and succinctly as possible explain my name. This time, however, Charlotte into Lottie was merely a footnote on the page of interesting names.

"La-uh-ah Brown?" Dr. Jamison stumbled over a name with a very confused look on her face.

"Dr. Jamison, it isn't La-uh. It's La Dash ah. Just like it's spelled, L, A, a dash mark, A, H. *La Dash Ah*."

I laughed so loudly I snorted. "She's got to be pulling Dr. Jekyll's leg," I whispered to Butch forgetting that this was no huge state school class, but a very intimate setting. An intimate setting where everyone could hear my comments. I could feel Butch's body language as he physically tried to distance himself from me as much as possible by shifting in his desk. In our short acquaintance we hadn't bonded enough for him to be willing to go down with my ship. At that point I did wish that I could have sunk and escaped the laser rays that two sets of very angry eyes focused in on me.

"My mother was a creative speller. She liked to think outside the alphabet, " said La-ah with pride as she turned from giving me the evil eye. And a second murderous look La-ah Brown sent my way told me, with no creative spelling required, that she did not like to be ridiculed. Great, my

29

first class and my lack of an internal filter system and a big, spontaneous mouth had gotten me my first enemy. Make that two.

After joining La-ah in a maybe-looks-can't-kill-but-don't-expect-an-A-in-this-class look Dr. Jamison continued. "Well, *La dash ah*, that is an interesting use of punctuation to create words. Next Charlotte Lambert."

"Here," was all I squeaked out. For the next year I'd be Charlotte to Dr. Jamison as going by an alias would be safer than drawing any more attention to myself in Dr. Jekyll's class that day.

-7-
Didn't See That One Coming

Living in close confines with other women can be amazingly fun when sharing cookie dough, clothes and gossip. However at 8:30 on Saturday morning after a week of stress filled classes and major social screw-ups it could have some drawbacks. In one week I'd shown my granny panties to the world, stepped in dog poop, been humiliated in the cafeteria, called my professor an unflattering nickname and gotten myself on the bad side of a creative speller. I wanted to sleep.

Stina and I had stayed up past two the night before sharing life experience and laughter so all I wanted was topull the covers over my head and block out the world. Instead I heard what sounded like a muffled New Year's Eve party taking place in the hallway outside my door.

There are a lot of morning people in this world. I'm not one of them. I hardly ever get angry. And even when I do I rarely say anything. But I was tired. I was stressed. And to top it off, it was my twentieth birthday and I was feeling a little homesick for my mom and our traditional homemade waffle birthday breakfast in bed. I wanted to sleep. Without thinking matters through, I flung my covers off and marched to door. Jerking it open I said through gritted teeth, "Could you please be quiet.

Some of us are trying to sleep in here."

It wasn't one of my finest moments. There stood the K's, the volleyball team and my three suitemates holding a cake.

A birthday cake.

A birthday cake with my name on it.

"Happy birthday," squeaked one of the K's as all the others stared like possums in the center of the road suddenly aware of the fate that was coming.

My birthday didn't feel so happy. Instead I wanted to slam the door, sit down on the floor and cry. Obviously my new friends had gone to a great deal of planning and work to make my day special and I had ruined it before it ever started.

Then Stina began to giggle. Stina should have been registered with the Center for Disease Control because she was the most contagious giggler I had ever met. Soon everyone was laughing.

"Note to the group," Olivia said, "Lottie Lambert is not a morning person. And she's not aging all that well either."

I must have said sorry a hundred times before the cake had been cut. And another hundred after.

"It's no big deal," Rachel kept reassuring me. "An 8:30 birthday party is rather lame. Sorry. It was the only time we could figure out when everybody would be here. The volleyball girls have to leave for a team outing the rest of the weekend and the K's have dates tonight. So, birthday cake for breakfast seemed like a good idea when we were planning the surprise."

"And we couldn't not celebrate your twentieth birthday. You're almost legal," Stina added.

This brought all kinds of remembrances about everyone else's birthdays as if they were in days of the ancient past.

Soon we were having cake and morning coffee. I opted for a Diet Dr. Pepper instead. Let me clarify instead of the coffee. I had my fair share of the cake.

With one last apology for shouting at them, I added, "Thanks so very much for remembering my birthday. I thought with being new and all no one would even know it was my birthday."

"So why did you change schools?" asked a K.

She caught me with a mouth full of cake and I choked. For the first time ever I was glad to have something caught in my throat as it got me out of explaining what I wasn't sure I could. That was until I feared that Rachel had decided to do an emergency tracheotomy with our cookie dough butcher knife. Fortunately, I quit coughing before she actually tried.

The volleyball girls began to make noises about having to go. I felt bad that they had gone to the trouble of helping to plan my surprise party and I was still thinking of them as an entity rather than individuals. Project for that week was to learn all their names.

"We want to give you our presents before we go," said the short brunette one. I think her name was Pam. Or was it Paula. No, I think it was Pat. I was at least sure it started with a P.

"Brenna, that's a great idea," Rachel replied.

Yep, I had some name cramming to do.

With that everyone began revealing gift bags. Identical gift bags. Pink striped gift bags.

"Olivia thought you might could use these," said one of the K's.

With that it dawned on me where all the pink, striped gift bags came from. I took the first and pulled out the skimpiest thong panties I had ever held. By the time I had opened all the bags I had a nice pile of the sexiest underwear ever and my face was pinker than all the little bags put together.

"Welcome to adulthood, Lottie Lambert," Olivia declared. "No more granny panties for you."

-8-

Not The Perfect Way to Meet A Guy

Entering the cafeteria, my thoughts were everywhere. I was wondering if people could tell I was no longer a teenager. Did I look different? I had practically gotten whiplash over the last few days making sudden stops at every mirror I passed to study my face to see if there was any change. So far none detected. Was I more mature? I had handled the thong barrage better than I usually did when I was embarrassed. I wasn't sure if they had been laughing at me or with me about the panty fiasco. But I decided to let it go and laugh along. That was something I hadn't been able to do when I was nineteen. Did I feel different? Not really, except for thong underwear. That definitely took some getting used to.

It was Spaghetti Day in the café. That's a good thing. College cafeterias are not known for their *haute cuisine*. But spaghetti was one food few could ruin. I took a big helping and added a Diet Dr. Pepper to counteract the carbs. Life seemed to be looking up. I finally felt old enough for college. I was making friends and feeling confident. Stina was waving at me from across the crowded room. She had a seat at her table and was pointing at it indicating I should come sit with her. I know it sounds so juvenile, so middle school, but even adults need to feel included and be at the "popular" table once in awhile in life.

I started weaving my way across the crowded room, looking toward my goal, when something amazing caught the corner of my vision. It was Mr. Gorgeous Of The Granny Panty Fiasco again. Close up he was more fantastic looking than I would have thought humanly possible. Then the most miraculous moment happened. He looked up. Our eyes met. My heart stopped. Maybe there really was such a thing as love at first sight. Okay actually fourth sight, but first time to ever make true eye contact. His picking my panties from a tree or seeing me dissed by Olivia weren't significantly adequate encounters to generate true love at first sight reactions. And my hiding behind statues and across the lawn didn't count, as he hadn't actually seen me. This first time was going to be for real.

We were within inches of each other. He smiled. I smiled. He started to stand like an old fashioned gentleman and began to speak. Suddenly, my plate of spaghetti launched itself into the air coming to rest on his luscious hair, his tight white T-shirt, and his lap (which I feel would be inappropriate to describe.) As I tried to catch the plate, I dropped my tray and my purse. The Diet Dr. Pepper joined its coconspirator the spaghetti on his lap. My purse spilled across the floor. And, oh yes, a big fat *super absorbent* tampon rolled right to his foot.

Death, where are you when so strongly desired?

Like a fool I stood there gaping, while the entire cafeteria thundered with applause.

I needed to do something, anything to fix this horrendous mess. I grabbed a handful of napkins and started to wipe spaghetti off of the poor food-drenched hunk not realizing until too late that I was trying to rub spots off of his crotch. I looked up from my task and our eyes met again. It

36

wasn't the romantic across the room eye contact of love at first sight like before. Rather I saw perfect green eyes filled with humor and a slight bit of terror. What couldn't have ever gotten worse just had. I dropped to the floor groping around for my purse and belongings. A spaghetti covered Mr. Gorgeous bent to help me pick up my things, reaching the tampon first.

It just couldn't happen that way. Our first ever meeting could not include me rubbing his privates and him handing me a tampon, especially a *super absorbent* one. The first thing my hand touched from my purse spillage was the stupid pink eraser Crazy Aunt Charlotte had given me weeks before that I had thrown in the bottom of my purse and forgotten. Just as he reached the god forsaken sanitary product, with tears in my eyes, I picked up the ridiculous eraser and said, "I wish, I really, really wish, I could do this over."

Instantly I was back in the food line.

What the . . .? I looked around. Mr. Gorgeous Of The Granny Panty Fiasco Now Spaghetti Crotch Incident was still sitting at his table in a clean white T-shirt. Stina was still at her table with the popular crowd, a seat still vacant for me. What could possibly have happened? Had the moment been so utterly humiliating that I had mentally snapped? Was this how crazy started? Did it begin at a point in time when the mind could no longer handle the hopelessness of the situation?

No one seemed aware that anything earth shattering had happened except me. Had I become as deranged as my Crazy Aunt Charlotte? Crazy Aunt Charlotte. Stupid Pink Eraser. It couldn't be. I looked down. The eraser was still in my hand. It wasn't possible. It couldn't have happened.

I stood there like a goob for a full minute. There couldn't be such a thing as a do-over. I had studied physics in high school. I never understood

37

much of it, but I knew that what had just happened was impossible.

Yet, there I stood in the same place I had been five minutes before. I stood and stared longer. I had to get a grip. I hoped I wasn't drooling all over myself. It was a dream. That was it. I'd just play along and then I'd wake up.

Okay. Time to wake up. I pinched myself.

The guy across from me looked at me like I was mental. Oh wait. I was mental. I thought I had reversed time. I had to keep it together for a while longer.

As normal life went ahead in the crowded cafeteria, a debate on the level of Lincoln versus Douglas was going on in my poor brain. Either I was as *loca* as Crazy Aunt Charlotte or I really did have a magic eraser. Which just couldn't be. Or could it? Had the big pink eraser worked? Was Crazy Aunt Charlotte not bonkers after all?

All my poor befuddled mind could comprehend was that the impossible had become possible. Time had started over. Life really was giving me a do-over.

In my peripheral vision I saw La-ah entering the cafeteria. As I wasn't the most popular person in her world at that moment I decided it was time to get moving. I'd wait until I was alone to finish my nervous breakdown. For the moment I'd pull from every ounce of acting ability I didn't posses to appear calm, cool and collected. I'd figure out what had happened later when I could cry, babble and drool on myself in private.

Obviously I wasn't having spaghetti. I changed to the hamburger line. It took longer to get it grilled, but less chance of a mess if dropped. And water to drink, please.

Stina approached as I was finishing with the condiments.

"I was hoping to eat with you, but I just remembered I have to run back to the room for the right notebook," she said. Then she turned back to look at me really hard. "Are you okay? You don't look so spiffy. Maybe you should sit down."

"No I'm fine," I lied. Not ready for the little men in white coats to come take me away yet. First I had to meet Mr. Gorgeous Of The Granny Panty Fiasco But No Longer Spaghetti Crotch Incident and then I could go bonkers.

"If you're sure. I'll talk to you later." And she was gone.

Food finally prepared, I was off to meet Mr. G.O.T.G.P.F.B.N.L.S.C.I., possibly soon to be shortened to Mr. Right. Turning to where he had been, my hands firmly on my tray, my heart dropped.

He was gone. I guess I had been in line longer than I realized. The moment had passed. Or perhaps in my redo reality, it had never been.

-9-

Mental Melt Down

"Mom are you sure you don't know Crazy Aunt Charlotte's phone number?" Yes, I had called my mom as soon as I returned from the cafeteria to the safety of my dorm room. I know I was a college student, an adult, but be real. No matter how old I got, when in a crisis mom was always who I called.

My first thought was to tell my mom everything that had happened, or maybe didn't happen after all. Maybe I was just going crazy. Too much stress. Too much frozen cookie dough. I must have shared too much of Aunt Charlotte's DNA. I hadn't had anything strange to drink. No weird pills. And no way I could explain over the phone to my mom the last thirty minutes of my life. I needed to come to terms with the situation. I had always had an excellent imagination. Maybe it had temporarily taken over. I desperately needed to talk with Aunt Charlotte.

Mom was talking. I tried to listen. My brain was racing and it was so hard to focus.

"I really don't have any idea how to get in touch with her. To be honest I don't remember ever calling her or writing to her. She just seems to always know when we're having a family get together. Must be another family member that contacts her." Then my mom gave a confused little laugh. "I hadn't thought about it much, but your dad and I were talking years ago and neither of us even know how she is related. Isn't that funny? She's always just been there. But she's not my mom's nor my dad's sister or aunt or cousin and your dad says the same. Maybe she married into the family? Except, I can't remember her ever not being there. So I guess she must come from my side of the family. Except your dad says the same thing." Mom could have gone on for hours on the topic of our family's genealogy, but I was having a crisis and it was taking every ounce of sanity left in me to sound coherent. I thought it best to get off the phone before I started to worry my mom.

"That's okay, Mom. If you should think of some way to contact her, could you let me know? I just wanted to thank her for a gift she gave me last summer." That sounded sane, right? It would please my mom that I was using my manners and thanking people, right?

"Oh, that's nice Lottie. What did she give you?"

It wasn't working. I had momentarily forgotten that my mom was a snoop. She wouldn't let it rest until she knew.

"My goodness, look at the time. I'm going to be late for class. Gotta go. Love you!" With a click I disconnected and set my phone to go directly to voicemail. I knew she'd call back soon.

"Are you okay?" asked Rachel. I jumped about three feet in the air and gave a squeaky scream. I hadn't heard her come through our adjoining bathroom into my room. "You look awful. Bad day?"

Always intuitive, Rachel knew that I was having a melt down. She was so wise beyond her years that I almost told her of my bizarre eraser and time travel experience. But then again we had known each other for

41

less than two weeks and I doubted, even with her empathetic spirit that she would believe me. She'd probably just pack quickly and look for a different suitemate or make sure to always bolt the door between our rooms. As much as I would like to confide in someone, I didn't want my new start to land me on the nutty list.

"Poop," was what I said instead. Actually I might have used a more descriptive noun, but it meant poop.

"Yeah, I heard about that the other day," Rachel replied with a sad smile. "Small campus, remember. Do we need to go shoe shopping?"

Leave it Rachel to see the silver lining in fecal matter. At least it would give us a reason to go shopping.

Reaching in the mini-fridge, Rachel retrieved two cans of Diet Dr. Pepper and a roll of cookie dough. Slicing off a chunk with Stina's big butcher knife, she sat down on my bed and motioned for me to sit next to her. My eyes didn't leave the knife. With a nut job in the room, that big honkin' knife was not the best of ideas. I'd get rid of it later before my mental capacity deteriorated any further.

"Seems your start over is going a little harder than planned," she began. Dr. Rachel Herz, psychologist extraordinary, was in for counseling.

"Two classes and I've already stuck my one foot in my mouth and the other foot in dog crap. Then in the cafeteria. . ." I barely caught myself before I mentioned the spaghetti fiasco that in reality had never happened—or something like that.

"Oh I heard about that."

There was a look of shock on my face. Maybe I wasn't the only one to experience the time change. Maybe Rachel wasn't just empathetic but in touch with all otherworldly occurrences. Hopefully together we could figure it out.

"Olivia's like that," Rachel continued. I was confused. I started to shout out, great you felt the time change too when I slowly realized she was referring to the Olivia-hunky-guy-table-incident from the week before. "Please don't judge her badly by that. She really is a good person and in most ways a loyal friend. Just not where guys are involved. As you get to know her you'll start to notice—how do I say this nicely? Well, she's not super academic. I mean, you heard us teasing her about flunking out of Spanish, when she grew up in a household of native speakers. That doesn't happen very often. Her whole life she has gotten by on her looks. I've met her family. Nothing she does seems important to them other than how she looks—and if she finds a rich husband.

"I hope you don't think I'm breaking any confidences, as that is something I will never do. To be a good psychologist I have to be trustworthy. Even more so to be a good friend," Rachel paused for a moment and ate a nibble of dough. "Anything I tell you about Olivia, or Stina for that matter, is something that is common knowledge. But as we are all living in close confines together, the faster we understand each other the fewer hurt feelings. So I'll fill you in on the most pertinent facts. You'll find that for all her beauty, Olivia has no self-confidence. She needs to feel control of her situation a little more than most of us. She's just as lost and confused as the rest of us inside that drop-dead gorgeous body."

For a second I felt better. My mom had tried my whole life to make me understand that everybody has their own sorrows and success and not everything that happens has to do with me.

But this insane time change ability did. Then reality hit again. I wasn't just a freak with a magic eraser. Suddenly with Rachel recapping all the horrid things that had happened to me over the past week I had an epiphany. If I could figure out how to harness the power of the eraser, I could have what I had always wanted. I could have control over all the situations in my life. No more dog poop on my shoes, or laughing at the wrong moment, or watching my mom chase down huge underwear on the campus oval. If I wasn't crazy then it meant that I had the power to change my destiny. Look out world. Life finally did give do-overs.

-10-

I'm Invincible

It didn't take long for me to find a reason to use my wonderful eraser again. Less than twenty-four hours in fact.

Being a junior in college, I knew better, but my only recourse to get out of the dreaded dog-poop-shoe Old Testament class, was to take a different section at eight. That's A. M.—as in the morning. Ridiculous. And needless to say my body agreed, because at 8:10 a.m. I rolled over to stare my traitorous alarm clock in the dial and realized I was late. I jumped up to head for the shower, but heard it already running. One of my other suitemates must have beaten me to it. What was I to do? I'd already missed the first day of the class because of rescheduling. I was already going to spend the next two weeks lost and confused. But I couldn't walk in late and unshowered.

Finally my brain woke up. It had worked once, might as well try it again. I dug through my purse and found my beautiful pink eraser at the bottom. I tried to remember exactly what I had done in the cafeteria to make it work. I thought for a moment and said, "Can I do this over?" Nothing happened. I asked again adding please. Maybe good manners were essential. Nothing. I asked again a little more demanding than beseeching. Maybe I needed to show that pink thing who was boss. Nada. It was starting to dawn on me that it must have all been a dream. A very real dream, but a dream nonetheless. I hadn't actually really changed time. I hadn't thrown my food on the guy of my dreams and then unthrown it. I had thought at the time I'd soon wake up and it would never have had happened. In some ways it was a major relief. I wasn't going crazy. The universe did function normally as always. But it had seemed so inexplicably real. Just as real as I felt right then sitting on my bed, late for class, holding an eraser. It had to have been real. For some bizarre reason realizing that my not changing time the day before made me feel more insane than when I actually thought I had.

It had worked. I knew it. Something was keeping it from happening again. Something in the sequence or the words or time zone. Maybe solar flares or the hole in the ozone had to be properly aligned for it to function. I was grasping at straws. Maybe it was a one-use magic eraser? Maybe I had done something to break it? Maybe it only worked when food was involved? Exasperated I shook the stupid thing, shaking it as hard as I could, and said, "Give me a do-over so I'm not late to class!"

This time my clock read 6:55 a.m. and I wanted to kiss it. It had worked! Then it clicked in my mind. Crazy Aunt Charlotte (I guess I needed to quit referring to her as crazy as I was the mental person talking to a desk accessory) had said just wave it around and ask. The waving it must have been vital to making it activate. Strange how relieved I felt. I was doing the impossible, but the realness of it reinforced my sanity. No time to analyze it then. Off to jump in the empty shower and get ready for a good start to a new class.

Sliding into class with five minutes to spare, I found a seat in the back by a very handsome guy. He wasn't the hunk from the cafeteria by any means, but he wasn't anything to sneeze at either.

"Good morning," he said in very cultured tones. In Oklahoma you don't often get spoken to in very cultured tones. This should be interesting. "I'm Geoffrey Hale." He reached over to shake my hand. I guess his mother had raised him right.

"Lottie Lambert," I croaked out.

"Are you new here? I don't seem to have made your acquaintance. I know practically everyone on campus."

"I'm a transfer, that's why I'm taking a freshman level class. Are you a freshman?" I asked.

You'd have thought I had asked if he tortured puppies. I thought for a moment he wasn't going to dignify my question with an answer when he said, "I'm a senior. I simply didn't have time in my schedule in years past." He said schedule all run together and slurry like a British person. It made me feel like asking for some Grey Poupon mustard.

The more we talked the snootier he became. I wondered if the class would ever begin. Then the most awkward thing of all happened.

"My schedule is rather packed, but perchance I might squeeze in some time and we might go out this weekend?" he asked.

Okay, I'm all for live for the day and seize the moment and all that. But in a three-minute conversation, now that was too fast. Yep, let's try that little eraser trick again.

Once again I was sliding into class with five minutes to spare. The seat was still empty next to Mr. Geoffrey Hale. And it could stay that way. I found myself a spot at the front. Oh how I loved that pink eraser. Life was good.

-11-

Dorm Life - Love It or Don't

Life had become so much easier with the ability to rewind. I must have used that wonderful, fabulous magic eraser daily for the first week or so. Like the day I forgot to bring my homework to *Señora Aburrida*'s Spanish class. Okay it was really Albert, but she was boring. No homework, no problem. One wave of Super Eraser and I remembered to bring it with me. Unfortunately, it wasn't a magical Spanish-speaking eraser and I still got a D on the assignment. Maybe I would have been better off trying to talk my professor into letting me turn it in late and getting some help from someone better at Spanish than Olivia.

But, try as I might, the eraser would only ever give one chance to make a change. I learned rule number two one frantic morning a few weeks later from Olivia and her diamond earrings.

It wasn't my fault. It was a normal frantic morning in our suite. Everyone had put off getting up until the last possible moment and then we were all frantic to get ready on time. Rachel was sitting on the floor by our full-length mirror drying her hair. Stina was bent over the sink brushing her teeth, while Olivia was leaned over her looking into the mirror putting on her third coat of mascara. I was hunting for a clean cami that matched my shirt. Maybe a slightly dirty one would have to do. So digging through my dirty clothesbasket, I heard the shriek of a banshee and the rapid flow of Spanish cuss words. Well honestly, I really didn't know what the words meant. We hadn't gotten to the swear words chapter in *Señora Aburrida's* class yet. The words could have meant peanut butter and jelly, but with the force they were coming out of Olivia's mouth it didn't take a Ph.D. in linguistics to hypothesize that they weren't nice.

"Sorry, sorry, sorry," Stina was responding at just a slightly lower decibel. "I didn't know they were there."

"Those are DIAMONDS!" Olivia responded as if that made a difference in the situation.

"Well, what were DIAMONDS doing sitting on the side of the sink next to the toilet?"

Time for Rachel the peacemaker to intercede. I don't think we would have ever lived through the year without blood being drawn if it wasn't for Rachel's never failing reason and patience. "It's okay, guys. Look someone just has to reach in the toilet and get them out. Oh gross, who didn't flush?" Then again in some situations even Rachel wasn't the best diplomat in the world.

I rapidly thought back. Oh crap. Well, I didn't crap, but I had forgotten to flush after I peed. Someone had been pounding on the door for me to hurry. I didn't wait for the jury to come in on that one. Not to worry. Magic eraser to the rescue.

"Hurry up in there," Stina pounded on the door.

Business done. I turned and flushed. No diamonds in pee now. Off I

49

went to dig through my dirty laundry for a semi-clean cami. It was only a minute later I heard the Spanish cuss words again. But how could that be? I'd done a do-over. That's when the realization came to me. I had flushed, but I hadn't thought to move Olivia's earrings. Just because I changed one thing, it didn't change the actions of the others. The earrings were still in the toilet, but thankfully not in a urine-filled toilet. I'd go back a second time and move the earrings. I tried the eraser again, but nothing happened. I tried again and again. I quit trying when Stina and Olivia both looked at me waving my hand through the air like I was one can short of a six pack.

Rules I had figured out. Number one—can't fix everything by doing it over. Number two—one use only in any situation. Oh and rule number three—I had to get out of the suite quickly before Olivia killed Stina and I had to testify at the murder trial.

Fleeing the room early left me ahead of schedule for class. That was a rarity. It was a beautiful September day. Some trees were just beginning to turn reds and oranges. Those that had leaves left. As is normal in Oklahoma there had been a drought in July and August, so most of the leaves had just turned brown and fallen off.

I cut across the oval to my Spanish class, trying to remember if it was nouns or verbs that were suppose to be conjugated and why. I didn't see him until I smacked right into his back. Books went everywhere.

"What the. . .?" were the first words Mr. Gorgeous ever said to me. They were beautiful. It was as if he were speaking lines from *Romeo and Juliet*, they fell so eloquently from his lips. "Oh, hey, are you okay? I'm sorry," he added to his soliloquy. He bent to pick up my books. "I guess I stopped short," he apologized, even though I knew it was my fault. What a gentleman.

Did I wittily reply, "Oh, no the fault is all mine and here's my phone number, and insurance verification." No, I just stood there gaping like a goldfish in a bag of water.

"I guess you knocked her mute," came a sultry voice from his side. It wasn't until that moment I became aware that anyone else was near, or even on the same planet. Miss swimsuit model, with silky black hair, six-foot long legs and ginormous boobs (they had to be fake,) was standing leering down her perfect nose (also, probably fake) at me, the mute. This black haired vixen was the epitome of the evil, conniving, manipulative other woman. She was so obvious that it only took six words out of her mouth and five seconds for me to come to that conclusion. "Oh, and you might want to zip your pants," she added with a stage whisper to be heard all across campus.

Mr. Gorgeous, down on his knees picking up my books, turned to look at me which gave him a straight shot at my unzipped jeans. And needless to say I wasn't wearing my granny panties that day.

I thrust my hand into my purse and waved my eraser with much more thrust than needed looking like a swashbuckling demented pirate.

So I wouldn't meet Mr. Darcy Jr. that day. There would be other chances. I just couldn't have him tell our future grandchildren how the day we met my pants had been unzipped and showing my new pink sparkly thong undies.

-12-

Jane Austen Vs. The Taliban

Overall classes at my new school went fine. My new Old Testament class wasn't much different than my old Old Testament class. But at least I wasn't known as dog-poop-shoe-girl there. I had tried to do that over, but again the magic only seemed to work on current happenings—it couldn't go back more than a few minutes or at most an hour.

Nineteenth Century Lit. was going to be a challenge with Dr. Jamison. Especially if I ever slipped and called her Dr. Jekyll again. Other than the monstrous pile of hard work and the fact that I hacked the teacher off on the very first day, it was the type of class in which I thrived. To be in an upper level literature class, where we could have deep and meaningful conversations over great literary works was like shopping with a $20,000 prepaid Visa card. Bliss. No more listening to inane, half-asleep frat boys make shallow or crude remarks about Madame Bovary's ovaries or that Mr. Knightly really was gay.

La—ah had decided to be forgiving about my first day's *faux pas*.

Even though we were different in almost every way possible, she was loud, confident and hilarious, while I was awkward, quiet and insecure, we soon found that we were kindred spirits, as our favorite girlfriend Anne (with an E) Shirley would have said. By the third week we were study buddies along with Kasha from the K's.

Once singled out from the herd of K's, I was able to see Kasha as an individual. She was darling cute, and when not giggling insanely and finishing her posse's sentences, she was actually quite intellectual. This I discovered one day while discussing the feminist movement as seen through the works of Austen and Bronte with her in class.

"Dr. Jamison, you keep talking how Jane and Charlotte wrote about the plight of women. Up until I took this class, I always just thought they wrote love stories of the happily ever after kind," commented La—ah.

"Oo and I so loved that Mr. Darcy," said Kasha. I think I saw Butch nodding his head in agreement.

"Austen and Bronte did write some page turning romances. And it is said that Austen had all her stories have happy endings because her life didn't. But let's delve deeper. If you look beyond the romance, why were our heroines in their dilemmas in the first place? They were either being expected to live off the kindness, or the lack thereof, of extended relatives. Or they were being forced into loveless marriages for financial security. Titles and lands were passed to the male heir. Thus, poor Elizabeth was almost forced to marry Mr. Collins to keep a roof over her family's head. Or Jane Eyre was sent to relatives, and boarding schools and hired out as a governess. We owe so much to the women who worked to give us equal rights here in our own century," expounded Dr. Jamison.

"Yet, marriage for necessity is still around," added Kasha. "And not just to pay back student loans." Everyone in the class laughed. "Look at the women in Afghanistan who are under the Taliban. They have to wear those cumbersome, stifling *burqas*."

"I saw on the news that they weren't allowed to see men doctors so they have one of the highest pregnancy death rates in the world, one out of eight," added Butch our token guy in the class.

"All because of modesty rules," said Kasha. "I must have seen the same report. It seems absurd in the 21st century. I know that there were many political reasons we went to war with the Taliban, but I always have been proud that our soldiers were able to make it possible for women to go to school and have some tiny freedoms in their own country."

"Preach on girlfriend," added La—ah. We had suddenly changed from a literature class to a tent revival.

"Amen sister," chimed in Dr. Jamison. That woman could morph personas so fast, like from super intellect to soul sister, at any given moment. Then she also could rapidly turn so wicked it was a wonder a house never fell on her. "How about you Lottie? What can you add to our discussion?"

Up until that moment my brain was just humming with a plethora of profound hypotheses, yet the moment she said my name I did my best imitation of Snooki on *Jeopardy*.

"Well, I um, I um, I always had the hots for Mr. Darcy, but Mr. Knightly was actually a kinder character." Did I really just say that? For the love of Jane Austen, I had to change something fast. I started digging for my eraser in my purse.

"Excuse me? Are you now looking for a better answer in your purse?" asked Dr. Jekyll.

I found it. Gave a wave and hopefully saved my dignity.

"How about you Lottie? What can you add to our discussion?"

I pondered for a moment with my best highly intellectual look on my face. "It's hard to imagine that there was a time when women couldn't inherit property or had to face a life of poverty if they didn't marry well. But, as my grandma loves to remind me that before the 70s very, very few women in the USA were considered for any job other than secretary, nurse or teacher. And even today women aren't always paid the same salary as their male colleagues." Good save, Super Eraser.

"Good point, Lottie. Sadly our time is over for today." With that she reminded us of our enormous reading assignment and that we needed to begin work on our research papers.

There I was, over a month into the semester, and with the help of my wonderful, fabulous magic eraser, life was finally going great.

-13-

Cookie Dough & Dishing the Dirt

Fall break had come and gone. It was amazing how fast the end of the semester was approaching. When all those papers were assigned back in August they had seemed so doable, the end of October they were suddenly impossible. As always I had procrastinated.

Fall break had already come and gone. I had twenty-two sightings of Mr. Gorgeous. Still no introduction. I had almost met him four times, but all in bad situations that had required a do-over. I had spied him in the cafeteria numerous times. Always with the "theater" crowd and that black haired skank. I found out from Olivia that she was also a theater major named Taylor. To paraphrase Olivia's description, she was not a very nice girl. Go figure. Twice I *noticed* him picking that nasty, trampy, Taylor up in his adorable red Miata. Once he saw me watching, but with a quick little flip of my wrist that scene was rewritten.

I spent some time looking for him on social medi I had been able to find him in photos of mutual friends. But he didn't seem to have his own page. Yes, I was a Facebook creeper. And a stalker. I either needed to find a twelve-step program to get over this fantasy perfect man, or I needed to call in the big guns.

I'm an American girl. I went for the ammo.

"You look a little stressed tonight," Rachel said after my fifteenth sigh while reading *Jane Eyre*. It was 11:30 and Jane was trying to figure out the mysterious secrets surrounding Mr. Rochester. I still had two chapters more to read for the next day's class and a paragraph for Old Testament to write, yet all I could do was wonder about a guy I had never even officially met. It was time to take a break from Mr. Rochester's secrets and get answers to a few questions from this century.

"I think we could all use a cookie dough break," Olivia declared as she went to the mini-fridge and retrieved the Holy Grail.

"Olivia, Stina, you two know everyone on campus. There's this guy. . ."

I was quickly interrupted.

"Tell me, tell me. Please don't say Geoffrey Hale. He is soooo stuck on himself. Every girl on campus thinks she wants to meet him and after two minutes changes her mind." Stina was on a roll. "And that British accent he uses is so fake. Why, he's from Talala, Oklahoma, for pity sake."

"I bet it's that Jacob Smith. He is cute. I'll give him that. We went out **once.** That's all it took," Olivia spoke as the all-knowing authority on men, which she was. "Nice guy, but cheap!! Took me to a restaurant and used a coupon and then asked me, me—Olivia Corazon—to leave the tip. Why I never. . ."

"Oh yes, you have," interrupted Stina.

"And we've been there to put you back together each time," added Rachel with sympathy, not ridicule in her voice.

"Well, not with cheapo Jacob-o," Olivia responded. "Enough about me."

That was a first. I'd never had a conversation where Olivia had decided that there had been enough emphasis on her.

Olivia continued, "So, who is the guy?"

I started to sweat. My heart was racing. It was absurd. There I was just asking about a guy, like the outcome of the conversation was crucial to my entire future. He was just a guy I had seen across the campus a few times (make that twenty-two.) Just an absolutely gorgeous specimen of the male species. Not that I've been staring. Just thought about him a few times. Okay every night for weeks. He was just a guy. And it was time I left the realm of fantasy and started on reality. Good or bad.

"I've noticed this guy once or twice on campus. I've passed him when I was late for class a few times."

"I didn't think you were ever late for class. You seem to have some built in clock that always makes you punctual," said Rachel.

It was hard to keep all the real time and do-over time sorted out when telling what had happened in a day which too often was coming off as if I were either crazy or a habitual liar.

I couldn't give them his name, although I had discovered it through my social media stalking. Instead, I tried to play it like I only knew a few facts about him. "Well, um. . . I think he might be a theater major. I saw him go into the auditorium a couple of times."

"Well, that narrows it down. Male. Theater major. That leaves about twenty guys," Rachel started the process of elimination.

"Oh, but she said he was cute," Stina added. "That eliminates about ten. Olivia, who are the hunk actors on campus?"

"What color hair?" she asked.

"Brown. With just the perfect highlights," I was blushing. How stupid. "Real highlights, not fake. The kind you wish the beautician could get just right in your hair."

"Height?"

"Perfect."

"What is perfect?" Stina giggled.

"You know. Tall enough to give that feeling of protection, but close enough to be able to reach up and kiss."

"I think you might have happened to see this guy more than a few times," Rachel said in her all-knowing voice.

I was beginning to feel like I was on *CSI Oklahoma*.

"Does he have a car?" Stina asked back in a just-the-facts mode.

"I think I might have seen him in a little red convertible. Maybe a Miata."

"Oh, honey child, I'm so sorry. That's Al Dansby," said Olivia with actual sympathy on her face.

"Oh Al. Yes, he is cute," agreed Stina in a sad voice.

Obviously the thing with the black haired fashion model must have been more serious than it appeared in my **not** stalking observations.

"What's wrong with him? Does he have a girlfriend?" I had to ask even though I didn't think I really wanted to hear the answer.

"You wish that was the problem. No, he's gay," responded Olivia matter-of-factly.

"You don't know that for sure," said Rachel. "He's never said he was. You know it's wrong to go labeling people just because they don't fit perfectly into your preconceived idea of how a man should act."

"He doesn't act gay," added Stina. "Um baby, he's so cute."

"Oh, but let's look at the facts. He's a musical theater major," said Olivia as she started counting facts off her fingers.

"That's not a guarantee. There are musical theater actors who aren't gay," responded Rachel. "Okay, I can't think of one off the top of my head. But I know there are."

"Okay, you may be on to something Olivia. It's true I've never seen him date anyone, although I doubt any girl would ever turn him down if he asked," added Stina without her usual bubble. "And he turned you down. No straight guy has ever turned Olivia down," Stina turned to tell me.

Well, that was that. My fairytale was just that. I thought I was going to cry. I had built this up so in my imagination. There I was feeling as if my heart had been ripped out for a guy whose name I had just learned and I had never met in my current time sequence. My friends were giving me that look—some sympathy, but more confusion. I had said I'd seen him around campus a few times, yet I reacted as if he had just broken off our engagement. I was pathetic. I could see it in their eyes that they thought I was either a drama queen or some horribly psycho love junkie latching on to any guy who halfway paid me any attention. This conversation wasn't going to happen.

And suddenly it didn't.

"You look a little stressed tonight," Rachel said after my fifteenth sigh while reading *Jane Eyre*. It was 11:30 again and I still had two chapters more to read and a paragraph for Old Testament to write.

"I think we could all use a cookie dough break," Olivia declared.

Mr. Rochester had his secrets and so did I. Al Dansby went in the lost cause file and the topic was closed before it was ever opened.

-14-

Coffee, Tea, or... Never Mind?

I left the room ahead of schedule for class that Monday morning. That was a rarity. It was a beautiful autumn day, not much wind. That also is a rarity in Oklahoma, not the beautiful day, but the absence of wind. I decided on the spur of the moment to make a quick trip through the student center for a cup of coffee. Not that I really liked coffee. I preferred Diet Dr. Pepper. But coffee looks sophisticated. At twenty I wanted to look adult. Mature.

It was my lucky day. No line. Actually quite empty as it was early and most intelligent people were still asleep, either in their dorm rooms or in classes, but snoozing nonetheless.

"I'd like a skinny cinnamon dolce latte," I requested of the poor work-study employee stuck with the early morning shift. I really had no idea what that was, but it sounded urbane. He seemed less than impressed.

"I'll have the same," came the most glorious, cultured, sexy voice from behind me.

"Sure, Al," the barrister replied, much more enthusiastic about his job than before. This gay thing was so unfair. I wanted a chance with the Al of my dreams, but no luck. In my mom's day the dilemma was always all the good ones were taken. In my day they all are gay. How could I ever compete with that? I thought I was going to cry right then and there. I was so deep in thought that it took Al repeating *good morning*, I don't know how many times before it sunk through into my gloom.

"Are you okay?" he asked. Not in that obligatory way that people ask when they don't really want a truthful answer and hope to not have to deal with an awkward situation. No, he asked as if he really cared. I must have looked like a mental case, tears starting in my eyes and my face getting all red and splotchy.

Up close he was even more magnificent than my memories, my dreams, my fantasies had remembered. I had to get away, fast. Even if he wasn't a possibility for me, I still couldn't stand the idea of making a fool of myself in his. . . oh so green eyes that were looking into mine. Breathe. Yes, that was what I needed to do, breathe. I had to grab that eraser and get out of that God forsaken student center before I threw myself on him babbling platitudes of how if he just gave me a chance I could make him straight.

I left the room ahead of schedule for class that Monday morning. That was a rarity. It was a beautiful autumn day, not much wind. Now that also is a rarity in Oklahoma. Yet, I wasn't enjoying it. Should I have stayed in the student center? Should I have taken the chance to have a conversation with Al Dansby? No, no point in attempting a relationship that just couldn't happen. No coffee for Lottie Lambert, and no Al Dansby either. Some things couldn't change no matter how many special erasers I had nor how many times I did the moment over. Some days life just hurt.

-15-

Things That Cry In The Night

A party in the hallway at four in the morning, even on a Friday night—actually Saturday morning—is inconsiderate. Especially since I obviously hadn't been invited and it had disturbed the most beautiful dream. Mr. Knightly, Mr. Darcy and Al Dansby kept morphing from one to the other, all desperately in love with me. Ah. Then somewhere in the background of absolute bliss came the shouts of a wild, debaucherous festival. We were suddenly at a nineteenth century ball. Mr. Darcy was asking me to dance. I should have been thrilled, yet I knew there was someone I wanted more. I looked over just in time to see Al Dansby making a move on Mr. Knightly. That was what had shattered my bliss.

I awoke upset. Couldn't he even be straight in my dreams, if not in reality? The fog slowly cleared in my brain enough to focus in on the actual noise in the corridor. It wasn't the sound of a happy party after all. I heard sobs, then Rachel's voice. I couldn't make out exactly what she was saying. It sounded like a loving mother trying to comfort a distraught child. I heard Stina trying to lighten the mood with, "You're better off without him."

"But, I thought he was the one. He promised," sobbed one of the K's.

I didn't have to listen any longer. We'd all been there and done that in differing degrees. He promised. "Trust me," he said. "You're the only one for me." "It's okay if we really love each other." Then out of the blue, the old heave-ho.

There was more murmuring. It seemed more K's had arrived. I heard Stina slip quietly into our room, trying not to wake me.

"I'm already awake. Which K was it?"

"Keesha."

"The soccer player?"

"Seems he was putting in some extra practice elsewhere."

"How bad is she?"

"Pretty bad. She's been sleeping with the guy for a month and now she finds out she's not the only one. He's been dropping Keesha off at night and then going out with that Taylor, theater witch, the rest of the night."

"Hope she was using some kind of protection?"

"Said she was. Nothing is fool-proof though."

Symbolic choice of words I thought.

I contemplated Keesha's situation and felt her heartache. "Sadly, there's no protection for a heart. It breaks every time."

-16-
Finally/Unfinally

Life went on. The ever-present Oklahoma wind grew colder. More assignments came due as the semester began to wind down. It wasn't my first time to finish a semester, yet every new beginning I vowed not to wait until the last moment to write all my papers. Every term I waited until the end. So I trudged across the campus, that cold November evening, with my head down walking at an almost forty-five degree angle to the ground, fighting my way against the wind, on a quest to make some library time before Thanksgiving break. Most everything I needed for my research paper was available online. However, Dr. Jekyll was a Luddite and required us to use at least three books, real books, in our work.

Didn't she know that no one used real books anymore? Yes, she knew. That would be what separated the educated from the masses, she had said when making the assignment. True Academic Research. At that point she got a maniacal gleam in her eye and I was afraid to press the subject further.

So I trudged uphill (okay it wasn't really a hill, just a little incline), in the rain (so it wasn't raining, but it could have at any moment) against the wind (it really was unbelievably windy) to the library. Suddenly I did it again—I ran smack into the most fabulous non-straight guy on the planet.

"I'm so sorry," I said. "I seem to always be plowing you down."

He looked at me with the most confused expression. "Have we met before?"

I had to think quickly. What had and had not been done and undone where he was concerned? It was so hard to keep all my different realities straight. Yes, I had spilled spaghetti on him and knocked into him and even talked to him, but only in my reality. In his time/space continuum none of those meetings had ever happened.

"Oh, no I guess we haven't," I stuttered.

"Well, then it is time we did. I'm Al, Al Dansby."

All I could do was gawk. "And this is the part where you tell me your name," he said with the most magnificent smile. It was the perfect smile of a confident man, yet there was a twinge of a mischievous little boy just at the corner. The kind of smile that made grown, independent, liberated women go weak at the knees. Absolutely lethal to me.

"Lottie. Lottie Lambert. Well, really Charlotte Lambert. But, my parents had some weird idea of using an old nickname for Charlotte and calling me Lottie. I never understood why they didn't just name me Lottie if that was what they wanted to call me in the first place." Why wouldn't my mouth shut! I just kept rambling. I was making an absolute fool of myself like some silly, pathetic, lovesick schoolgirl. This just couldn't happen. My hand was reaching in my bag for my handy dandy eraser when I realized he was still smiling.

"Well, Charlotte Lambert, commonly known as Lottie, as it's rather freezing out here, could we continue this conversation over in the library?"

The library was one of the oldest buildings on campus. It gave the true ivy-covered redbrick college feel to the campus. I usually felt a sense of awe and reverence when walking through the door, knowing that on the shelves were books by centuries of famous authors. Yes, real books. Perhaps, although I didn't want to admit it, I did agree with Dr. Jekyll, just not on cold windy nights.

That evening the place could have been full of live pigs and molasses and I wouldn't have noticed. I knew it was futile to attempt a relationship with Al Dansby, but we could be friends, maybe even good friends. That would at least give me the chance to spend time with him. My inner voice kept warning me to walk away, walk away quickly. I was going to get my heart pulverized and I wasn't going to feel the least bit sorry for myself if I did. (Rachel's Psych class would have a field day with my schitzo brain.) Nevertheless, my illogical persona was winning. I would pursue a futile relationship and deal with the disappointment later.

"So Lottie, what brings you out on such a blustery evening?" he asked as we entered the reading room with its old burgundy leather couches and mismatched chairs. His voice sounded so cultured — slightly British. Not all snooty and fake like Geoffrey Hale, but like smooth, dreamy melting in my mouth butter. The real stuff, not margarine. He definitely wasn't from around *these here parts*.

My brain knew that this was where I was supposed to respond. My tongue hadn't gotten the memo. My eyes just stared. I could have sworn my traitorous eyelashes fluttered. I was going to have to have an inner body conference soon about working on getting my different parts to be team players. Finally I came up with a witty response.

"Research." Yep, that's me Charlotte "Lottie" Lambert. One minute I can't stop my mouth and the next it's on strike.

"Oh, well this is a good place for it," Al Dansby replied. "I guess I should let you get with it," he said. Did I detect a slight longing for a reason to prolong our conversation or was I projecting my own desires on

67

his simple statement? I needed something profound to extend the moment.

"Okay," was what my stupid mouth came up with. OKAY!? What was I thinking? I needed to ask him for help or suggest coffee. Instead I had just mumbled okay. There I was with my inner being wanting beyond words to connect with Al Dansby, but no words would come. Instead my inner turmoil and outward awkwardness made me come across as cold and unfriendly. I was practically dissing him. Then again it was probably for the best to not start a no-win relationship no matter how badly I wanted to try.

"It was a pleasure to make your acquaintance. I'm sure I will see you around," he said as he turned to go.

I had blown my perfect opportunity. I grabbed my purse and started digging for my eraser, my lifeline to hoping I could change the last two-minute conversation and say something that would make him stay. But, I couldn't find it. I remembered with frustration that it was in my other purse from the afternoon. No chance to change the past. I was stuck like every other mortal, with only one timeline and no alternate responses. It didn't feel fair. I wanted my do-over. I had come to expect this ability and felt cheated when I couldn't. Was I really about to through a temper tantrum like a two-year-old simply because I had to live a segment of my life in the original time sequence like the rest of the world?

Lurking in the back of my mind was a slow revelation that I had become spoiled. Maybe I was relying too much on magic and not enough on my own abilities. I didn't like contemplating the fact. So I didn't.

For the moment I would have to rely on my own witty resourcefulness, which were hovering on empty. I was a goner. The moment had passed and he was walking away. And still I stood there my jaw hanging open like a mouth breathing dweeb and nothing witty or smart or even audible came forth.

I started to make a frantic run to get the eraser in hopes there would be adequate time to redo the whole meeting.

I stopped short of the sprint when miraculously he turned back and gave me an unsure smile. "I know you're really busy and I have to get to a meeting myself, but maybe later, if you get your research done and you don't have to do anything else majorly pressing," and then he gave a self-conscience laugh, "What I'm trying to say, but not doing a very efficient job at, is would you like to, maybe, if you can find the time, go get some coffee—with me that is—later this evening?"

Stop, Lottie, I told myself. Think. Don't blow it. Just say yes. Keep it simple. Play it cool. "Sure, I'd love to. I only have a few hours of work. I'll be through by 8:30." Yep, I was so cool.

"Usually I'm not done in the theater until twelve or one when we are in production. But tonight is just a theater club meeting. We should be finished about 8:30."

I gave a smiling nod. I sure hoped I wasn't drooling on myself. Then ol' Mister Reality checked in. Why was I so elated? Nothing had changed. Sure now I would get to know Al Dansby, but that would only make things worse. He was still unobtainable and I was still ridiculously infatuated.

-17-

Nobody Ever Said That Life Was Fair

Waiting is one of those tiresome activities that takes no effort, yet still leaves you exhausted. So there I waited in the reading room of the library, for a coffee date with a guy that I sadly knew I had no future with. Yet, I anxiously waited still.

No research had been done after leaving him earlier at the library. Rather I had rushed back to the dorm for a quick wardrobe update, mouthwash, make-up touch-up and more deodorant for good measure.

"I thought you went to the library?" Stina said when she saw me back in the room. She and Rachel had just returned from a nutrition run to the grocery store, more cookie dough and Diet D.P.

"I'm going out for coffee with a guy."

"Well, finally. You've been here for four months and no dates. Not that they haven't been interested. So who is the lucky dude you finally consented to spend some time with?" asked Stina moving a pile of clothes off of her bed to sit down. It had taken a few dry runs to find the right outfit for coffee. One that said this is no big deal while at the same time making a statement that would last for a lifetime.

"I hadn't realized I was putting guys off. No one has asked." Okay actually a few had, but with a time manipulation I had rewritten those moments so that I wouldn't have to turn them down. But Stina didn't know that.

"Oh, some have been interested. But there just seemed to be a glass wall there. I've had the distinct feeling that there was a broken heart in your recent past," came the clairvoyant Rachel. "I'm glad you're willing to start disassembling that wall."

"Disassembling—who says disassembling?" Stina laughed. "Rachel sometimes I think you're morphing into a psych textbook."

"Well OMG, let me use some hip talk. Boom, boom chica boom," beat boxing Rachel began to do the worst imitation of a rap singer on the planet. "It's time for some major destruction to that invisible obstruction."

"Oh pleaaaase, no more," I moaned.

"I'll only stop if you tell me who the fortuitous young man is," said Rachel, as Stina mouthed the word fortuitous and rolled her eyes.

What would they say? The gay conversation had never happened. I had erased that. Now they would tell me again. How un-fortuitous. But I was not in the mood to listen to reason. I was going out with Al Dansby, gay or straight. Let them say what they wanted.

"Al Dansby," I finally choked out. I saw the quick look they exchanged. I wouldn't have noticed it if I hadn't known what was coming.

Strange how when you know what is coming, it often doesn't.

"Oh he's gorgeous," Rachel said.

"And a fantastic actor. I saw him last year in *Les Mis*. He was Marius. He was so awesome," chimed in Stina. "And a really nice guy. We've had a few classes together and he is always such a gentleman."

71

"I'm surprised he asked you out," said Rachel. Oh no, there it was. She was trying to think of a nice way to let me down easy. I gave her a questioning look. I didn't trust my voice to talk. "He never dates. I think it's because he's so shy," she continued. "That's a weird thing about him."

"You're right," Stina confirmed. "He can get up in front of hundreds of people and be magnificent, but one on one he really isn't very confident. He must really have the hots for you if he dredged up the nerve to ask you for coffee."

Where was the gay thing? I had avoided this guy for over a month because it wasn't possible and now all they say is he's shy?

"What time are you meeting him?" Stina asked.

A look at my cell for the time and I knew I'd better book it or be late. "Gotta go."

"Don't worry. We'll wait up," laughed Stina.

"Waiting for all the juicy details," added Rachel. "Just one thing Lottie. Don't say anything just yet to Olivia."

"Yeah, she has a few issues, as Rachel would say, with Al," said Stina.

Here it comes. The bad news. I looked to Rachel for affirmation.

"Yup, he's the only guy who ever blew her off." They both exchanged a knowing smile and I left on that note. Off to find out if maybe there could be a potential where none had been before.

Rounding the corner from the dorm I suddenly remembered I had forgotten my special eraser. I sure didn't want to go to such an important rendezvous without it. Hurrying back to the room, I was stopped by the conversation I heard through the door.

"Should we have told her?" It was Stina's voice.

"I just couldn't. She seemed so happy," replied Rachel. "Let's see how things go. Maybe she won't even like him."

"Sure, one cup of coffee and she might figure it out for herself," replied Stina, not bubbling for once.

I slowly withdrew my hand from the doorknob. So they did think he was gay after all. Half of me was angry that they hadn't been honest with me. The other half was grateful that at least I would have a chance to find out for myself. But as good or as bad as the evening would go, it wouldn't be done over. I wasn't about to go back in that room right then and know that they knew that I knew what they had been talking about.

So there I sat impatiently waiting in the library reading room. Trying to look nonchalant. Okay, he was five minutes late. That was fine. I hope I didn't look too eager. I checked my cell phone for important texts. There were none. I fiddled with it looking like I had important texts anyway.

Ten minutes late. How long did I wait? People kept passing by. I knew that they didn't know that I was waiting for a "date" that didn't seem to be coming. So why did they keep looking at me like I was pathetic? I had read all my emails, even the spam folder. Still no "date." Fifteen minutes. I should have scraped together whatever self-esteem I had left and slunk out of the stood-up date level of *The Inferno*. But then again maybe his meeting had run long and if I left he'd think I didn't like him and ruin everything. There was a war going on in my head and it was taking no prisoners. Then she came in—all long legs and flowing black hair. I tried to look very busy.

"So I told Al," she said loudly to her friend obviously forgetting she was in a library. However, I wasn't going to file a complaint as she had my undivided attention the minute she said Al. "I couldn't go with him and Butch tonight. I guess they went on without me."

Butch? Tonight?

73

"Oh, hi. I didn't see you over there in the corner," said Ms. Long Legs. "Are you okay? You look a little flushed."

I couldn't respond.

"Oh, cat got your tongue. Well, I'm Taylor and this is my BFF Taylor. Isn't that funny."

"We're both named Taylor," said Taylor number two, with shorter legs and definitely a nicer aura. "Isn't that ironic that we are best friends with the same name. We met the first day of school and it was like well, so easy to remember her name, cause, well it was my name." Taylor two laughed. Number one didn't. I had the feeling she had heard the story before. "In fact at last count I found fourteen people named Taylor here on campus. Girl Taylors and boy Taylors. And that's not counting the ones with Taylor as a last name."

Thing One cut her off, "So, now you know our names, and probably more than you wanted to know about our history. What is yours? And please don't say Taylor."

"Lottie, uh my name is Lottie," I finally stammered out. "Nice to meet you." My mother would be proud that all those manners she drilled into me as a child weren't wasted.

Thing Two was ready for a pleasant chat. Thing One simply gave a smug smile and started to walk on.

"Well Lottie, I guess we're going. Hope to see you around. Don't forget, my name is Taylor. Easy to remember," Thing Two added as she hurried to catch up with the alpha queen canine.

I guess eighteen minutes is how long I should have waited. I was replaced by a guy named Butch. It was time to quit waiting. Not just for the evening, but for good. The whole "romance" with Al Dansby was just a figment of my imagination and was not ever going to happen no matter

74

how many different time space realities I could create.

I was back to my dorm by nine and luckily the entire suite was empty. I grabbed my trusty eraser. It was time to undo this sad evening. "Do your stuff, my little friend." I instantly found myself standing outside my door, holding the doorknob, eavesdropping on a conversation between Rachel and Stina.

"Should we have told her?" It was Stina's voice.

"I just couldn't. She seemed so happy," replied Rachel. "Let's see how things go. Maybe she won't even like him."

"Sure, one cup of coffee and she might figure it out for herself," replied Stina, not bubbling for once.

My trusty friend had failed me. I couldn't go back far enough and undo the fact that I had told them about my not-to-be-date. Now I had an hour to kill. The library was definitely off the list. I went out the back door of the dorm thinking I'd go for a walk. It was too cold and windy. I went back in the dorm. Couldn't do laundry, as I would have had to go back into my room to get it first. Maybe one of the study rooms would be vacant— someplace to sit and be alone and feel sorry for myself. I was in the mood to throw myself the biggest pity party ever. It would make Mardi Gras look like a one-year-old's birthday party.

The basement study room was full of the K's cramming for a test. Gratefully they didn't see me looking in the door. I went up to the first floor. Busy also. No studying going on, just some couple making out. I guess when someone told them to get a room, they didn't clarify that it shouldn't be a study room. Seeing another happy couple was just great for my self-esteem bucket that already had a big hole in it and was leaking everywhere. Off to the second floor. Busy also. Since when did so many people in college start studying so much? Third floor. Finally a dark and deserted room.

I entered the room. No need to turn on the lights. Depression prefers the dark. It was the perfect place to let go and have a good cry. Wow, I must have been really upset. I was crying in stereo. No, someone else was crying too.

I asked the dumbest question on earth, "Are you okay?" Obviously if someone is crying they are not okay.

"I'll be fine in a minute," answered Olivia's voice from the corner. "Just don't turn on the lights right now."

We both sat and sniffled for a moment. I could smell the distinct aroma of alcohol in the tiny room. We all knew that Olivia was a social drinker. She wasn't unlike so many other college students I had met over the years. But tipsy on a Tuesday night at nine sitting alone in a study room, that is starting to sound more like a problem than a party. Finally I broke the ice. "Which of us is going to tell our tale of woe first?"

"You first," Olivia whispered.

"It's silly really. Here's the condensed version. I met a guy this evening that I've been trying to get to notice me for months. He suggested we meet later and go get coffee. Then he didn't show up, and the over-sensitive, pathetic loser that I am overreacted. So he changed his mind. Should have been no big deal. It was just coffee.

"Wow, saying it out loud really does show how pathetic I am. It was just coffee with a stranger," I concluded.

Olivia's response wasn't what I expected. "Yes, but he still hurt your feelings." Olivia paused for a moment and then continued. "Our feelings aren't always logical. Rachel's been helping me for the last two years come to grips with that. You're a romantic, Lottie. I could see that in you the first week we met. You love your literature with dashing men and happy

76

endings. You've lived your life in a family of happy endings. And I'm sure some day you'll get your happily-ever-after. You're kind and caring and you deserve it."

"Don't we all deserve a happily-ever-after?"

We sat in the silence a while longer until Olivia spoke. "A fairytale. That's it. We all grow-up thinking life is a fairytale. That is until someone ruins it for us. If you haven't noticed, I drink too much." She gave a sad snort of a laugh. "Rachel's been telling me that for a year now. But it helps. Not her telling me that. That doesn't do anything but make me feel worse about myself. The drinking helps, some."

"How?"

"Dulls the pain. If I drink enough it goes completely away. But just for a while. Then it comes back. Sometimes worse, cause I do stupid things when I'm drunk. I tend to hook up with any guy who comes along. Only the gay ones turn me down." She paused and then whispered, "Or the really nice ones."

The quietness returned. My gut reaction was to tell her everything would be fine. But for once in my life I kept my mouth shut. How did I know that everything would work out? I didn't even know what was wrong. I had a friend in high school whose sister died. He said the hardest thing was living on without her. The second hardest thing was putting up with all the concerned looks and unsolicited platitudes of how it was *God's will* and *it was all for some divine purpose*. He taught me that sometimes the most comforting words are the ones not spoken.

"It always comes back." Olivia was talking again. I'm not sure if she was actually talking to me or herself. "Maybe in a nightmare. Or just a sound. Smells also. There are just some smells that bring it back instantly."

"You've lost me there."

77

"You're so lucky," Olivia said with a little hiccup. I was beginning to realize she'd had more to drink than I had first thought.

"Everyone just sees the Beautiful Olivia Corazon. The Beautiful Olivia Corazon adored by every guy on the planet. They don't know that she's never had a guy that loved her. They only see the beauty on the outside. They don't realize that inside is just a broken little girl."

This conversation was going way deeper than I had expected. How could Olivia have anything tragic? She was perfect and every guy on campus would agree. Something bad was wrong. I thought seriously of going to find Rachel, but I didn't want to leave Olivia alone.

"I was happy until I was seven. I don't remember my dad. He left when I was so little. I don't remember him at all. He left. Just left." Again the silence entered the dark room. "My mom and I had each other. We were happy. Then *he* came along. My mom thought he was her knight in shinning armor. That lasted less than a year."

Olivia gave a gut-wrenching sob. "Lasted until she came back unexpected from Christmas shopping and caught him molesting her eight year old daughter. Wasn't the first time either. I was so scared. And he'd threatened me if I told. He didn't just threaten me. He threatened that he'd hurt my mom. And he told me she wouldn't believe me anyway. I was just a little girl. I didn't know what to do. I was so scared."

I was stunned, sickened, saddened. Nothing in my middle class, SUV, piano lessons world had prepared me for this. Sure I'd read stories about abused children. But they were other people. Not my friends. Not Olivia.

"My mom called my uncles and once they showed up, I never saw that perv again. I heard he was killed in a hit and run later that week. I know it was just a freak coincidence, but I still always wondered if my uncles had something to do with it. I never asked. They never told. All I knew was he could never come back." We sat in silence for a few more minutes when a tiny little girl's voice asked in whisper, "So why didn't I ever feel safe again?"

I knew I needed to say something. To give some sort of support. Instead I did what I always do in a crisis situation. The wrong thing. I just stared at her like she was a freak show attraction.

"Why did I just tell you that? The only person besides my family I've ever told was Rachel. Crap, I always say too much when I'm drinking. Now you'll be giving me those tragically sympathetic looks all the time. The walking on eggshells—oh so sorry for Olivia looks."

It wasn't what I was thinking. I was thinking how badly I wished I could fix things, go back to when she was eight and protect that sweet little innocent girl. But, she was already regretting baring her soul to me. Now every time she saw me she would know that I knew. Olivia had had enough hurt already in her life. At least I could fix that one thing.

"Olivia, your story is safe with me," I said as I waved the eraser.

The basement study room was filled with the K's. But, I had a much more important mission. I pulled out my cell phone and hit Rachel's number. Fortunately, she picked up.

"Olivia is in the third floor study room and she looks upset. Maybe you had better go talk to her."

"Thanks Lottie. I'll go right now. I'm just down the hall. This time of the year is always hard on her," Rachel said and hung up.

-18-

Perspective

"You never did tell me how your date went."

It was after midnight in our dorm room. I thought Stina was asleep until I heard her voice in the darkness. "With all the drama with Olivia, I forgot to ask how your date went. Sometimes I just lose my patience with Olivia and all her theatrics."

"Don't be too hard on her," I advised.

"Oh, come on Lottie. You're just too nice. I love Olivia, but she does bring a lot of her problems on herself. She goes out and gets drunk and then wonders why bad things happen. She needs to grow up."

I couldn't be too hard on Stina. Until my earlier chat with Olivia in the dark study room I would have agreed in an instant. Olivia on the surface was what all of us wish we could be. Beautiful beyond comparison with the ability to attract any guy she wanted. But the surface is only that, the surface. In the layers below she was still that terrified eight-year-old little girl who had no control over the horrifying events in her life. Had that loss of control made Olivia into the totally-in-control-of-all-guys person she had become?

How did I get that across to Stina without betraying a confidence that actually never happened for anyone but me?

"I think things go deeper. My mom always taught me to love people as much like Jesus as possible. It isn't optional. And the pricklier they are usually means the more hurting they are inside. The prickles stick both out and in. I used to get so frustrated with her when she said that. But the more I live, the more I know that everyone needs someone to give them unconditional love."

"Lottie, you're right. But can I just vent about it a little bit longer? I'll be nicer tomorrow," said Stina with a tiny bit of bubble coming back. "And by the way. Love that word prick-les." Stina was laughing again and I joined in. Guess that was a word from my childhood that didn't quite work anymore.

It was quiet again. Stina had distracted herself about Olivia and forgotten again about my not date. Good.

"So how was your date?" came a perky voice in the darkness.

"It didn't happen."

"Oh, sorry. What happened? Did you change your mind? Did Olivia's drama mess this up for you? I'm going to be mad all over again. This was so important to you. Does she ever think about how her problems screw-up everyone else's lives?"

"Simmer down missy. It wasn't Olivia's fault. I didn't see her until after the not date. He just didn't show up."

"Oh."

"Yeah."

"Bummer."

"Yeah."

"Maybe he got hung up at his meeting?"

"I waited eighteen minutes. I would have waited longer, but that Taylor with the black hair and long legs came in talking about how he had invited her to go with him and a friend and she had turned him down."

"Maybe you were the friend?"

"No. Butch."

"Oh." In the dark room a light was dawning in Stina's head. I knew it was coming now. "Well, it's good that you learned he was undependable before you got involved. He just wasn't the guy for you."

"No, you're right. Al Dansby was just a passing fantasy—not the guy for me." So why did not-the-guy from our not-date give me so much real hurt.

-19-

VIP Turkey Missing

Thanksgiving. A time of traditions. There were certain foods we only ever ate on that day, some sort of orange Jello with maraschino cherries, green bean casserole and sweet potatoes with pecans. Usually the pecan topping got eaten off and the sweet potatoes left behind. The irony about the menu was that everyone complimented the dishes, yet we never served them any other day except on Thanksgiving Day.

Then there was family. My brother Jason and three teammates were home only for the day before returning back to Norman and practice. Jennifer and Jessica, a.k.a the twins, had been thrilled for ten minutes when I got home late Tuesday evening, but I hadn't seen them for more than fifteen minutes at a time as their social schedules were packed. Their past two hours had been consumed with finding inventive ways to attract the attention of our brother's friends. The rest of the usual suspects began arriving by 10:30 in the morning.

Uncle Harold was there. He's the one never to stand too close to, as he spits when he talks. On the other side of the living room was his ex-wife, Aunt Maude. They were divorced over fifteen years before, but in our family once you're family you're always family. So at every family function they both would come and pretend the other wasn't there. And we all pretended that everything was fine. Hey, it's awkward but it worked.

Next to Uncle Harold was his new wife, Vanessa. Okay they had been married fifteen years—do the math and understand the situation—but in family vocabulary she would always be the new wife. And she wouldn't ever be *Aunt Vanessa*, just Vanessa, "new wife."

People kept arriving: cousins, second cousins, cousins twice removed on Fridays with a full moon, friends and sometimes I suspected complete strangers who heard that the Lamberts put out a great spread on holidays. Hey, if the Obamas can have gatecrashers at their parties, the Lamberts could too. But none were the notorious relative I desperately needed to see. In all my years, she had never missed a family occasion, yet that was the Thanksgiving Crazy (or maybe not so Crazy) Aunt Charlotte decided to go AWOL.

By noon there were around twenty relatives gathered in the den watching the football game and too many cooks helping to spoil the broth in the kitchen. My mother was in a panic because the turkey wouldn't get done and was receiving every imaginable sort of unwanted advice on remedies for the situation.

"Maybe we could stick it in the microwave," was Vanessa's suggestion. Obviously Uncle Harold hadn't married her for her cooking skills. One look at her cleavage and it didn't take a rocket scientist to figure that one out.

"Humph," was Aunt Maude's thought on Vanessa's culinary input and most anything else about Vanessa to be truthful. "Just turn the heat up to four-fifty. It'll get done sometime. What time did you put it in?"

To escape that brewing discussion I decided to wander to the front door once more and check for my crazy aunt's arrival. She still wasn't there. On into the den. There were plates of *hor d'oevoures* everywhere. I didn't understand why my mom was stressed about getting dinner on the table. Nobody was going to starve in the Lambert household that day.

My dad scooted over to make room for me on the couch. "Lottie, have a seat and enjoy the game with us. I've barely talked with you since you got home. How do you like your new school?"

"There are parts of it I love and others . . ." at which point I was interrupted with shouts of "TOUCHDOWN!!!!"

"Sure didn't see that coming so quick," my dad said.

"That boy can just fly down the field," added Uncle Harold. Soon everyone was giving his own play-by-play and color commentary. I decided to wander on to another spot.

It was like my family knew at birth that I would be the odd-man-out. My parents, Julie and Julius, named my brother Jason and the twins Jennifer and Jessica. I'm Lottie. What, were there no "J" names left on the planet? My mother always tried to placate me with, "But, honey, Lottie was always my favorite name." That doesn't work when you're ten and being constantly reminded by the other J. Lamberts, and equally observant people in the community, that you are an L. I felt like I should have had a big scarlet "L" on my forehead for Loser Lambert.

There were a lot of ways I never fit with my family. I didn't like football. That could be termed blasphemous in Oklahoma. Nothing against sports, I just didn't get the point. Why was so much time and effort, not to mention money, put into moving a ball past another person to get it to a pre-specified location, while normal everyday people morphed into raving lunatics in the stands as if their shouts could change the outcome of the game? Needless to say, a significant portion of my childhood was spent with me whining as my family was packing off to see my siblings in yet another of their ballgames or gymnastic meets always in search of the next competition.

Maybe that was the problem. I wasn't competitive. My brother's room was filled with trophies and plaques. The twins also had their share of medals, certificates and newspaper photos and clippings. Me—nada, never. In my entire life I had never won anything.

To be completely honest I hardly ever entered anything that could be won. I contemplated so many times entering the writing contests at our library or my school, but was terrified the judges would laugh at my work. As long as I kept it too myself, I could always believe that I was a fabulous author.

I guess I was competitive after all. It slowly dawned on me that I needed to give my family a break about their sports obsessions. We all had things that we felt passionately about. They just weren't the same. That didn't make the other person's passion any less justified. Sadly it had taken me twenty years to start to understand that concept.

I wasn't having the most thankful attitude that Thanksgiving and decided it was time to make a mental adjustment. My life was good. My family loved me, even if I didn't fit in perfectly. I had my health. I had my new friends at school. I had shiny manageable hair, and if I listened to commercials that was crucial for a happy life.

"Turkey's done," came the shout from the kitchen. Wow, I must have been at my private pity party for an extended length of time or Aunt Maude had turned the oven up to the nuclear blast setting.

"Can we wait for half-time to eat?" asked my dad.

Oh no, here it came. "Julius Andrew Lambert," my mother said. Including the middle name. "I have cooked for three days to get this feast together! You can TiVo that game! It's not OU playing! It's not that important!"

"I was just giving you a hard time dear. We're coming," said my father. Would he never learn that there are just some things that were not joking material? My mother's Thanksgiving dinner was top of that list.

***

We all ate more than we should have and then had seconds. Pig fest. It was great.

With the men folk back at the TV, the womenfolk began the cleanup ritual. Equal rights would never exist on Thanksgiving Day.

Mom was digging in her stash of old Cool-Whip containers to find enough to store all the leftovers, while Aunt Maude was filling the sink with hot, sudsy water. Every year she and Mom would have an argument about the dishes. Aunt Maude was a rinser. One of those who practically washed the dishes before she put them in the dishwasher. Mom believed that was why you bought a dishwasher—to wash the dishes. Mom was a scraper. Just scrape them and put them in. Let the machine do the work. Rinsers and Scrapers do not work well with each other. We needed a distraction before the confrontation began.

"Where was Aunt Charlotte this year?" I asked.

"Now, that's strange," said my mom, head still submerged in the bottom storage cabinet searching for containers. "She never misses a holiday. Did anyone hear from her?"

"She's so spacey, maybe she's doing the holidays on the moon this year?" giggled Jennifer.

"Or with some tribe in Africa?" added Jessica. "Oh, mom that's my phone ringing. Can I please have it back now? Please. Dinner is over." My mom had confiscated the Double J's cell phones before the meal in order to have a call/text free meal. She reluctantly gave the girls back their lifelines to civilization.

Suddenly the kitchen seemed claustrophobic. Jason and friends had entered. "Mom, just wanted to tell you goodbye," said Jason putting on his coat.

"It was a great meal Mrs. Lambert. Thanks for including us," said one of the teammates while the others nodded in agreement.

"Do you have to go already?" Mom asked, knowing that they did.

"We have a team meeting first thing tomorrow to view some films."

"Mom, that was Jeremy on my phone. He was wanting me to come over to his house later for dessert," said Jessica.

"Well, you better go. There's not much food here," said my mom. I doubt she meant the sarcasm to show as much as it did.

With that all my siblings were out the door. The room filled with aunts, friends and Vanessa suddenly felt empty—lonely. And for a second I saw a sadness in my mother's eyes I'd never noticed before. It gave me a Rachelesque insight. We were all leaving her. Even on holidays there was no time for mom. Jason couldn't even come home for more than the time it took to inhale a meal and the twins couldn't stay in place much longer. Life moved on too fast. For a brief second I saw through my mom's eyes— toddlers and tweens and teenagers going through her life. Then we were all but grown-up. And gone.

"Happy Thanksgiving, Mom," I told her as I gave her a spontaneous hug.

"Thanks baby," she said, almost in tears. "You know you always were my favorite." Once again the kitchen was full of laughter. That was a Lambert tradition. We all were my mother's favorites.

"And you were always my favorite too," I replied.

-20-

Unreality vs Reality - Reality Zip

"It was a nice day," my dad said later as just Mom, Dad, and I sat in the den by the fire. All the various relatives had left. The dishes were done. The enormous amount of leftovers had been put away or given away.

"Yes it was," said my mom as she sipped her cup of tea. "I think next year for Thanksgiving we'll go on a cruise and let someone else do the cooking."

"You said that last year," I reminded my mom.

"And the year before," Dad added. "Well, I'm all tuckered out. It was a hard day of eating and watching football and then eating some more. You womenfolk don't stay up all night gabbing," Dad said as he made his exit.

"This is the nicest part," said mom. "I'm so glad you're home Lottie Bug."

"I haven't heard that name in a while," I said with a smile.

"Come sit close and I'll share my afghan with you."

I moved over on the sofa with my mommy, just like I was three again. Life was a lot easier then.

"I feel like we're in one of those coffee commercials," I laughed.

"So, Lottie Lambert, decaf or regular?" my mom played along. "Seriously, I've missed you. I thought after two and a half years I'd get used to you not being here all the time. But some days I just miss you more."

"I miss you too, Mom. Especially when I have to do my own laundry or eat cafeteria food."

"It's been so crazy since you got home. Now we have peace and quiet. And at least an hour before the Double J's get home. So, tell me about your new school. Have you made new friends? Do you like your classes?"

"Yes, I have made some wonderful friends. Yes, I do like my classes. You already knew all that from phone calls and texts. Ask what you really want to know."

"Okay, have you met any cute guys? Did you ever get to talk to that one you thought was really hot? What was his name?"

"I've met lots of cute guys. Just not the right one."

"Lottie, you've got to give them a chance."

"I know mom. I just don't want another episode like I had with the skank at OU. I'm making sure this time not to get hurt."

"I guess it is time for some wise momma words. I heard this saying once. I don't know, maybe it's a famous quote. But, it is some good advice. 'A ship in a harbor is safe. But that's not what ships are made for.' Lottie Bug, you've got to step out there and live your life, whether it is to find Mr. Right or just meet some nice guy and have fun. Not every guy is deceitful and malicious like that jerk at OU. Some are pretty special, like your dad."

"My daddy sure is special." I was thinking of poor Olivia and how evil in the form of her stepfather had shattered her innocence. I wanted so badly to confide this with my mother, but I couldn't. It wasn't my story to share. It was a conversation that had never happened and yet it weighed on my heart every time I looked at my beautiful suitemate—which made me all the surer that it was better that she didn't know that I knew. What a burden it must be: not just the horribleness of having a tragedy in life, but to be constantly reminded of it by the over-sympathetic and pitying looks that surround your everyday.

"Lottie, what's wrong? You look heartbroken." Yes, it was better for me not to know, as every thought I ever had instantly played itself out on my face. A poker player I would never be.

"I'm okay, Mom. Just a sad thought. You know my transparent face better than anyone."

"Now my little tugboat, who is this guy you definitely don't like and will never go out with?"

And so I told her about Al Dansby, trying to make sure I only told the things that had happened in our current reality. Which wasn't much. Because of the do-overs all that had really transpired between us was him helping my mother get my granny panties out of a tree, and him asking me out for coffee and not showing up. Not much of a love story in our current time sequence. What I couldn't tell my mom was the spark of electricity there had been as our eyes met for the first time, before the flying spaghetti. Or how gallantly he picked up my books and the kindness in his words before Taylor announced that my pants were unzipped. Or how beautiful his voice was as we ordered coffee together in the student center. Those wonderful encounters that set my heart racing should have been the beginning to our happily-ever-after, yet they were just part of a fairytale that never happened.

When I finished my short narration, my mother had a perplexed look on her face.

"Oh," she said. "I'd say he seems nice, but I guess not, as he stood you up. I'm just confused, Lottie. Not much to him but one conversation."

Right then I decided to explain to my mom about the magic eraser. If anyone would believe me, she would. If I could explain to her how I kept redoing bad situations, she'd understand.

But she wouldn't. No sane person could ever understand. It was just too farfetched. Only a crazy person could believe it, and she hadn't shown up for lunch.

"You're right mom. He's just a drop dead gorgeous guy who doesn't have the common decency to tell me if he's not going to show up for coffee. Who knows, he's probably gay anyway."

On that my mom gave a rip snort laugh. "Oh, Lottie. That's a different prospective. I hear the garage door. The girls must be home." And as usual, the moment they returned the world quit revolving around me, and went back into its *proper* rotation around the twins.

-21-

Empty Platitudes and Purses

The break ended too fast as always. The weekend had been taken up with an Oklahoma sacrament, the annual OU/OSU football game. My family made the holy pilgrimage to Norman without me. Although I did want to enjoy the tailgating festivities and see my OU friends, I just didn't feel like seeing the ex-boyfriend or enduring the know-all looks from his friends. A quiet weekend of catching up on term papers and Lifetime movies was more therapeutic. Wounds were healing, but it would take more than six months to recover from the ex's deceit.

I returned to campus in panic mode, as there were only two weeks of school left to finish papers and finals. My first evening back major trauma erupted in the K's suite that had nothing to do with boys or clothes—a rare occurrence.

"No, no, NOOOOOOO!!!!" screamed Kyra. "It just can't be!"

We all ran out into the hallway to see what had happened. Who had died? Who had been dumped? Was it rapture time and we'd all been left?

Kyra sat slumped in the floor of the hall cradling her laptop like an infant. The other K's surrounded her with empty platitudes and words of sympathy.

"I can't believe it," Kyra sobbed. "Not a week before finals. It just can't be."

Kasha asked what the rest were too afraid ask. "Did you have your files backed up?"

"No." And then came the loudest sob of all. I discreetly slunk back into my room. Kyra needed space during this time of mourning. What we all hoped would never happen, yet we always knew could, had become a reality for poor, poor Kyra. Her computer had crashed and she had lost all her term papers.

I looked over at Stina. She was frantically inserting a memory stick into her laptop. "There but for the grace of God go I," she said. "It's backup time." I quickly followed her example. I felt bad that Kyra didn't have a magic eraser too. But wait, maybe I could help her out. Where was mine? I'd rewind the last hour and just nonchalantly remind her to back her computer up and *voila* she wouldn't lose all her work after all. I reached in my bag for my trusty friend. Not there. Wrong purse, I remembered. I'd put it in my red one when I went home for the break. Red purse. Red purse. Where was my red purse? I would not have a meltdown. It had to be there somewhere.

"Have you seen my red purse?" I asked Stina.

"Not recently. Let's see, I borrowed it two weeks ago to take to that party. But, I brought it back. I promise I did. I did, didn't I?" Stina said losing confidence the more she spoke. She jumped up and started pulling dirty clothes out of the bottom of her closet searching for the purse that only thirty seconds before she was sure she had returned.

I was doing likewise in my closet. There was that black cami I had been looking for and somehow my silver hoop earring was in there too.

But no red purse.

"I'm trying to remember. Yeah, you did. I used it last week. Think. Think. Think, what did I wear it with?" I mused. "I used it on Monday."

"Yeah, it gave just the right pop of color with your black pants and jacket," said Stina suddenly channeling Stacey on *What Not To Wear*.

"I remember, I was so pleased with how that outfit turned out, I took it home to wear on Thanksgiving. But, then I went with jeans and a hoodie. It was just one of those kind of days."

"The big question here. What did you do with it when you got back?" prodded Stina.

I grabbed my car keys and started for the door to go and look if it was still in the trunk. Then it hit me. I didn't bring it back. It was all still hanging in my closet at home. No red purse. No magic eraser. No way, no how could I fix Kyra's computer disaster.

The look on my face must have been horrific because Stina said, in her most comforting tone, "It'll be okay Lottie. You can borrow my Coach knock-off if you want. I know it's fake, but most people never realize it."

I was texting my mom before Stina could finish her generous offer of the loan of her most favorite accessory. Ding went my phone. My mom had texted me back. Yes, my purse was there. She'd keep it safe for the next two weeks until I came home for Christmas. Ding came her next answer. No she would not drive it the three hours to school. I could just use one of my ten other purses.

Two weeks. I sat on my bed stunned. Until three months before I never even imagined the ability to redo life's mistakes. Without it I felt like a Greek god who had become mortal. How could I cope? I was afraid to leave the safety of the dorm without my trusty friend. I didn't have six hours to spare from studies and finals to drive home and get the eraser. I tried to figure out the math. If I did over part of the time, it wouldn't make any difference. A six-hour round drive was still a six-hour round trip, no matter how magical my school supplies were.

"Woe, you must really be attached to that purse. You look like you lost your best friend," said Stina with a nervous giggle. I must have had a scary, tragic look on my face. It was time to get a grip. I could survive a short time in the present. I'd just have to be very careful where I went. What I did. Who I talked to. Oh crap! That had never worked for me before. I doubted it would work then.

-22-

Being Mortal
Once Again

Of course I overslept the next morning and headed out for class in the first thing I could find to throw on—dirty yoga pants and a hoodie. I was such a fashion statement in the making. I slunk into *Señora Aburrida's* class five minutes late realizing I had the wrong notebook.

"*Señorita Lambert. Buenos días. ¿Porque estás tarde? ¿Siempre estás aquí temprano?*"

I had no idea what she was saying. I just smiled and said, "*Sí.*" Half of the class died laughing. The other half looked as confused as me. When I had had my little pink friend I had gotten into the habit of waiting until someone translated and then rewound class so I could look like I understood. To be honest I wasn't learning much Spanish, just how to be quick on the draw with the redos.

Things progressed in much the same pattern throughout the day. Perhaps I had grown just a little codependent on my pink helper? I had become lazy at watching what I did or said as I could always fix my mistakes. For the next week and six days (not that I was counting, of course) I would have to be ever vigilant.

After my disaster of a Spanish class, I headed back to the dorm in hopes of a quick shower and clothes that didn't smell of a two-week-old workout. Hurrying, as I didn't have much time for a miracle transformation, I didn't see him coming until we were face to face. Sweet Mother of Pearl, he looked good. I didn't. Nowhere to hide. No way to change things. But it didn't matter as "Morning," was all Al Dansby said and then he walked on by.

I pondered that encounter for the rest of the day and then the night. What had that one word meant, "Morning." By the next day at lunch Stina, Rachel, and I had analyzed and dissected that brief encounter to every subatomic particle.

"I think he was just embarrassed about standing you up for your coffee date," was Rachel's diplomatic hypothesis.

Stina kept insisting, "You looked so bad, he didn't recognize you."

"But he sounded miffed. Or almost disappointed. He was the one who didn't show up, not me. What would he have to be all huffy about? He didn't sit there for eighteen minutes and then have that skanky Taylor come in. . ." Oops. Had I said too much? Taylor had only come in the first reality not the second because in the second I never went. Fortunately everyone was too busy hypothesizing on Al's "morning" that they weren't listening to me anyway.

"Maybe he had just been running late. He said he had a meeting. They always go over," said Rachel still trying to be the peacemaker.

"But then he could have asked someone if they saw you. How long would he have expected you to wait?" countered Stina.

"Maybe he sent word with someone and they couldn't find you," said Rachel.

Or maybe they did find me, but being the warm fuzzy soul that she wasn't, she didn't tell me. Was it just me, or had Taylor made a point of talking loudly about Al and Butch when she knew I was there? Could she be so deceitful that if Al had asked her to tell me he was running late, she wouldn't tell me? Yes, yes she could. Then all of the sudden I had another epiphany. I had shown up the first time. But then I did it over and I never went. Maybe he came later and I wasn't there. Originally I had talked with Taylor, which I had almost just blurted out to my friends, but then I hadn't. She could have reported back to him that I wasn't there. And ironically she was telling the truth. Anyone he might have asked would have reconfirmed that I wasn't there. With my little flick of an eraser I had changed from being the stood-up-y to the stood-up-er and probably had erased any chance of being asked out for coffee with Al Dansby ever again.

-23-

Just Six More

Six more days until Christmas break started and I hadn't had too many major catastrophes. Just four tests left to do and OKMU's annual Christmas dance to attend. Then I was off for the next four weeks to eat fudge and recuperate.

"So, what are you going to wear?" Stina asked for the third time. "I'm wearing this little black dress I borrowed from the K's. Not sure which one it actually belongs to. Don't think they know anymore. They're all the same size and they seem to just have a community closet. Maybe you could go find something down there?"

A school-wide dance was still a novelty to me. (Dorothy, you ain't at the state school anymore.) I hadn't made plans to go. Since it was my first year at OKMU, I hadn't realized that it was the social event of the year.

"No date. No dress. I think I should just stay here and study. I have finals all next week. I need to study," came my insecure, self-pitying reply.

It didn't work with Stina. "Grow-up girlfriend. WWJAD?"

"What would Jesus Do?" I asked very confused, as I don't remember Jesus ever going to a Christmas dance even though it is His birthday.

"No, silly. What Would Jane Austin Do? Or Emily and Charlotte

Bronte? Make your heroes proud. Be a real woman. Go without a man."

"Easy for you to say. You have a date," came my whiny reply.

"And so do you," said Rachel to the rescue as she came in our room. "My date, Trevor, has a brother, Will, who is coming to visit for the weekend and needs a date. I know it's last minute, but we can double. It'll be fun."

"Moldy cheese and stale crackers, I've hit the bottom of the loser barrel. A last minute blind date!"

"It will be fun," Rachel insisted.

Stina joined in. "He can't be too bad. Trevor's a sweetheart. Everyone loves Trevor. I'm sure his brother is great too."

"It will be fun. We'll be together," Rachel kept insisting.

***

Oh yeah, it was fun. Nobody ever bothered to mention that he was sixteen and still in high school. Now four years between the ages of twenty and twenty-four isn't a big deal, between forty and forty-four is nothing. Between sixteen and twenty? The Grand Canyon. So there I stood next to Mr. High School, zits and all, trying to make a conversation that didn't make me sound like a geriatric asking the kiddy about what he wanted to be when he grew up,

I'd spent the day trying to study for a Spanish exam that I knew I was going to fail, while Olivia and Stina tried to work a miracle on me. They did a fairly good job as fairy godmothers. I had on Olivia's emerald green, perfect for a Christmas dance, Free People flowy gown. Stina had put my hair in some amazing bun-like creation, with just the right amount of wispy hairs loose. A look in the full-length mirror and I was delighted. Maybe it was a good thing that Rachel and Stina had convinced me to go to the dance after all. I felt like a princess until the toad showed up with his brother.

As they had said, Trevor was a sweetheart of a guy. Notice no one ever described him as handsome, because he wasn't. A little overweight. A computer nerd. But with such an outgoing fun personality, he was liked by all. His brother was his spitting image *sans* the fun personality and the liked by all. Whoever said "two out of three ain't bad" never met my date.

"Ain't there no beer here?" were his first words entering the dance. "I thought that college parties always had kegs."

"I'm sure there is some hidden somewhere, but aren't you sixteen?" I gently reminded him. I was not about to get arrested for encouraging the delinquency of a minor.

"Freak," (Okay he didn't really say freak, but there are some words I just won't repeat.) "What kind of college party ain't got no beer?"

"A classy one," came Trevor's reply. "For once Will, just shut-up and have some fun. I didn't bring you here to get plastered. You could have done that at home standing out in a cow pasture with your so-called friends."

I sensed a reoccurring family conversation and thought that it would be a prudent moment to walk over to see the K's, giving Trevor and Will some quality brother time.

The K's all looked fabulous. Who would have known that just two hours before they were all frantically changing and re-changing their dresses for the optimal wow factor.

"Yes Kaylee, your cleavage looks alluring without looking slutty," Kasha was saying as I approached.

"Hey Lottie, you look awesome," they turned in unison and said. It was always scary when they did that one combined mind thing.

"So how is the blind date?' Kyra asked. "Is he a hunk?"

At that moment I felt a clammy hand on my bare shoulder that started to work it's way down my back. I tried to step away and bumped into Kyra.

"Hey, babe," (Did he actually just call me babe, like some lamo seventies movie?) "Thought I'd lost you. Now who are these luscious ladies?" asked Will, AKA my date from hell.

I spent the next hour dodging groping hands and cliché dialogue. It was time to fake a headache and leave the party. Hiding behind one of the numerous Christmas trees decorating the ballroom, I was desperately devising an excuse to leave, **without** my date. Glad we hadn't driven there, as heaven only knows what he thought he could get off a college woman in a car.

"Do you always hide behind the shrubbery?" came the voice of my daydreams and my nighttime fantasies. There he stood, looking straight at me. I think he had a suit on. I'm sure he was dressed. But I couldn't take my eyes off of his magnificent green eyes. There was a twinkle there that wasn't just the reflection of the Christmas tree lights.

"I was just admiring," your eyes almost came out of my mouth. Quick save. "I was just admiring the ornaments on the tree," I said never looking at the tree.

"Yes, they are amazing," he responded, not looking at the tree either. Then he smiled that mischievous but shy little boy smile that made my toes curl and other parts do unmentionable things. "I love Christmas. And Christmas trees."

"And ornaments." Was it me or had time simply frozen around us as we were partaking in the most wonderful, stimulating, witty conversation I had ever heard?

"I'm glad to have found you here tonight," he broke eye contact. I could breath again. "I wanted to talk with you about the other night at the library. . ."

"Hey, date! There you are. 'Bout never found you over here behind this here tree," interrupted Will as he flung a proprietary arm around my shoulder.

Al's beatific smile disappeared. "Oh sorry," he stammered. "I see you're busy. Well, Merry Christmas," he wished me with all the joy of Scrooge before he spent the night with the ghosts of Christmas past/present/future.

Back home in a red purse in my closet was a simple eraser that could fix the entire situation. But it was back home in a red purse in my closet and not in my hand. Instead, I watched helplessly as he walked away. The room was a swirl of colorful dresses, sequins, and Christmas decorations. All I saw was his retreating black suit. It simply couldn't get any worse.

But it did.

What was Taylor of the long legs doing? She was dangling some sort of greenery over Al's head. Mistletoe. No, she couldn't. No, he wouldn't. But she did. And he did too. And it wasn't any little peck. Then there were cheers and catcalls.

The party was over for me.

Merry Christmas Lottie Lambert. After I had blown my chance with Mr. Dansby it turns out he definitely wasn't gay after all.

-24-

Have Yourself a Merry Little Christmas Not

"I thought the new school was supposed to make her happy," came Jennifer's voice through our adjoining wall. All these years and those two still didn't acknowledge that I could hear everything they said from their room to mine.

"She seemed happy at Thanksgiving. Maybe she F'd her finals," answered Jessica. "Bummer she didn't meet some hunk and fall head over heels and forget the loser from OU."

"Hey is that my nail polish? I didn't say you could use it. Ooo but it does look great," said Jennifer, distracted by shiny fingernails. That's the Double J's. Sweet girls, but easily off task where shiny objects, or nails, were involved.

Wake-up call to Lottie. It was time to quit moping around the house. I hadn't realized I was such a downer. Time to put on a happy face. My mom had worked too hard to make Christmas Christmas for me to ruin it.

I hadn't had a chance to talk with Mr. Dansby before I left. He seemed to have dropped off the planet after his passionate display with skank girl. I only caught a glance of him once and wished I hadn't. He was busy trying to cram Taylor's luggage into the back of his tiny Miata. Mission accomplished and then the two of them drove off into the sunset. And I climbed into my reliable old Camry and headed for home.

"Hey Lottie Bug," came my mom's voice, drawing me back from my sad reverie. "I've got to run to the mall for two more gifts I forgot. Go with me. We'll have fun." And we did. It's hard to stay unhappy around my mom at Christmastime. She kept me as busy as a mother of sextuplets without a reality show for the next two weeks. We shopped and lunched. We wrapped gifts and delivered cookie baskets. We gathered around the piano and sang Christmas carols and then drank hot chocolate by the fire. Home was good. Maybe I was just the normal middle child, but my mom could make even normal children feel special.

By New Year's Eve, I was tired. Over the holidays I had seen every relative ever invented, except the one I needed, Aunt Charlotte.

"Mom, I think I'm going to skip the church's New Year's party."

"Are you okay, Lottie? You're not getting sick are you? I heard that the neighbor boy has strep. I saw you out there talking with him two days ago. I hope you don't have strep. Although if you have to be sick that is a good one to get, because you can get an antibiotic and be well in just twenty-four hours."

"Whoa, mom. I'm not sick. Just tired. Maybe a little melancholy."

My sweet, loving, intuitive mother nodded. "I understand. After a while it gets old being the one with no one to kiss at midnight. Been there done that. But it will happen," she said giving me a hug. "I thought I'd never meet your daddy. I was an old maid of twenty-two when he finally came along." She laughed. "But, I'm glad I waited. He was worth the wait. And you'll see. When the right one comes along he'll be worth all those

106

lonely midnight countdowns."

But what if he had already come along? Maybe even a few times. But I had done it over to the point it would never happen.

***

The weeks before Christmas had been full of activities and festivities. After the new year began everyone went back to their old routine. Jason had only come home for Christmas Eve and Day and then went back to his apartment in Norman. For all practical purposes he no longer lived at home. The Double J's had to go back to their last semester of high school on the second of January. They were not pleased that their break had ended so abruptly, but were over-the-moon excited about finishing high school. They couldn't wait to head off to OU the next fall. Dad was back at work. I'm not sure if he ever mentally left it. Mom was between jobs at the moment. Her current plan was to become an interior decorator. She had taken a few classes at the local junior college. It was a phase. Before that she had taught school, worked in a bank, ran a tutoring agency, worked in a daycare, sold make-up, even cleaned houses while putting my dad through his MBA. I asked her when I was little why she changed careers so much. Usually I got some vague answer about being bored, or wanting a higher salary. Once when I was twelve I asked again, and demanded a real answer.

"Do you really want to know Lottie? Why do you want to know?" She had answered my question with questions.

"You seem pretty good at so many things, but you never seem to stick with it until you get really good at it," I answered and then realized as usual, I had hurt her feelings. "I'm sorry mom. I didn't mean that you aren't good at things, it's just that . . . Well,"

"It's okay Lottie Bug. You're very perceptive as usual. To be honest,

107

I'm not sure what I want to be. Okay, that's not totally true. I know the one thing. But it's not culturally acceptable."

Oh no. My mom wanted to be a stripper or worse. I wasn't sure if I wanted to know anymore, but I had to ask. "What?"

"What I really wanted to be was a mother. You know like June Cleaver -- please tell me you've heard of her." All I could give her was a blank look. I didn't think that she went to our church and I knew there was no Mrs. Cleaver at school. "Okay, bad example. Let me explain. Once upon a time. . ." That earned her a very teenagerish eye roll. "Women got married, had babies and then stayed home and took care of them. Sometimes that was wonderful. Sometimes that was very hard, because they didn't have money, or they didn't like the whole motherhood gig. Women couldn't get good jobs. Mothers in bad marriages had to stay in them because there was no way they could earn a decent living and take care of their kids."

"I know mom. We studied the Middle Ages in school. What's that got to do with you?"

"It wasn't just in the middle ages. Fifty years ago it was like that in America. Back in your grandma's day. But I grew up in the seventies. Peace, love all that. I never knew a time when girls couldn't get a job or even wear pants to school."

"What are you talking about? Wear pants to school? Did they go naked?" I laughed at my witty tween self.

"How quickly things are forgotten. Your grandma had to wear dresses to school. They had all kinds of complicated rules about it having to be at a certain temperature before they could wear pants. And get this," she laughed, "No one wore jeans!"

"Prehistoric! But mom what has that got to do with you and a job?

You weren't born in grandma's day. You could do any job you wanted."

"That was the problem. The pendulum had swung so far the other way that any educated girl felt she had to have a career. Stay home moms were seen as lazy parasites."

"Harsh."

"Okay, maybe not that bad. But almost. I had a degree. I was a motivated individual. I should go out into the workforce everyday and leave my babies in a daycare. That worked great for a lot of my friends, but not for me. I always felt torn in two. When I was at work I worried about my babies. When I was at home I worried about work. Ever since Jason was born I've been trying to find the happy medium. The perfect job that also lets me be the perfect mother. Needless to say I haven't found it yet. In the process I think I've driven your poor father crazy."

"Didn't have far to drive." We both gave a conspiratorial laugh. "Don't worry, Mom. Soon we'll all be grown. Then you can have a great career with no kids at home to worry about."

The look on my mother's face that January second, as my twin baby sisters set out for their first day of their last semester of high school, reminded me that my mom was about to retire from her favorite career, motherhood.

"Let's go do Starbucks," she said as she watched the Double J's pull away from the house. "I need some strong caffeine."

-25-

It Was A Dark & Stormy Night

It was sleety and windy moving back into the dorm the middle of January. Ice was beginning to cover all the roads—and every other surface for that matter. I was glad I had made it back to OKMU before it had become too treacherous. Hopefully it wouldn't ice so badly that it knocked out the electricity. That was common in Oklahoma ice storms, and life without the big E could quickly become the big B—boring.

I made it to the main door of my dorm just as it was opening. Good thing as I had my arms full of clean clothes. Bad thing, it was being held by Mr. Dansby himself and I wasn't the only one he was holding it for. Right behind me was old Thing One—Taylor.

"Oo, thanks Al. I didn't think your little bitty car was going to make it through this sleet. That sure was an adventure," she all but purred. I was confused, because I thought her kind barked.

"Thanks," I murmured as I slid through the door.

"Lottie? Is that you behind those clothes?" he asked. "Did you have trouble driving? I'm glad you made it okay. I. . ."

Standing there in the freezing cold I felt warmer than I had in weeks. Our eyes locked and once again I felt I could believe in instant love.

Instantly that beautiful moment was shattered as Taylor slithered between us. "Who is your friend, Al? I don't think we've ever met. I'm Taylor."

"Lottie," was all that came out of my mouth.

"Oh my lord, aren't you the girl whose undies went flying in the wind the first day of school? Al, don't you remember that? We were walking across campus and saw some lady frantically chasing them all over the place. We laughed so hard." Taylor was laughing not at the story, but at me. Al looked like he would prefer to be back out in the sleety storm permanently over being a hostage between the two of us in Asbury Hall.

That just couldn't be happening. I was embarrassed enough for myself, but strangely more empathetic for how Al felt as he stood there awkwardly holding the door open as if looking for an escape. He'd already made it clear with that infamously passionate kiss under the mistletoe, which was forever seared in my mind, that he preferred Taylor over me. I'd just use my magic and help out. No use both of us being miserable. I could be miserable enough for two on my own. My hand reached in my pocket. My trusty eraser did its stuff.

It was sleety and windy. I would just stay in my car a few minutes longer. No need to hurry. There they were. Miata pulled up. Taylor and Al up the steps. Door open. Door closed. Wait five minutes. Al back out the door. Back in the Miata. Little red Miata pulled away. Time to get out of the car and start another semester at OKMU.

-26-

That's The Night The Lights Went Out In Oklahoma

Cozy. That was one way of describing it. A typical Oklahoma ice storm. No electricity, no idea how long it would be off. The only heat to be found in our four-story building came from the one lone fireplace in the parlor, a plethora of lit candles (in a building where fire code stated that candles were illegal) and the hot air from some two hundred girls gossiping. Without electricity what else could they do?

Classes didn't start for another day still, so a party atmosphere was prevalent in Asbury Hall. Stina had organized an impromptu spades tournament next to the fire. The volleyball team was staying warm with an indoor volleyball match in the basement hallway. Through the dim shadows I saw Rachel leading a group therapy session in one corner of the parlor. Olivia was speed texting in the other. I saw her slip something out of her purse, take a sip and put it back. I guessed that was one way of keeping warm. I hoped she didn't go overboard, but sadly knew she would.

After witnessing the Taylor/Al/tiny Miata incident a few hours earlier I wasn't in the sociable mood. Maybe I needed to move over into Rachel's corner and get some mental help. No, there was just too much togetherness for my rotten mood. I needed some fresh air.

After bundling up like Nanook of the North, I headed out for a slip-slidey walk to who knows where. Just anywhere to be alone. Although the sleet had stopped, after about three minutes of the bone chilling Oklahoma wind I'd had enough fresh air, but I didn't feel like going back to the dorm. Across the street I could see the music rehearsal building. One thing my grandma had always preached was that music was the best stress reliever known to women. Well, next to chocolate. And as I didn't have any chocolate handy, there was a rehearsal hall available. Off I went to the music building. If I were lucky I could use one of the practice pianos. I wouldn't have to worry about anyone hearing my inadequate skills, as no one with any common sense would be there on a night like that.

The door was unlocked, but no lights were on. Duh, the electricity was off there too. The check-in desk was empty and the whole building seemed deserted. I'm sure if my life had been a movie there would have been scary music playing and the people in the audience would be saying, "Don't go in there alone Lottie." But it wasn't and I went. Thankfully, no man with a mask and chainsaw jumped out to get me.

The first floor of the building was made up of about ten practice rooms. Each room was just big enough to hold an upright piano and a bench. Nothing spacious. Supposedly they were sound proofed, but in actuality it only muffled the sound.

I didn't go in the first room. Or the second. Like Goldilocks, I went all the way to the back looking for the best fit. The room most secluded from the world. It would have been pitch dark if not for the glow of the full moon reflecting off of the ice covered landscape shining through the window. I was in the mood to play my saddest songs. I was no virtuoso. Although I had taken piano for six years and could play adequately, I never felt comfortable playing for others. I loved Broadway show tunes, so I started to play "Maybe" from *Annie*. It's sad yearning for what wasn't was exactly how my heart felt. Soon I was singing along and feeling the release of all the pent-up frustrations I had felt since the not-coffee-date.

I finished the last word of the song, "Maybe," when there was a slow clapping applause at the doorway. I screamed bloody murder and hoped I hadn't wet myself. I had been so absorbed in the music I hadn't heard anyone enter.

"I'm so sorry," came the voice of a dream, not a nightmare. "I came to get in some practice and heard you playing. I didn't mean to scare you. I should have realized I would scare you. Are you okay?"

"You're just lucky I didn't have a can of mace on me," I laughed, trying to regain my composure.

"You play quite well," said Al Dansby. "Are you a music major?"

That got a snort laugh from me. Oh snap. I snorted. "No, English. That is I'm an English major. I just play the piano for therapy." I was doing it again. Talking nonsense.

"It's the best therapy I've ever found," he agreed. "Maybe that's why I'm here tonight."

Awkward silence. I wanted him to stay and talk. But my brain had locked up. No mental file would open. "Please don't leave." Was that out loud? Had I really said that out loud? Of all the stupid pathetic things to say. Where was my eraser? I had to fix that blunder. But it was back in my room.

"Okay," he said.

He said okay. Now think brain and don't mess up again.

114

"Do you play duets?" he asked.

"*Heart and Soul.*"

"Scoot over a little and we can play some mean *Heart and Soul* and then, if you're lucky the ever popular but technically demanding *Chopsticks.*"

I loved the fact that piano benches aren't very big. He played the bass cleft, I the treble. It all seemed perfectly natural.

"I liked *Annie*," he said.

Who was this Annie chick I wondered. I thought I only had to worry about Taylor. And what was he doing bringing her up? Was he trying to make sure I knew up front there was someone else in his life? I'd have to do something about both of them.

"You know the musical," he laughed at my confused expression. "You were playing *Maybe* from it. Not my all time favorite. A little too girly. I suppose *Phantom* or *Les Mis* are. But *Annie* is a great play about never giving up hope."

"What do you hope for?" I asked amazed how easily we were talking in the moonlight. Usually by this point in a conversation I had put my size seven in my mouth, but in the stillness and the moonlight everything seemed safe. Safe to let my guard down and be vulnerable.

"All Christmas break I've been hoping. . . ," he stopped playing his part of the song. I followed suit.

"Me too."

"Strange, I've really only talked to you that time in the library and too briefly at the dance. I must apologize from making such a spectacle of myself. Sometimes I can be just a little bit theatrical." Al paused for a breath and a depreciating laugh. I was about to start over explaining my date from hell when he began speaking again. "But, I feel like I've been almost running into you all year. Or maybe after you. Even though I haven't. It's like I instantly knew you," he said giving furtive glances my way as he spoke.

I wondered. Did minute traces of events remain even after I redid them?

Slowly he took over the whole keyboard and began to gently play a song. I recognized the tune, but couldn't place it until he gently began to sing about enchanted evenings and finding his true love.

This so couldn't be real. There I sat in a moonlit room, while the guy of my dreams serenaded me with the most romantic song from *South Pacific*. If I had had a room full of Harlequin Romance writers working for weeks they couldn't have written anything this perfect. Then it happened. The ridiculously super efficient Public Service Company of Oklahoma went and got the electricity back on. Light flooded the entire building. The spell was broken.

"That was beautiful," I whispered suddenly self-conscious in the bright lights.

"Thanks. That's the play we're doing this semester. I'm playing Lt. Cable. He doesn't actually sing that song, but somehow it just..." he stopped talking and looked flustered.

"I'm so very sorry," he said starting to talk again.

"Huh, for what?" I asked.

"For standing you up at the library. I was stuck in a meeting about the musical. Taylor said she would tell you I'd be late, but she said she didn't find you. I guess my description wasn't good enough. I couldn't remember what you'd been wearing. I told her to look for the prettiest girl around." Then I swear he blushed.

"The music rehearsal building is now closing," came a disembodied

116

voice. I was so engrossed in our conversation I jumped thinking it was the voice of God, but then realized it only came from the building's P.A. system.

"Guess we have to go," I said. Neither of us moved from our bench.

"Guess so."

"**Maybe** another time?" I asked.

"**Definitely**," He answered. "Can I walk you back to your dorm?"

I would like to say we had a leisurely stroll back across campus. But it was a freezing, windy night in January in Oklahoma. We both walked as fast as possible, trying not to slip on the ice, hunched against the elements. At that pace we reached the dorm much too fast.

It was too cold to loiter on the steps, so we stepped into the foyer.

"Charlotte Lambert, English major, commonly known as Lottie, thank you for an enjoyable evening. We should..." Al Dansby's beautiful voice was cut off as the outside door burst open and Olivia staggered through.

"I think I'm going to be sick," Olivia declared and then she was. Right on top of the new boots the Double J's had given me for Christmas.

***

"Lottie, I'm so sorry," Olivia apologized for the tenth time. "I'll buy you new boots. I'll buy you two new pairs of boots. I guess I ate something bad."

We all played along, but we knew it wasn't what she had eaten but what she had drank that made her blow chunks on my new Frye boots.

A split second after the upchuck Al had made his exit. The look on his face declared that he wasn't good with vomit.

"Forget the puke for a moment. Tell us, Lottie," demanded Stina.

"Yeah, give us all the details. Where have you been for the past two

117

hours and how did you end up with Al Dansby?" demanded Rachel.

"I thought he was gay," added Olivia prone on Stina's bed with a wet washcloth on her forehead.

I proceeded to give them the high points of my enchanted evening.

Stina kept interjecting, *How romantic's*, throughout the narration. Rachel kept analyzing the situation. Olivia kept mumbling about there should be better rules defining gaydom. I just kept thinking how other than Olivia's last meal on my boots there was nothing in that evening that I would ever want to erase.

-27-

Call Me?

My evening had been enchanted, but the next day wasn't. Would he call? How could he call? I hadn't given him my cell number. How would he find me? If only I had left a glass slipper, but sadly glass slippers were in short supply during an Oklahoma ice storm. And I really doubt he wanted an upchucked-on boot.

After hours of panic, common sense set it. He had walked me home. He knew where I lived.

The day wore on. Books to buy for my new classes. Forms to be signed by my advisor. Stina and I had to catch up on all that had happened in our lives over the past month apart—all the details that we hadn't given each other in our daily text messages and Snapchats. It was a busy day, yet in the back of my mind, out of the corner of my eye, I kept looking for Al Dansby.

By evening I was a basket case again. I had sat in the cafeteria for an hour and a half at dinner picking at some disgusting thing they billed as an enchilada. He never came through. I finally gave up my vigil and headed for the dorm when the cleaning crew started moving tables to vacuum.

Stina wanted to go to the movies. It was our last night without homework, but I wasn't in the movie mood. I would never confess that I was afraid to leave the dorm. Afraid that if I did he would come by and I'd miss him. I was roaming the room like some pathetic caged animal.

"Lottie, sit still. You're driving me crazy," said Kasha. She and two other K's, Rachel, and Stina were primping for a girls' night out to the movies. Seems ironic how much time they spent to look fantastic to go and sit in the dark, but hey, it's a girl thing. They were off to see some vampire thing they'd all seen before, but once was never enough. "Just call the guy. It's a new millennium. You can call a guy yourself."

"I can't."

"Why not? You're a liberated woman."

"No, I can't. I don't have his number."

"Oh. Well, don't worry. He'll call you."

"Can't."

"Doesn't have your number, huh?"

"It was a little too awkward to exchange technical info with Olivia's stomach contents on my feet.

"Have fun at the movies. I'm going for a walk." And that I did. I walked by the music rehearsal building three times hoping that we might just casually bump into each other. No Al Dansby there.

For once there was no wind blowing. It was a nice evening to be out. That's the craziest thing about Oklahoma weather. It changes. The day before we had sleet, the next sun. My mom always said our weather was like a metaphor of life—things might be bad, but in a day or two it would melt away and be nice again. What she didn't add was that after that day of sun it would be sleety again. I kept walking. As I rounded to the back door of the fine arts building I heard voices.

"Thanks Al. I had the most wonderful time," said Taylor all gushy and sultry.

I turned the corner to see her arms around Al's neck like a baby anaconda. Al Dansby's neck. His eyes met mine for an instant. I felt like an enormous fool. He must have thought I was some pathetic stalker seeking him out just because we had had a chance conversation the night before. His eyes looked anything but pleased to see me. Obviously there was something going on between him and snake woman. But she didn't have a magic eraser and I did. Redo time.

"Lottie, wait," was all I heard. Then, I was back in front of the music rehearsal building. I was tired. A walk wasn't a good idea after all. Time to return to my dorm and get ahead on my reading for my Lit. class. I'd probably end up graduating *Magna Cum Laude* seeing as how I was going to have plenty of time for studying that semester.

-28-

And Then There Were Three

"Hey girlfriend, how was the movie? Did all the werewolves take off their shirts again to your approval?" I asked Stina, when she came back at midnight.

"Ooo baby. And the funniest thing is all the cougars in the audience drooling over jailbait boys on the screen. Love that movie," laughed Stina. "Any vampire action around here tonight?" she asked. One look at my face told her the answer. "Bummer. He's probably just busy. Those theater people are always practicing something. Didn't you say he has a lead in the next musical? I'm sure he had some rehearsal or something."

Or something was right. First I had spent a semester thinking he was gay and unobtainable. I find out he's straight, but straight into the arms of super gorgeous octopus woman.

"Well, here's some news to put priorities back into perspective," said Stina. As she was talking Rachel and Olivia came through the bathroom passage to join our gab session. "Keesha didn't come back this semester."

"Only three K's. That just won't work. All out of balance," observed Olivia.

"Where is she?" I asked.

"Prego," came Stina's reply. All the joy gone from her voice.

Rachel gave a heavy sigh and sat down on the end of my bed. "I thought she was before Christmas. She said she thought she had a stomach virus. Some rare type that only happens in the mornings. Mr. Soccer Player—old love 'em and leave 'em."

"I just don't get it. She said she was using protection," came Stina's naive little voice.

I gave a sad laugh. "Come on we all know it doesn't always work. Ask my mom. That's how she ended up with my little sisters. After that she took dad to the vet for the old snip, snip."

"So what is Keesha going to do?" asked Olivia. The mood in the room was like that of a funeral. In a bizarre sense it was. The death of the K's as we knew them. The end of Keesha's childhood. Yes, we all wanted to be adults and mature, but not instantaneously.

Rachel filled us in. "She dropped out. Just too much stress to try and go to school full-time right now. Kasha said she is looking for a job and taking some classes online. They're only sophomores so she wasn't even half way through with her degree."

"Is Mr. Soccer helping out any?" I asked. Always the romantic, I was hoping for a happy ending.

Stina rolled her eyes. "Phew, no. He's still dating that skank Taylor. According to Kyra he tried to claim the baby wasn't even his. Called Keesha a slut and said she'd been sleeping with every guy on campus." At least there was a little justice in that Taylor was cheating on him also. Sadly, with Al Dansby. Made me despise her even more.

123

Olivia was hot. "We all know that's a lie. That scum. That lousy soccer-playing scum. If I could just get my hands on him."

"Run him over," I murmured. Olivia shot me the strangest look. Then she looked at Rachel.

"Fortunately Keesha has a wonderful mom who's going to help raise the baby. Without her I don't know what she would have done. She doesn't have any job skills to get anything more than a minimum wage job and with paying for a babysitter she wouldn't make any money. Could have ended up homeless," said Stina

"It just isn't right. We think we have progressed so much since the days of Jane Austin, but let's be honest. That LSPS" which the lousy soccer-playing scum affectionately became known to us from that moment on, "gets to go on and live his life with no interruptions and Keesha's entire world has changed. It's just not fair," I ranted.

"No, life just isn't fair very often, princess," said Olivia in a world-weary voice. "It's just not fair."

-29-

IT

"So have you ever done IT?" asked the little voice in the darkness. It had to be one in the morning when we had finally gotten lights out and to bed. I thought Stina had been asleep for some time as I lay there wishing and dreaming and worrying.

"Stina, where did that come from?" I countered.

There was a moment of uncomfortable silence. Then Stina said, "With everything with Keesha. It made me realize it could so easily have been me."

"But you're not even dating anyone. Especially not a tool like that soccer player."

Stina sighed. "Back in high school. There was this guy. I was seventeen. I was in love. Next thing I knew we were in the backseat of his car and it was over in less than four minutes. Not at all like the movies, not at all. Just awkward and messy. I felt so stupid. It wasn't even a nice car," Stina finished with a mirthless giggle.

I had no idea how to respond. I knew that most people my age had had a least one sexual encounter. Most a lot more. But somehow I never would have thought that Stina had. She just seemed so innocent.

"Two weeks later and two more quickies and then he dumped me. He was a senior and I was a junior. Said he wanted to go off to college with no ties. I was crushed. I really thought he loved me."

I could hear the tears in Stina's voice. Our sweet, bubbly Stina. Almost four years had passed, yet it still hurt her.

"I haven't dated a guy seriously since then," she continued. "Just felt so betrayed. Don't ever want to feel that way again."

"I'm sorry."

"Not your fault. Thanks anyway. It's just that I could have gotten pregnant at seventeen."

"Didn't you use any protection?"

"No. Didn't know how. I was a good girl. Nobody teaches good girls how to protect themselves. Good girls don't have sex."

"No, they just get pregnant." It was quiet again.

"So? Have you?" Stina asked again.

"No."

"Oh, I thought that was what the whole OU guy was about."

There in the darkness I began to unburden my soul. It was amazing how easy it was to tell Stina about the hardest event in my life. Maybe knowing Olivia and Stina's stories helped me put my own experience into perspective. Although heartbreaking and humiliating it didn't compare to Olivia's terror or Stina's disappointment. Maybe it was just that it was a story that was easier to tell in the dark.

"Yes, it was. Same story just a different twist. We dated about a month. He kept trying to get me to do *it*. Not saying I didn't want to. But, I wasn't ready. I wanted the dream. The magical moment. You know — the beautiful four-poster bed, white curtains blowing in the breeze. And a knight in shinning armor that you know will still be there the next morning and the next year. Not some backseat and four minutes." We both gave a sad laugh. "I was prepared. My mom made sure of that when I turned sixteen. What she didn't realize was that a lot of my friends were already doing it at fourteen. But she tried, bless her heart."

"So, why did you leave OU?"

"It was a catastrophe. He said, his actual words, 'Lottie, this relationship has to move to the next level.' Then he gave me an ultimatum to put out or get out. I finally told him no way, no how until marriage and that didn't seem very likely. You should have seen his face. He was mad. Like I'd gypped him out of something. Like I owed it to him. Needless to say we broke up then and there."

"So, why did you leave?"

"Cause he didn't stop there. He was out for some sort of demented revenge. He got on my Facebook page—I didn't know he had my password. He put this horrible status that—well—it was vulgar all about how much I enjoyed having sex with him and a bunch of other guys. He also put my phone number on Craig's List for kinky stuff. Then he told anyone who would listen how I was bad in bed and that's why he dumped me."

"What a ..."

"Yeah, my reputation shot in record time. How could I undo that? I had to close my Facebook account and get a new phone number. My brother Jason was going to beat the crap out of him. But I talked him out of it. It would have gotten him suspended from the team and wouldn't have changed anything. I'd have still gotten the looks, the smirks. Suddenly, I had guys lining up to go out with me because they thought I was easy. I even had a guy I barely knew lean over and tell me during class not to worry if I was bad at sex—not the words he said, something too disgusting—said he'd teach me how to be better if I'd go out with him. It was just gross. I had to get out of there."

"The girl always seems to lose."

"I don't get it, Stina. What do you mean?"

"It's the girl—every time. Look at you. You left a great school to get away from a D-bag idiot. You're the one that life became unbearable for, not him. You had to change your life, not him. Just like Keesha. She's gone. Her life has changed forever and the LSPS just gets to go on like nothing ever happened."

We laid there in the silence pondering it all. Stina was right. When things went bad it always seemed the girl had to make the changes while the guy went happily skipping down the road of life.

I thought Stina must have gone to sleep when I heard a little voice again. "He should have anyway."

I was totally confused. "He who should have done what anyway?"

"Your brother. He should have pulverized the scumbag."

"I told you, it wouldn't have solved anything and could have gotten Jason kicked off the team."

"Yeah, but it sure would have felt good," said my loyal friend.

"Yeah, it sure would have," I giggled. "Anyway, I left there older and wiser."

I heard someone walking down the hall bouncing a ball. Volleyball girls must still be up.

Stina sighed. "I hope someday I can trust again."

"Me too," I whispered. In my mind I no longer saw the scum from OU when I thought of trust, instead a pair of green eyes over a beautiful smile. "Me too."

-30-

You Don't Bring Me Flowers

Two days I could handle. Three, getting stressed. But by day four and no Al sightings or communication I was having major withdrawals. It was time to give up. Non-gay Al Dansby was obviously hooked-up with SW (aka skank woman, aka Thing One, aka Taylor.) I mean why not? She was what guys wanted, tall, beautiful and willing.

"No word today?" Stina asked at dinner. One look from me told her the answer. We were getting almost as scary as the K's at non-verbal communication. "Doesn't the guy ever eat? We've been staked out here in the cafeteria for days spending over an hour at every meal and he hasn't come through."

"We are not staked out. I just eat slow," I said, in denial. Honest truth—I hadn't eaten much all week. Slow or fast. I just played with my food, looking for his golden brown hair. No luck. "Anyhow, it's a pointless venture. I saw him and SW with my own eyes. It's so just not going to happen."

Stina gave a Stina giggle. "Yeah, just keep saying that while you continue canvassing the campus for an Al Dansby sighting. Well, pokey eater, I have things to do and places to go. I'll see you back at the room. And remember what my mom always told me, 'A woman without a man is like a fish without a bicycle.'"

"Thanks for those wise words you Gloria Steinem wannabe."

Stina gave me a sad smile. "Just wanting to remind you to believe in yourself. Something we all need reminding of some days.

Out of the mouths of Stinas do come very wise words some days. Not most days, but some. I had to quit being so lovesick pathetic. Time to go get on with life without a bicycle.

It was a nice day for January, only a little wind. I thought I should get some exercise so I started on a walk. Turning the corner I realized the wind had just been blocked by the building. It was there alright, strong and with a bite to it as usual. Maybe a walk wasn't such a good idea. Up the front steps of the dorm, which I seldom used, and in the front door.

There he stood in the foyer in all his perfection, holding a single red rose. I'd either died and ended up on a pathetic reality show, or my prayers had been answered.

He turned to look over his shoulder to see who had just come in the door. His face was a mixture of glowing and dread. Find that color in your Crayola box. I gave him my biggest Colgate smile. He was there. He cared. He'd even shown up with flowers. How could it get any better than that?

"Oh, Al, you're here," came a voice from the lowest pit of hell. "And you brought me flowers. How nice," said Taylor looking like a modern day Scarlett O'Hara walking down the stairs.

Life can be bad sometimes. Sometimes it can get worse. But that had to be the ultimate worse. Being all ready to get flowers from the man of your dreams just to realize he wasn't there for you.

Instant tears of frustration, humiliation and any other -ation I could think of sprang into my eyes. This so wasn't going to happen. He'd made his choice and I wasn't going to stand there like the loser duffuses at the Bachelor Rose Ceremony.

"Lottie, wait," he said. But I didn't. The power of the eraser worked its magic. Even if things were never to be between us, at least he didn't have to see me being all drama queen about it.

It was a nice day for January. Only a little wind. I thought I should get some exercise, but not by going on a walk. Instead a good cry in my room would burn off the same amount of calories, I decided as I entered the backdoor of the dorm headed to my basement sanctuary.

-31-

Noteworthy

Life always feels better after a good cry. And two Snickers bars.
And a Diet Dr. Pepper. And some cookie dough. All shared with three
good friends. And then wait four days.

A week had gone by with no Al Dansby sightings. At least none that
anyone other than me would ever know of. I had kept my trusty eraser
friend always close at my side making sure I wouldn't accidentally run into
the man of Taylor's reality. Three times it had happened, but I had quickly
fixed the situation. I was finding interesting alternative routes for getting to
and from class. I just wasn't up to hearing his voice, or some lame words
of how we could be good friends.

I had just finished the most recent dodge/do-over by entering in the
main dorm entrance rather than the back as for some bizarre reason Al had
been standing next to the back door earlier.

"Hey, Lottie," called Kasha as I entered the foyer. "Waz up?"

"Not enough. You working the desk tonight?"

"Yup. Trying to get *Madame Bovary* read. Have you started yet?"
Like last semester, Kasha and I were in the same Lit. class, again with Dr.
Jekyll. Second week of school and she already wanted an essay on a book I

hadn't finished reading. I couldn't get past Madame Bovary and her lovers. SW's face kept appearing in my thoughts and I wanted to sling the book across the room.

"Started, not finished. I forgot you worked the desk. I don't usually come in this door unless it's after hours, to sign in."

"Obviously. Look at your mailbox. Ever think of getting your mail?

She was right. It was stuffed with junk mail and flyers. Guess I should check it more often, but who of importance used snail mail anymore? Email or text seemed to get the word out. If it was really important it could be Snapchatted. I grabbed the pile of junk and stood next to the trashcan sorting it. Credit card applications. Didn't they know that they weren't supposed to solicit to college students anymore? Yeah, right. Flyers for a dance from the week before. Guess I missed that. Hey, what was that? An actual letter written by hand. What could that be?

The front said, "*Ms. Lottie Lambert - English Major, Basement, Asbury Hall.*" Okay, I was intrigued. I went to sit in the parlor to open it.

Lottie,

I enjoyed our duet last night and hope that we can do it again, soon.

I didn't know how to get in touch with you, as I didn't have your phone number or email address. Then I remembered there was this archaic form of communication called a letter. Rather inefficient, but better than smoke signals.

133

As I don't have your number to call you, could you call me if you'd like to go out. If you don't call I'll understand.

Al Dansby

There in the bottom corner were both his email address and phone number.

He liked me. My heart was a flutter. The world was right. I swear I heard birds singing. He liked me. He hadn't forgotten me. In fact he had written to me the very next day after our piano interlude.

THE VERY NEXT DAY. Oh crap! The letter had sat in my mailbox for over a week. He had been waiting for me to call, and I hadn't.

"Good news or bad news?" Kasha called from the desk. "I heard you gasp all the way in here so it must be something."

"Great news. Just the wrong time. I have got to check my mailbox more often." With that I was off to my basement room to get advice on how to proceed.

***

My first impulse was to grab my phone and call. Always being one to follow my first impulse that was what I did.

"You have reached the cell phone of Al Dansby," his magnificent voice said. "I am either unable to answer your call or am screening calls and you didn't make the cut. Either way please leave a message at the beep."

What to say? What to say? I hung up. Oh great, it would show my missed call. I'll just erase that. Flick of the eraser and start again.

My first impulse was to grab my phone and call. This time I wouldn't. I'd play it cool. I'd text. What to say? Keep it simple.

134

"Hey, Lottie. What cha doing?" asked Stina as she came in the door followed by Rachel, Olivia and Kyra and Kaylee.

"You feeling okay? Is there a reason why you're standing in the middle of your room holding your phone in one hand and a piece of paper in the other?" asked Rachel.

"You look really flushed," observed Kyra.

"Oo baby! You heard from Al Dansby! Didn't you!" bubbled Stina.

I didn't trust my voice. I just held the note up for them to see. Olivia took it and began to read it out loud.

Lottie,

I enjoyed our duet last night and hope that we can do it again, soon.

"Whoa momma! 'Our duet.' What is that code for?" asked Kaylee.

"How poetic," said Kyra. "Our duet. So much nicer than say, 'Hey it was great hooking up with you.'"

"Keep reading," demanded Stina.

I didn't know how to get in touch with you, as I didn't have your phone number or email address. Then I remembered there was this archaic form of communication called a letter. Rather inefficient, but better than smoke signals.

"Why didn't you give him your phone number?" Kyra asked. Four sets of eyes turned to look at Olivia. "Oh, yeah. Forgot about Miss Blow Chunks' timely arrival."

"Keep reading!" demanded Stina again. She was losing her patience.

As I don't have your number to call you, could you

135

call me if you'd like to go out. If you don't call I'll understand.

There was a collective sigh in the room. Rachel expressed the unanimous thought. "How romantic. There's just something about a handwritten note. So old worldly."

"So sweet," said Stina.

"So a week old," said Olivia. "Why have you been carrying this around for eight days and not telling us?"

"I just got it! Well, I mean I just got it out of my mailbox. I never check my mailbox. Who uses a mailbox? But there's no point in it now. I saw him giving Trampy Taylor a rose days ago. He's already over me and on to the next." I just wanted to cry. My mail retrieval incompetence had made me miss the romance of a lifetime.

Kyra and Kaylee locked eyes. "We need to go check our mail," they said in unison and fled the room.

Olivia read through the note again. "So Lottie. What are you going to do?"

"Obviously by not responding for more than a week, he's thinking you don't like him, but that he could move on to another girl so fast. . . not possible," hypothesized Rachel.

"Oh, he probably feels stupid now for writing it. Maybe that's why he hasn't come to eat. Afraid he might run into you," said Stina with sympathy for the note writer.

"Think, women. What is Lottie's best plan?" General Olivia took charge. I had never seen her in a leadership position before. But as matters went, Olivia was our resident expert on the male species.

Stina held up her hand. "She has to call him as quickly as possible."

"There's no point in it. You all aren't listening. He's moved on to

136

Skank Woman," I moaned.

"Definitely she has to contact him," agreed Rachel with Stina totally ignoring my comments. "But what does she say? She has to explain why she hasn't called."

"That's crucial," agreed Stina.

Slapping a pencil down like a riding crop Olivia added, "Yes, but she doesn't want to look all needy, whiny. Somehow, in very few words she has to give him the message that she got the note and would like to pursue the relationship."

"But he's dating Taylor now! I saw it with my own two eyes. Why can't you all get that this train has left the station and I missed it!" No one was listening to me.

My cozy little dorm room had turned into the command center of a war bunker. I thought that I was beginning to hyperventilate. Olivia handed me an old McDonald's bag. "Breath into this," she said. "You can't call him wheezing like that. He'd think you were an obscene phone caller.

"Now ladies let's get a plan and get it into action fast," Olivia continued.

Kasha came running into the room. "The rose wasn't for Taylor. I saw him there the other day with it when I was working the front desk. She did come by and say something about thank you for the flower. But he just laughed and said not this time. He waited around about an hour and then threw it in the trash and left. I didn't know who he was waiting for and he never said."

Then Kasha got an intrigued look on her face. "How did you know about the rose, Lottie? I never saw you come through."

I was busted. And stupid. If I hadn't used that stupid eraser he would have given me the rose and we'd be on our way to happily-ever-after.

Instead it was in the trash, just like our future.

"Rumors," I stammered. "Gossip and rumors. You hear everything that happens in this building."

An hour later I was putting the plan into action. The general agreement was that a text message would be the safest. I could simply say,

Sorry to not be in touch sooner. Your note was waylaid and I just got it. Call me when you have time. If you've changed your mind, I'll understand.

The only flaw was it then left me waiting for him to call—or not call. I guess it was only fair, as I had made him wait for more than a full week to hear from me. My biggest fear was that in those eight days he had changed his mind. That might explain why he had been locked in an embrace with Taylor behind the fine arts building. He had found someone else to play a duet with that was more *prestissimo*.

I had to retype the message three times before I had everything spelled right. I hit send. We all stared at my cell. Waiting. Waiting. Waiting.

Two hours later. Still waiting.

Stina sat on her bed doing some weird complicated math problems—one reason why I was an English major. Only basic math required. I sat on my bed staring at *Madame Bovary*. Was I just being a foolish romantic like Ms. B.? Living my life thinking that the love stories in real life could ever compare to those in novels? Would I just live my whole life hoping for a happy ending that wasn't coming?

"Lighten up there Lottie," said Stina. Was she now able to read my mind? "The look on your face is tragic. Give the guy some time to call back."

"I wasn't even thinking about him," I lied. "I was just reading about poor Emma Bovary and her devastating affairs."

"Yeah, right," Stina snorted. "He'll call."

"Do you really think so?"

"Any guy who would actually go to the bother to write you a note will call. Think about it. That note was a lot of work. First he had to find paper and pen. And a real envelope. Who has an envelope available? He probably had to make a special trip to Wal-Mart just for supplies to write to you."

Stina logic made me smile. She was right. A note was much more work than a text message. So why didn't he call?

"Should I call him again?"

"You haven't called him have you? I thought we agreed on texting?"

There I had done it again. Confused the two realities. "I meant text him again." There quick save.

"Wait."

"Wait," I repeated.

"Wait," we both said in unison.

By eleven o'clock I had given up. Despair was taking over. I might as well go to bed and dream of an Al Dansby that I would never have. I was brushing my teeth with my phone next to me on the bathroom counter. Yes, hope springs eternal. It started to ring. I went to grab for it with a mouth full of toothpaste. Spa-lop my phone took a dive into the toilet. Had the diamond earring episode not taught me anything about leaving things on the counter next to the toilet?

"Oh my fig newton!" Stina screamed from the doorway. "That could have been him!" And it will be I thought. I ran from the room, snatched my purse from the floor and started digging. "What are you doing? Do you have an extension in your purse?' Stina asked utterly confused.

139

Finally, I found my trusty eraser. My bosom friend. My help for all happiness. I might have swung it around a little harder than need be, but it worked.

I was back on my bed reading. It was 10:55. I thought about brushing my teeth, but I'd put that off for just a moment. Precisely at eleven o'clock my phone began to ring. Stina was bouncing on her bed— two thumbs up.

"Hello," I said, my voice cracking.

"Lottie are you alright?" asked my mom. "Your voice sounds scratchy."

-32-

A Watched Phone Never Rings

There was a lot of time to think the next week, as I sure wasn't spending it on the phone. He didn't call. Looking back, I started to realize how many chances I'd had to get to know Al Dansby, but for my fear of ever looking foolish I had changed time and missed opportunities. And I was still doing it. I saw him three more times on campus, but dodged him with my mini time machine. I just couldn't face him knowing he knew that I had texted him and he hadn't texted me back. I felt so sixth grade.

It had been a full two weeks since my enchanted evening when Olivia, Stina and Rachel came into my room all dressed in black like burglars.

"Hey, I know tuition is high, but I didn't know that y'all had taken on an illegal profession to make ends meet," I said looking at them bewildered.

"We've been on a reconnaissance mission. We're ninja spies," announced Stina, pulling some leaves from her hair and then striking her best ninja pose.

"What?"

Olivia pulled out her iPhone. "We've decided something had to be done about this Dansby business. You're obviously not getting over him."

"That's for sure," said Stina.

Rachel added her clinical diagnosis. "You have been extremely despondent lately."

I didn't think I had been that bad. In fact I had been making a special point of not sighing loudly and only sniffled in the shower.

Stina added, "We decided to do an intervention."

"What?" That was all my poor befuddled brain could come up with.

"We have been monitoring Al Dansby's movements for the past two days," said Stina. I felt like I was watching a very low budget *Mission Impossible*.

"Point one—we found out," said Olivia reading from her iPhone screen. "He does not live on campus. Thus, the reason for not seeing him in the cafeteria. We did observe that he eats there on Wednesdays, due to a schedule conflict that keeps him from being able to leave campus for lunch."

"I found that out from La—ah. She works the lunch shift at the cafeteria this semester. I also found out he favors mystery meat over salads, but likes tacos best," Stina said so proud of her super sleuth abilities.

"He owns a condo," said Rachel not to be outdone. "Did you get that? *Owns* a condo four blocks away. I Googled to find that."

"Ladies, this is almost scary. Doesn't this count as stalking? Isn't that illegal?" I asked trying my best to sound like I objected, but really hoped that they had found out why he hadn't called.

"Not if he doesn't notice," said Olivia back in General mode.

"Currently he is in the play that starts in four weeks, so every evening this week he has been at play practice."

Stina held up her hand to speak. "He's playing Lt. Cable. I snuck in to watch the practice. He sure can sing."

Olivia consulted her IPhone again. "Here's the most important info we've uncovered so far. He broke his cell phone."

"Yeah, we got that from Butch," chimed in Stina.

"Butch thought it was so funny. Al told him he had been carrying his phone everywhere because he was expecting an important call," Rachel was saying, when Stina interrupted, "That would be your call! He was waiting for your call!"

"But," Rachel resumed telling the story, "he went to grab for a call and dropped it in the toilet!"

"Just like someone did my diamond earrings," said Olivia through gritted teeth.

Rachel held her hands up as the peacemaker, "Let it go Olivia. We got them out. Fortunately there was no pee in the toilet so they were just fine after we sanitized them.

"Back to the matter at hand. Al told Butch who told Stina and me that Al is from California and his phone was on a plan from there so he had to get his dad to get him a new phone and his dad was out of the country for work and once he got ahold of him getting a new one seemed to deal with something to do with overnight shipping and losing all his phone numbers and text messages."

Olivia was back in charge. "So you see, he never got your message."

We all sat there for a solid two minutes no one saying a word. Three hopeful faces stared at me. Finally I spoke as if in a trance. "He never got my message."

143

"Nope, never," they all three said with Stina nodding like some crazy bobble head doll in the back of a car going down a dirt road.

I had been such an idiot with that stupid eraser. If I hadn't made sure that he didn't see me all this time, he could have told me all this himself, without the *Get Smart* crew having to go into action.

"General Corazon, Sir." I saluted and asked, "What is our plan of attack?

-33-

You Say Stalking, I say Conveniently Located

Deodorant ads lie. It did not turn up a degree when my pits—and the rest of me—were totally stressing as I tried to get up the nerve to enter the theater door. I would have turned around ten different times and left if three ninja stalkers hadn't been hiding in the bushes forcing me to proceed. Five times I contemplated using my fickle eraser. But the track record so far on my trusty friend wasn't so perfect. Yes, sometimes it had gotten me out of extremely humiliating situations. But, it had also allowed me to miss so many opportunities to get to know Al Dansby and who knows what else.

Two deep breaths, and no do-overs. I was off to see this encounter through whether it worked out for a happily-ever-after or just the crushing end to a dream that was just beginning.

Okay, maybe three deep breaths. Four. Oh, I was getting lightheaded. I heard a rustling from the bush patrol. "Get in there now," came the order from Commander Corazon.

I made my way to lurking in the empty dark back row of the theater.

145

There were a few actors still on stage, but practice seemed to be over.

"Who's up for the Coffee Corner?" came a voice from backstage.

Different replies of "I can't. Got to go study." and "Sure wait for me." came from different areas of the stage.

"How about you, Taylor?" asked Butch as he walked on stage.

Taylor looked around expectantly until her vision locked on a lone figure sitting at the rehearsal piano on the far apron of the stage. "Are you going, Al?" she asked in her disgustingly purry voice walking over to him and ruffling his amazing hair. My knees turned to Jello. My heart felt like I was running a marathon and green, jealousy steam was coming out of my ears. How was I going to rectify the cell phone/text message debacle if he went to coffee with her? Was I right after all? Had he not called because he had already moved on?

"Not tonight," came the melodious voice of my quest.

In your face, Taylor of the long perfect legs. He doesn't want to go out with you. I was practically doing the happy dance in the back of the theater.

"I have a paper to write. Give me a rain check, okay?" the beautiful voice continued. My happy dance wasn't quite as perky anymore.

A war was going on inside my poor cranium as Taylor left the stage with the rest of the cast and crew through the backdoor. He had just said he had a paper to do. He had asked my archrival for a rain check. Did anyone really say rain check? And how could he make it sound so sexy to say such an antiquated phrase? Analyzing every detail of the past two and a half minutes, trying desperately to decide whether to go forward with our plan of attack or call a strategic retreat, I heard someone near the doorway clearing her throat. "If you don't get your skinny butt up there right now and talk to him, I'm gonna come in there and grab your boney hand and drag you up there myself," came La—ah's forceful whisper through the door. The ninjas must have called for reinforcements.

During all the various and drastically different conversations that had been taking place, Al had sat alone at the rehearsal piano, randomly playing bits and pieces of different tunes.

Four steps down. I hesitated. I had never realized what a huge auditorium it was. I was groping for the handrail, trying not to miss a step in the dimly lit room. The only lights on in the vast room were a few working lights on the stage. I heard La—ah clear her throat again. I took five more steps. I felt like I was playing some eccentric form of Mother May I, hoping for a yes you may, not a go back to the beginning. More throat clearing. It was starting to sound like a tuberculosis ward in the hallway. I had to speed things up.

Al began a new tune. One that gave me hope. He had very slowly morphed into "Maybe," from *Annie*. Maybe he hadn't given up on me. Maybe he still thought of me. Or maybe it was just a very catchy tune that got stuck in your head and wouldn't go away. I was hoping for option one or two. It gave me the courage to make it to the apron of the stage.

That's when I tripped over someone's book bag in the floor of the first row and whacked my head against the edge of the stage.

-34-

How Romantic, Just Me &Al And Stina, Rachel, Olivia, and La—ah

"Lottie, are you okay?" said an angelic voice. Had I died and gone to heaven? Or had I just knocked myself out being the klutz queen of OkMU?

Option B, of course.

"Stina, call 911," came the command from the General.

"She's coming around," said Al. "Lottie, can you hear me? Are you okay?"

"The Godmother's outside. We should take her to the hospital," came Rachel's decisive voice.

All I could see was Al Dansby's face, actually three of them, staring down at me. Bliss. All three Als looked so concerned. How nice. My brain wasn't working. I kept trying to say I was fine. Instead, I just kept looking at Al. He was down to two faces. Finally there was only one.

"Hospital. Now," decided Al.

"Looks like she tripped over some moron's bag," said La—ah.

"That would be mine," said a very guilty knight in shinning armor. My brain kept saying that's okay. But my mouth wasn't in on the act. Instead, I just mumbled something incoherent. I wasn't sure if it was the brain injury making me unable to talk or being so close to the man of my dreams. If ever I should have done something over that was the time. But my brain wasn't only not talking to my mouth, it was on the outs with my hands too. I had dropped my purse a few feet away, and I couldn't reach it even if my body parts were speaking to each other.

"Can you bring my stuff?" Al asked. "I'll get Lottie. She needs to see a doctor and fast. Brain injuries should be taken seriously." With that he lifted me up. Wow. If my brain could have functioned, I would have been worried that I had something major wrong with me, or that he would think I was too heavy, too fat. Instead, all I could think was how romantic. He just swooped down and picked me up like Rhett and Scarlett. And off we went to our chariot of love. Or Rachel's beat up old Ford Windstar commonly known as "da Godmother." At least there was room for all of us, including the ninja force. We even had room for Chuck Norris, but he didn't show up.

***

"I'm okay. Really," I finally was able to say when we reached the emergency room doors.

No one believed me.

"You're seeing a doctor," said Rachel.

"We're not having you die on us like that beautiful movie star lady who hit the tree skiing," said Stina.

La—ah joined in, "Never take a brain injury lightly." And the discussion was on about all the famous and not so famous people, including La—ah's Great Aunt Beatrice, who died from unattended brain

149

trauma. The fact that she was ninety-seven didn't play into the equation, or so the story went. I only half listened. Al carried me from the car to the hospital entrance. I could walk for myself by then. But why? Here was the world's most amazing guy willing to carry me. And he smelled so good. I'd enjoy the ride while it lasted. A nurse with a wheelchair met us at the door and the glorious ride was over.

***

After an hour of waiting, x-rays and me begging them not to call my mom and have her come, the conclusion was a concussion. No need to stay in the hospital. No treatment unless I displayed more symptoms. Sometime during the evening Rachel was allowed to go back in the treatment room and had become my surrogate mother. The doctor gave her the list of signs to look for and put her in charge.

It was well after midnight when we all piled back into da Godmother and headed back to campus. I was delighted to see that while I had been back with the doctors Al had remained with the rest of the ninja force.

"Al, put on your seatbelt. Nobody rides in da Godmother without proper restraint," said Rachel.

"Oh, sorry. I don't know why, I'm horrid at remembering to use a seatbelt. Thanks."

Restraint seemed to be the theme for what was supposed to have been an Enchanted Evening. In no way had this turned out to be the romantic interlude of all our strategic planning. Just Al and me—and Stina and Rachel and Olivia and La—ah in the world's oldest minivan with Sonic and QuikTrip trash at our feet. No intimate moment to share our deep passionate feelings. I felt like I was on a rerun of *Big Love*.

"Can you drop me at the theater?" asked Al. "I need to pick up my car."

150

Fail.

As we cruised into the back parking lot of the theater building, Al began to gather his evil book bag. Obviously, he was looking to make a quick escape the moment da Godmother came out of warp speed.

The car stopped. No one moved. Four ninjas tried to melt into the upholstery in order to give us some privacy.

"Hum, Lottie," Al looked at me expectantly. Here it came. He would ask me out—or propose. No probably not propose. He'd save that for a real date. He looked at me with beseeching eyes. He wanted something that only I could give. He spoke again. "Um, I need to get out your door. This one doesn't work."

"Oh, yeah. Sorry."

I opened the only sliding door that worked and crawled out of the middle row seat so that he and his book bag could get through. As I turned to get back in the van, he took my elbow and turned me to look at him.

"I'm really, really sorry that I left my ridiculous book bag on the floor and made you trip." He paused. There was that mischievous little boy smile again, like he knew he was going to time-out, but hoping to charm his way out of it. "Do you think. . . that maybe. . . we could go on a proper date? No emergency room and," he glanced back over his shoulder, "no ninjas?"

All I could do was nod my head. Ouch that hurt, but it was worth it.

"I'll call you tomorrow."

"You don't have my number." I was panicked.

"I do now. Olivia gave it to me on a note while you were in the emergency room. Rachel gave it to me on an index card. And Stina jotted it down for me on the back of a hygiene pamphlet. Oh and La—ah wrote it on my arm." He pulled up his sleeve to show my number written in big black Sharpie reaching from his wrist to his elbow. "Don't worry, I won't lose you. . . I mean your number."

-35-

He Didn't Call

"Lottie, Lottie wake up!"

I was in the most fabulous dream. A dream where I was dressed in a flowing gauzy white gown and Al was wearing a white piratey shirt, half open. Like those pictures on paperback romance novels. And he was carrying me across the threshold of some amazing. . . And then someone was pounding at my door, which echoed in my concussed head. It was Saturday morning. Serious sleeping time. Somebody was going to die.

Kasha came bouncing into my room, followed by Kyra and Kaylee. "Look, look!" they all kept saying together like a bunch of yippee dogs when they meet you at the door. Kaylee was holding a take-out bag from the Coffee Corner, Kyra held a cup of coffee, and Kasha held some daisies.

"I was working the desk and he came in," said a very excited Kasha.

"He brought you breakfast," said Kyra.

"And flowers," said Kaylee.

By this point Stina was up and out of bed also. "How romantic," she chimed in.

I was about to say, I thought so too, but before things went too far I had to check one basic fact. "He who?"

"Al Dansby!" they shouted like a chorus of demented cheerleaders.

All I could do was smile.

Sometimes life is good. And then it gets better.

But very, very seldom did it get as good as it was that morning.

I opened the bag. There was a blueberry bagel and a banana muffin and a doughnut and a raLSPSerry torte. Also, most importantly, a note.

Lottie,

I hope you are feeling better this morning. I still feel dreadful for leaving my book bag in your path. I thought you might like breakfast in bed, but seeing as how your dorm isn't co-ed I'll drop it off at the desk.

I wasn't sure what you liked, so I sent a variety. For some bizarre reason I thought you liked skinny cinnamon dolce latte coffee. Don't know why, but hope I'm right.

Al

He remembered my coffee order from a time that never really happened. (Wow, I'd never had a guy remember even when it did actually happen.) I wondered, as I had since the whole impossible magic eraser adventure had begun, how much could really be erased. Even if it changed time did residual thoughts still remain somewhere in the very recesses of others' minds?

The room had gotten really quiet. I looked around to see what had happened. Kyra was eating the muffin, Kasha the donut, Stina the torte and Kaylee the bagel.

"Can I at least have the coffee?" I asked, pretending to be angry, but in such a happy mood even food thieves couldn't bring me down.

All of a sudden a cell phone began to ring. I went flying across my bed to my dresser to grab my phone. Taking a deep breath I went to answer. But the ringing kept on. It wasn't my phone.

"Oops, that's me," said Kasha sheepishly. "Hey, . . . oh yeah. Sorry. Yeah, I'll be right there." Kasha hung up and then started dying laughing.

"What?" we asked.

"I have to go back to work. I got so excited about Al bringing you breakfast, I just left the desk without thinking."

With that a trio of laughing K's left the room.

-36-

A Whole New Chapter

I was finishing drying my hair, very gently with my sore head, when Rachel came rushing into the room.

"Did he call?" she asked breathlessly.

"Better," Stina answered before I could. "He brought her breakfast. Isn't that romantic?" Stina finished with a heavy sigh. I wasn't the only one enjoying my new romance. It was if the whole wing of our dorm was basking in the wonderful aura of hopeful bliss. All I could do was smile. I'd been doing that a lot all morning.

I always loved romance novels growing up. From the sweetness of *Cinderella* to those bodice rippers with half-clothed men on the front, nothing made my heart melt more or my toes curl tighter than, after hundreds of pages and when it looks all hope is lost, the girl finally gets the guy of her dreams. And then the book ends.

It's so not fair. I've read for hours and hours and invested all my emotions to get to the happily-ever-after and then it just ends.

So what happens after the end? He liked me. I liked him. I had spent so many hours hoping and dreaming of ways to get to this point, but this was a whole new chapter. The best chapter? Who knows. It's the chapter the authors never write.

What if after getting to know me Al decided he didn't like me after all? Or what if he did and I suddenly realized I didn't like him? Maybe I was not actually infatuated with the real Al Dansby, but the fantasy one I had created in my own overactive, hormone-driven imagination? What if he expected sex? On the first date? What if I wanted it and he thought I was slutty? And if I didn't, would there be a second date? What if he was okay with waiting but after dating for weeks or months or even just a few days he changes his mind? What if we find we have nothing in common, nothing to say to each other? What if he's a bad kisser? What if he thinks I'm a bad kisser? What if I really am a bad kisser? What if his dad doesn't like me? What if he finds out I don't floss regularly? What if...?

"Lottie, what's wrong?" Rachel asked. I guess my poker face was a tell-all book again. "You look like you're getting ready to have a panic attack. Where is that McDonald's sack we used last time? Everything is working out just like you wanted. What in the name of heaven and Hugh Jackman is wrong with you?" she asked again.

I had to get a grip. My ninjas had gotten me this far. I'm sure they could help with the rest.

"I don't know what happens next," I said in a small, bewildered voice.

Stina giggled. Rachel laughed out loud. Olivia yelled from the adjoining room, "Can you guys be quiet in there! Some of us need our beauty sleep!"

-37-

Getting To Know You

"It sure is nice weather we're having today," he said.

"Yeah, not much wind," I replied. This just couldn't be happening. I had tried for months to get Al Dansby to notice me, without me making a catastrophic fool of myself, and this was it? We were sitting there in a lovely restaurant while the candlelight flickered, talking about the Oklahoma weather?

Silence. I knew what he was thinking. It had been a mistake. He wanted to find an excuse to leave. Ever since he had picked me up for our date he'd been glancing at his text messages and looking at the ground. He was regretting our date, our whole start of a relationship. He had been so eager and now, he wanted an out. I knew he did. I started to dig in my purse for my trusty magical friend. I'd just do this over and cancel the date. Save us both a lot of embarrassment.

"Lottie," he broke the silence. "I'm sorry,"

Oh no, here it came. He was apologizing for asking me out and then he was going to end the date. WHERE WAS THAT STUPID ERASER?

He kept talking while I kept digging. I was going to have to learn to make sure that my magic escape route was always easily accessible. I needed to buy a purse with a special magic eraser pocket built right in for just such emergencies.

"I was so elated that you would go out with me tonight. I . . . um . . .," he kept struggling for words and looked down again at his phone. Obviously he couldn't find a nice way to say, *This ain't gonna work.*

Instead he said, "I'm so happy to be with you that my brain doesn't seem to be communicating with my mouth." And then came that mischievous, but shy little boy smile again. "It was so much easier to talk to you in the dark." Pregnant pause. Was it going to turn into the whole nine months? Should I ask the waiter to turn the lights out? But then he was talking again. "I know we barely know each other. It's strange, because I always seem to feel like I've known you longer. But, I do know that I want to get to know everything about you. Not just what you think about the weather." With that he gave a relieved laugh and million-watt smile and continued. "I have a confession to make." He paused and looked at his phone again.

For the past ten seconds things had seemed to be going well. We weren't going to talk about the weather and then suddenly he was confessing. What? Was he already engaged to someone else? Was it one of those third world country childhood betrothals?

My fingers finally touched that pink eraser, when he spoke again. "I am a little bit shy. On stage is easy because someone else has written all the lines and I simply repeat them. But in real life I have a very hard time thinking and speaking at the same time." He gave an embarrassed laugh. "I can't believe I'm telling you this, but I wrote down some things to say on our date on my iPhone and then I lost them and I keep trying to find that app and it was making me even more distracted and making it even harder to think of the right thing to say. So then all I could think about was the weather and . . . can we start again? Without the meteorological updates?" Al gave a sheepish smile and I dropped the eraser back in my bag, glad that I hadn't undone what promised to be a great evening. I had to learn not to be so trigger happy with changing time.

"I think this is the point where we start to play twenty questions," Al suggested. "You go first."

Twenty questions. Try twenty thousand. Where to start? *Will you marry me?* would probably be too pushy. I'd start with something more generic.

"Where are you from? You don't sound like most of the people around here." Oh that sounded stupid. He didn't sound like the people around here, he sounded glorious.

"Whelp, little lady," he said with his worst Oklahoman accent. "I reckon I do sound a little foreign as I'm not being from around these here parts." With that he laughed and returned to his luxurious voice. "I'm from California."

"Oh, but . . . well, I don't know. There's something a little different."

"You should go into linguistics if you picked up on that. Yes, I am a little different." Oh no, now he's going to tell me he's a vampire. Or gay. Or a gay vampire. "My mother was from London. I spent some summers there with my grandparents. So, there are some times—some little phrases that I use that sound not quite from around these parts."

"My turn. Where are you from?" he asked.

"Just down the road a fair piece," I said with my best Okie accent which wasn't hard as I always said everything with an Okie accent. "I moved a whole three hours away from home to go to school. I've lived in Oklahoma my entire life. In fact the same house since I came home from the hospital at birth. Pretty boring, huh?"

"No, not boring. Settled. Secure. It's a nice place to live."

"How does a guy," a gorgeous, sexy, accented guy, "from California with a British mother end up at OKMU? Do you have the world's most faulty GPS?"

That got a laugh out of him. Oh, and what a laugh. Not a loud, barky laugh that seemed fake, or a snorty, wheezy laugh that sounded geeky. No, just the perfect masculine, deep laugh. Yep, he even laughed perfectly.

"I came for their theater program. OkMU has the best theatrical department anywhere except the coasts."

"But California? That's movie world. Wouldn't you find better schools there?"

He was quiet for a while, deep in thought. Like there was a lot more to the story, but unsure how much he wanted to tell me, someone he barely knew. "Let's just say, I needed my own space. Next question."

Oh great, now I'd blown it. One, okay maybe two if being really picky, down on my twenty questions and I'd already made him defensive.

"Favorite food?" I asked hoping that was safe.

"Tacos."

"La—ah was right." Oops, did I say that out loud? "I mean, she just was observing what people prefer in the cafeteria one day." Bad cover.

"I guess I'll take that as a compliment that my eating habits make the daily news. Tune in tomorrow for my favorite drink."

"Mine's Diet Dr. Pepper."

"I like coffee. No let me correct that. I love coffee. I live for coffee. Don't ever come around me in the mornings before I've had my coffee."

That sent my brain on a short fantasy trip of what would he look like in the mornings before his coffee, with just PJ bottoms and tussled hair and a little bit in need of a shave?

"Lottie, you okay?"

Oh crap! I hoped I wasn't drooling on myself.

"I seem to have lost you there for a moment. Are you sure your head is okay from yesterday's accident?" he asked, concern filling his voice. Fortunately, we were distracted by the waiter who came to take our orders. I've no idea what I ordered. Some sort of food. I assumed he did too.

"Back to our questions," he resumed after our order was taken. "Tell me about your family."

"That will cost you more than one question." I proceeded to tell him of my siblings and my parents. I tried to explain my life as the middle child without sounding whiny about it. I didn't tell him of my extended family. I didn't want to scare him off.

He seemed mesmerized with my boring life. "It must be great to have a brother and sisters. I'm an only child. I always wanted a brother."

I opened up and confessed to him something I had never admitted before. "I have always said that it would be wonderful being an only child. Sometimes in really loud shouting matches with my sisters," I laughed. "But deep down I don't really mean it." There I was saying out loud to a guy I barely knew what deep down in my heart I never had wanted to admit. For all my moaning and complaining about being the normal, un-special middle child, I really did like my brother and sisters. Some days I even loved them. "They are what make my family, my family. And Christmases and snow days and family vacations would be pretty dull without them.

"Now tell me about your family." It was my turn to make demands.

"Not much to tell. There's just me and my dad now."

"Oh, divorced? That happens a lot."

162

The look on his face was so sad. It must have been a really messy affair. I wished I hadn't brought it up.

"No. Not a divorce," he began. "My mother. She was so special. You'd have loved her. Everybody loved her. My dad always did. Still does." He paused and took a deep breath. "She died when I was fifteen." He stopped talking for a moment. Again, deep in thought. It seemed he was trying to decide if he should confide in me his deepest hurts or keep it simple. After a moment he looked me in the eyes and continued. "She had cancer. You always hear how awful it is to have someone you love die of cancer, but you don't know until you've actually lived it. They don't die all of sudden, but every day, a tiny bit, right before your eyes and you're helpless to do anything about it. It's like there is a murderer right there in the room and nobody can stop him. Everyone is powerless, helpless." He stopped and took a drink of coffee. His hand was shaking ever so slightly. I sensed that he was telling me thoughts that he didn't share often or with just anyone. My heart ached for him. "We all knew it was coming, yet we pretended—hoped—prayed she'd get well. Always knowing that she wouldn't. She struggled so hard, kept taking all the drugs they gave. Sometimes it seemed that the cure made her sicker than the disease. My dad felt guilty for giving her medicine that didn't seem to work. But what was the alternative? Just give up? She couldn't eat or sleep. By the end she was so emaciated even her friends wouldn't have recognized her. Except when she smiled. She had the most beautiful smile."

"Is that where you got your smile?"

I was rewarded with a melancholy version of his glorious smile. "Yeah, everybody always says I look just like my dad. Except when I smile. Then I'm all my mother."

We sat there for a moment in silence. Strangely it wasn't awkward.

163

Then he looked into my eyes and smiled. "You'll love my dad. He's special too."

Not as special as his son, I wanted to say. But, I was trying to play it cool. Also, I was trying not to cry.

We spent the next two hours playing our version of twenty questions. The music montage of life. All the endearing smiles and laughs as some wonderfully syrupy romantic song played. I've always loved those in movies. But also wished that they would slow the happy times down and let me experience them. This time I did. I learned what his favorite song was.

"I just love that Michael Bublé song. 'Just Haven't Met You Yet.' All last semester when I'd hear it, it would bizarrely click in my head like there was this someone special that I knew, even though I hadn't met her. Or should I say you, yet."

That comment totally made my heart race and my toes curl. But, there it was again. That tiny lingering fragments of feelings left from a do-over, of remembering a meeting that hadn't happened in his reality. I also wondered, as I hadn't really allowed myself to wonder before, if doing time over wasn't hard on others. Did it leave them with confused, déjà vu feelings that could never be explained or resolved? I didn't wonder for long as he was on to his next question.

"What is your favorite book? Writer? Movie?"

"That's three questions."

"I know. I thought I'd try putting them all together and hope I could get more than my twenty in." Little did he know he could interrogate me until forever and I wouldn't complain.

"Hmm, book? Anything by Jane Austen, of course. And Agatha Christie. But I'm also a *Harry Potter* freak. I almost went into depression

when the last book came out and I knew there wouldn't be any others."
Now to tell or not to tell? I also was obsessed with *Twilight*. But for some reason, guys didn't want to hear about it.

Al took a sip of his coffee. I think he was on about his tenth cup. We had been there a while. In fact that pause made me look around and realize we were the only people still in the restaurant.

"I thought you would like *Twilight*. Most people who like Jane Austen do," he said.

"Busted."

Then he looked around the room like an undercover spy, making sure there were no bugs or surveillance cameras. "I'll make a confession to you. But if you tell, I might have to kill you."

Oh no. Here it came. The something bad. That's how I'd felt since the breakfast in bed had arrived. This was all too good to be true. Any time he'd confess to some major obstacle that would doom our chances of being together forever.

Then he gave a very sheepish smile and said, "I've read them too. And I didn't hate them. But, if you ever tell anyone, I'll deny it.

"Now favorite movie," he continued.

"That one's easy. Anything with Alistair Dansberough in it. They're always so good. Did you ever meet him in California?"

Suddenly, Al seemed to realize what I had known for awhile, but didn't want to mention, the restaurant was empty. "We probably should go. I think they want to close up.

-38-

Some Things Are Worth Doing Over

"So Lottie Lambert, English major, I've had a perfectly enjoyable evening," then Al corrected himself after looking at his watch, "night, or actually it is getting to be morning."

"The best," I gushed. I would never learn to play it cool, but for once I didn't want to. I was having the best evening, night, well actually morning I had ever had and I hated for it to end.

There we stood at the front door of my dorm. Both of us not wanting the date to end, but knowing it would. Would he try to kiss me? Would I let him? Did I want him to? That question was easy, YES. But, would he think I was easy? I know that in movies now-a-days people sleep together after just meeting, often before they even exchange last names. That wasn't my upbringing, not even my style. I was taught commitment and respecting myself. And my breath. I had just remembered that I hadn't had any kind of mint or gum after dinner. Was I garlicky? I hoped I didn't have broccoli in my front teeth. I was starting to panic. And just being silly, because I hadn't even eaten broccoli or garlic. I was safe. Oh, but I did have black pepper. That could have been stuck right in my front tooth and

I'd never have known. Was I going to hyperventilate? Oh crap and then he'd think I was jumping to the heavy breathing without even a kiss. Should I use my eraser and get us back to the restaurant so I could check my teeth in the restroom mirror?

"Lottie, are you okay?" He seemed to be asking me that question a lot. It was time to get a grip.

I nodded yes. And smiled. With my lips closed, in case of the pepper thing.

"Like I said, I had a nice, no strike that, a fabulous time tonight. I hope to see a lot of you."

"Me too." I don't know why I ever thought I could be a writer, because as a speaker I was never very eloquent. 'Me too' was all that I could come up with.

Al stepped a little closer and took my hand. "I'm in this play right now. And when we're in production I'm extremely occupied with practices," Oh crap. I had misread everything. He was trying to find an excuse to not see me or at least not that often. "But," Oh a BUT, I loved a but (the one t kind not the two t's kind, although his two t kind was mighty fine.) "If you don't mind odd hours and unpredictable times, I really would love to spend more time with you."

I just nodded. And giving caution to the wind, gave a full teeth smile.

With that, he stepped even closer and took my other hand. "I know this is our first date. Although as romantic as the atmosphere was, I wouldn't count our trip to the emergency room as a date." There was that mischievous smile again. My knees were going to melt. "I was hoping, well, wondering, . . . wishing. Lottie, may I kiss you?"

"Yes, yes you may." And he did. It was the perfect kiss. Just the

167

right amount of pressure with just a tiny bit of a nibble and . . .(oh sorry, TMI.) Anyway it was the perfect kiss.

"I'll call you tomorrow," he said as he went to open the door for me. "Don't worry, I've still got your number." Then he pulled back his sleeve. "Sharpie is very hard to wash off."

I floated into the foyer. Life was good. Fortunately the lobby was empty, as it took me a full two minutes to regain any sense of composure. Then my hand was in my bag snatching up my trusty friend. There were many things in life I wanted to do-over in order to change them for the better. But, some things in life are just too good to only do once. So with a flick of my wrist I was back on the front stairs staring into Al's beautiful green eyes.

Hearing, "Lottie, may I kiss you?"

I loved that little pink eraser.

-39-

A Woman Scorned And Her BFF's

Floating. I did a lot of that over the next few weeks. The only work my magic eraser was getting was to do instant reruns of wonderful moments. But, I had to confess, that even though doing a first kiss a second time was fantastic, it's still not as good as the first. Knowing what to expect takes away some of the firstness of it and then it was really just a second kiss. Which was still pretty awesome.

It was late on Thursday evening. I was floating down the hallway, on my way to meet Al after his rehearsal. My mind was anywhere but in my head. So, it took a few seconds before I saw Kasha sitting on the floor in a little enclave of the hallway. She was reading something on her laptop and softly crying.

I knelt down next to her and asked that dumb American question yet again, "Are you okay?"

"Yeah," she answered. Why did we always do that? We could be standing there with blood pouring out of our bodies, a limb severed off and still we'd say we were fine.

"No you're not. What's wrong?"

"It's not me. It's Keesha. She's so lonely and miserable. I was just reading an email from her."

Keesha. It had been over a month since we all got her pregnancy news. After the seven-day wonder, we seemed to forget about her and go on with our happy lives. So sad, but so true. Maybe that was the hardest part of all of being a teenage mother, the loneliness. Keesha's friends went on having their exciting adventures while her life was on hold—alone. Dealing with the overwhelming stress of being responsible for a new life coming into the world, and at the same time feeling guilty for wishing she could go back to her pre-pregnancy happy-go-lucky days. At least she had one true friend who hadn't forgotten her, Kasha.

"There she is, stuck in Kansas. She's already gained almost twenty pounds. Twenty pounds! Her clothes don't fit and she doesn't have money to waste on new ones. Twenty pounds. Way too much for being in her fourth month. But she says she's bored and unhappy and nothing to do but eat. And then everyday I see that jerk soccer player strutting around campus, always some other fool girl with him. He's not fat. His ankles aren't swelling. He didn't have to move back to Kansas. Urgh. I just get so mad. One of these days I'm just gonna walk right up to him and slap that smirky smile into next month."

"I think we need a little project," said Olivia. I jumped. I hadn't heard her approach. "The ninja troop solved your problem Lottie, now it's time for some retribution for ol' mister soccer."

"We can't run him over!" I said before thinking.

Again Olivia gave me an intense look. I tried to put on my most innocent, I know nothing about your past face, as I possibly could. I guess she bought it as she continued speaking. "I'm not planning anything illegal. Gosh Lottie, what kind of person do you think I am? Well, not majorly illegal. I mean if we castrated him, we'd go to jail. So that's off the list."

"And egging his car is so middle school and won't change anything. So what are we gonna do?" asked Rachel. Where had she come from? "I heard you all out here plotting a plan and I knew I wanted to be in on it too. Any ideas?"

"Not yet," said Olivia back in her commandant mode. "This one will have to be perfect. Some way to screw-up his life, like he did Keesha, but in a way that it doesn't come back to bite us all on the butt. This will take some major planning. First we'll start with surveillance. We need his schedule. Who he's with, when, where? Anything we can find out."

"The K's are on it," said Kaylee. What another materializing person? Note to self. Never have a confidential conversation in our hallway, as it was becoming apparent that anything said in that area was heard by all.

"We need his phone number and any passwords, logins and pertinent information we can find," the General continued. "Stina," last to join our importune conference, "you're the best at computer espionage. See what you can find." Then turning to Rachel. "Dr. Freud, you get into his psyche. Find out the thing he values the most. We already know he's a horn dog, with no scruples when it comes to women. Now we need to know his ultimate weakness. His Achilles heel."

The look in Olivia's eyes was almost maniacal. Maybe our plan of sabotage on the LSPS wasn't such a good idea. She was out for blood. Not just revenge on one self-centered, egotistical jock, but on all of the evil, manipulative, predatory men on the planet. She was out for revenge for her eight-year-old self and any others like her. Then again, maybe it was time for some of those wronged women to be avenged. All I knew was that I would be holding very tightly to my magical friend in case anything should

171

get out of hand and we needed a rapid redo escape route.

-40-

The Green-Eyed Monster

One thing I had learned in less than a week of dating (oh, that sounded so nice, dating, I think I'll say it again, dating) an actor was that rehearsals ended when they were done, no matter what the clock on the wall said. Al had invited me to go for coffee after his practice, ending time TBA. But I didn't care. Al Dansby was worth the wait any day.

I quietly slipped into the last row of the auditorium and sat to watch patiently wait. It was still two weeks before the show went up. That was a theatrical term Al had taught me. Plays didn't start. They went up—as in, the curtain goes up. I also learned that thespian meant actor. Go figure. To while away the time I opened my laptop and tried to focus on my newly motivated writing career. I had started a short story about a girl who almost didn't meet her Prince Charming because she was too obsessed with always seeming perfect. Yes, art was attempting to imitate life, but once Al came on stage my fingers quit moving across the keyboard. His voice, his face the way he moved totally consumed me.

It was the first time that I had made it in time to see Al's big scene. It was a good thing too that I was able to see it without a crowd of people. I'd forgotten a lot about *South Pacific*. I'd watched it once when I was in middle school on DVD with my mom. I knew that Al was playing Lt. Cable and he had a Tonkinese girlfriend.

There stood my man, in half a military uniform. For some reason his shirt was on the floor. That was my first viewing of his chest. Nice. Just the right ratio of muscles to hair. But, what was he doing topless on stage? And he was singing the most beautiful, romantic ballad about a girl who was younger than springtime. It was melt your socks steamy as he kept singing and reached out to gently stroke her hair. That's when I realized that wasn't any regular Tonkinese girl. It was skank woman, Taylor. Oh and it just kept getting worse. He kept singing and they kept getting closer. Then they were kneeling on a blanket. Where did that come from? Smashed together! And then they weren't kneeling anymore. They were lying down—TOGETHER. It was getting dark in the theater. I wasn't sure if that was because of the stage lighting or I was about to pass out from rage.

After at least three hours the song finally ended. The stage was black, but I was definitely seeing red. I didn't remember this part on the DVD. Obviously my mom had fast-forwarded through it as it was a little too risqué for her middle schooler.

"That was great!" came a call from the front row. I guess that was the director. I felt like standing up and yelling, "I object."

The director spoke again, "Bring up some light."

I couldn't agree more. And some clothes. And some space between them. The lights came back on and Al, my Al Dansby was still laying on that blanket with that woman. Finally, he sat up.

There was a long technical talk between Al, the director and SW I didn't understand it. My brain wasn't functioning for all the steam coming out of my ears. As quietly as I could, I left. I was going to have to do a little rethinking. I wasn't sure if I was cut out to be dating an actor.

***

Al found me an hour later, sitting on the bottom step outside my dorm. He didn't talk at first, just sat down.

"It's rather cold out here," he began. Then I knew it was coming. "Are you okay?" Yep, like I said, that phrase got used a lot. But this time I wasn't going to say fine when I wasn't.

"I came to rehearsal."

"I know. I saw you leave."

We sat side by side for a few minutes. He was right. It was cold out there. I'd been so upset, I hadn't realized until then.

"Why did you leave? I thought we were going to go for coffee."

Did he really not get it? Was I just so unsophisticated that I couldn't handle watching the guy I liked, really, really liked, make out on stage with another woman? And not just any woman. A drop-dead-gorgeous-cheats-with-other's-boyfriends woman. I didn't want to have this conversation. I reached for my purse to find a *timely* exit.

Al took my hand from my purse. "Please, don't leave. We've barely started this relationship. But, Lottie, I really want it to work. There's something here. Something special. When I look at you, talk to you, am near you. I really want this to work. But, you have to tell me what you're thinking. You have to tell me what is wrong."

Relationship. He had said relationship. That sounded permanent, sound, secure. He was right. I needed to quit running from any awkward situation. I needed to quit changing time and follow through on the hard

175

parts. I needed . . . to start talking, because he was looking at me like I was a deaf mute.

"I'm sorry I left. I didn't know that you even knew I was there."

"The slamming close of the seat and the door, kind of gave you away." He gave a little smile.

"Oh." I thought I had quietly slipped out.

"So, I'm waiting. Why did you leave?"

This was hard. I didn't want to sound all controlling and jealous. But he needed to know.

"I've never dated an actor before."

"Okay." He still looked very confused.

"Alright. I feel stupid. But you were holding her and kissing her and singing to her."

"Yes, that's how the show goes." The guy was obtuse. No light bulbs at all were coming on in his brain. I was going to have to just spell it all out.

"You don't get it, do you? There you were with your former girlfriend. The look in your eyes was just smoldering. You looked so. . . so . . . Well, I was," then nothing would come out of my mouth.

"You were. . .?"

What was I? I felt angry and hurt and scared and just a little bit out of control. It was a feeling I'd never felt so strongly and confusingly in my life.

"Jealous," I whispered. I was glad we were outside with only the street lamps for light as my face was glowing as red as Rudolph's nose.

Al was stunned for a moment and then gave me his most glorious smile. "That's the nicest thing I've ever heard."

That so wasn't the response I was expecting.

He reached over and gave me the softest kiss on my cheek.

"Jealous. I don't think I've ever known a girl who cared enough to be jealous." Al scooted closer and put his arm around my shoulder. It felt good in so many ways. "But, point number one. Taylor is my friend. Never was and never will be my girlfriend."

"But I saw you leave and come back together for Christmas break."

Al looked a little startled and then gave a mischievous smile. "I didn't know you were stalking me."

"I wasn't. Just a small campus and I was strategically located," I countered trying not to blush.

"Lottie, Taylor and I are both from California. So I just gave her a ride to the plane. That's all. We've known each other for years. She's a good friend and a good actor. That's all. I think she's dating some soccer jock anyway, even though I don't think he's even good enough for her. I'm sure she's going to get hurt, but she won't listen to me," he finished sounding more like an older brother rather than a lover.

"Now I guess is the time for Acting 101 class. The smoldering eyes and the loving looks, that was acting. That's all. It's like a choreographed dance. We've worked for weeks on blocking all the moves and emotions to make it look real. But it's not. I promise."

"But it looked so real."

Al gave an ornery smile. "I'm a good actor."

"I feel like such a fool."

"No, you're a wonderful girl, who's never dated an actor before. Now let me tell you something else important. When I die in the play, I don't really die either."

I reached over to touch his cheek. "I'll cry anyway." That got me a chuckle and a kiss on the tip of my nose.

177

"Your nose is cold. Let's go get some coffee. I'm having withdrawals. It's been almost three hours since I ran out of the magical elixir backstage."

Hand in hand we walked the few blocks to the Coffee Corner. Life can be so sweet. Al was humming a tune I didn't recognize as we walked.

"What song is that?"

Al stopped and thought a moment. "I'm not sure." He hummed a few more bars. "Must just be one of those things in my head that I'm not really sure where it came from. Do you ever get that?"

"Hmm, I guess." I had no idea what he meant, but I'd agree to make him happy.

Al chuckled. "Now you think I'm mental. Sometimes this year I've thought I was losing it myself. I've had some of the most bizarre, vivid dreams. I'd almost have sworn they happened. But they didn't."

"I've done that before. Like dreamed I bought new shoes, and then went to put them on the next day and realized it was only a dream. A wonderful dream." I giggled. "I like shoes."

"My dreams weren't so normal. I've had this dream about someone. Like someone just out of my line of vision. And I simply couldn't find her." Al stopped walking and turned to look at me. "Maybe my subconscious knew you were coming." Then he gave a big laugh. "I also dreamed someone threw spaghetti on me in the cafeteria. Some dreams are just weird."

-41-

Homework Vs. Romance

Al and I had been an official item for two weeks, three days and two hours and forty-five minutes, not that I was counting, complete with a Facebook status change to *in a relationship*. It was scary to me how quickly we had fallen into the couple thing. One minute (okay the one minute thing had happened more than once) we met and then we clicked. I'd always dreamed there was such a thing as love at first sight, but I was also mature enough to know that dreams are just that. Dreams.

Most of our *official in a relationship* time had been spent with Al in play rehearsal and me up to my ears in a Lit. paper that was rapidly becoming due. Homework stoppeth for no man (nor woman), even those in love. Thus, my Thursday evening would be spent in the library while Al was just a few buildings over in the theater.

Literature is wonderful when reading much-loved books like *Anne of Green Gables* or *Little Women*. Or authors that make you think deep, seldom thought feelings like Dostoevsky or Sinclair. It is drudgery when trudging through *Moby Dick*. (Be honest. Has anyone ever actually enjoyed *Moby Dick*?) Even worse when your sadistic teacher wanted an in-depth analysis and comparison of the *Dick* and the *Old Man in the Sea*. Nothing in common but water. And by the end of both stories, I couldn't have cared less if they all drowned.

I sat in the library contemplating using that as my thesis statement, while checking my email, Facebook, Snapchats, and text messages every couple of minutes. Just in case Al had a break and thought of me. I was pathetic.

"I only have shore leave for fifteen minutes. So I snuck out the back door," said Lt. Cable who had stealthily sat down next to me. I love a man in a uniform. "How's your paper coming?"

I looked at the blank screen of my laptop. "Okay, I guess," I fibbed. I didn't want to confess that my mind had been out to sea, but not with the old man or Moby. Rather on a little island in the Pacific with a certain Lieutenant.

Al reached up to gently touch my cheek. Things were looking promising. "I wanted to catch you and let you know, we're going to be extremely late. The first two acts were dead tonight. Completely dragging. So after we finish, we're starting over."

"No Coffee Corner tonight?"

"Sorry. Can we meet for lunch tomorrow?"

"I can't. I have a study group lunch. What about supper?"

"We're starting rehearsal early, so we're having food brought in on the set."

"It's a busy time."

"Very busy. But this play will go up in a week. And it only runs for two weekends. Then I'll be free."

With a peck on the cheek he was gone. Back to his Tonkinese fling and I was back to M. Dick. Being an item was great. Being one with time to spend together would have been even better. Well, the least I could do was double the little time that we did have together. Out came my trusty friend and Al was back next to me for an instant replay.

"I only have shore leave for fifteen minutes. So I snuck out the back door," said Lt. Cable who had just sat down next to me. "How's your paper coming?"

"Fine," I lied again. Did that make me a pathological liar if I kept repeating the same lie in different realities? "So your rehearsal isn't going so well?"

Al gave me a deep look. "Wow, you are perceptive. We have just barely gotten to know each other, yet you seem almost to read my mind already. Scary." I was going to blow it. Soon he'd think I was some psychic freak and run for the hills. Then he gave me that magical smile and touched my cheek again (the one on my face, in case there was any confusion.) "A very nice scary. Yes, the show is really dragging."

I needed to remember to play by the original script.

All too soon, with a peck on my cheek, he was gone

-42-

Holy Smoke

Halloween is supposed to be the time of terror, with skeletons, witches and vampires (and not the sparkly kind.) Friday the Thirteenth is the day to hide in your room afraid that luck will run out. But no day holds the terrifying suspense, that intense fear of the unknown, that ultimate dread of what might not happen—no day is more horrifying than February the fourteenth—Valentine's Day. Monsters can only kill you. Valentine's Day can break your heart.

For years I had dreaded that day. Back in high school it had been a major status symbol to receive flowers delivered to the school. Woe be it to the pitiful boyfriend who didn't. Many a budding romance dissolved due to the lack of floral arrangements. By my sophomore year, after picking up a sobbing freshman up the year before, my mother knew to always send me anonymous flowers on that fateful day.

Finally, the fates had changed my destiny. I had a boyfriend. Valentine's Day had become a day of anticipation, not dread. So then why was I more terrified than ever before? Why? Because the stakes were suddenly so much higher. Not only did I have the wonderful anticipation of receiving the perfect valentine from the perfect guy, I had to give the perfect valentine to the perfect guy. What a perfect dilemma.

"Something to do with coffee," Stina suggested. It was two days before the fateful holiday. Great minds were converging in our dorm room for a strategic planning meeting.

"He does like his coffee," Rachel agreed. "But is that romantic? **We** need something so special, so unique. Something . . ." Rachel was stumped. As were we all. This discussion had been going on for over an hour and lord only knows how many calories worth of cookie dough had been consumed in the name of romance.

"Guys are impossible to buy for," repeated Olivia. "We all know the one thing they want."

Stina came to Al's defense. "Not all guys. There are some good ones. Right, Lottie?"

"Lottie?" asked Rachel.

"See he's already been putting the moves on you. Hasn't he?" Olivia demanded.

I hadn't really thought about it until that point. I was so caught up in the magic of first love I hadn't noticed that for the first time ever I was dating a gentleman. Sure we had had some major snogging in the stacks, but no trying to slip his hands where they didn't belong. No trying to sneak a grope in the pretense of a hug. No staring at my cleavage instead of my face.

"Earth to Lottie," Stina said with a worried giggle.

"No, no he hasn't," I finally said. "Wow, isn't that amazing. He truly is the perfect guy." I was gushing all over the place.

"Or gay," Olivia snorted.

"Time to get back on task," teacher Stina interjected. "Maybe it isn't a gift, but something thoughtful that will make the day special. What is his schedule like on V. Day?"

"Class all day and then play practice all night. We are planning to meet for lunch. He has no other free time all day."

"If only you could create time," Stina pondered aloud wistfully. I snorted a quasi-hysterical laugh. If only they knew how close that was to the truth.

"Girlfriend, sometimes you are so abnormal," Olivia said once again giving me that wondering look.

***

So the day had arrived and our plan was put into action. I had one addition to the plan that the rest of the crew knew nothing about. I was sticking to that magic eraser like cat hair to black pants. At any slight sense of failure there was a magical redo ready to be done.

The day started earlier than planned. That's what fire alarms do.

"Oh my gravy! What is that?" Stina shouted over the noise. It was three a.m. That would be three in the MORNING. I had a dilemma. Which was better: to get up at that ungodly hour and be safe, or stay in bed and take my chances that it was a false alarm and not a real fire? Stina made the decision for the both of us.

"Lottie, get up! We have to go out!"

We scrambled to find sweatpants and shoes to throw on. It was February, cold and dark.

"This place had better be burning to the ground, or someone is going to regret it big time," I was griping as we went up the stairs and out.

Fire trucks had already arrived, complete with hunky firemen. Not that I was looking, of course. The majority of co-eds seemed more stressed by the firemen seeing them without their make-up than the possibility of our temporary homes going up in flames. Suddenly, there was one more red vehicle zipping up to our dorm. A little, red Miata. And a frantic knight in shinning armor came leaping out. My first thought was to hide so he wouldn't see me with frizzled hair and black mascara rings under my eyes. Instead I started to use my magic eraser. Only one problem, it was in the dorm. I contemplated running back into the possibly burning building to retrieve it. But one look at his face changed that plan. He looked frantic, vulnerable, even scared. I could hear him asking everyone if they knew where I was.

"Al, I'm okay," I shouted as I rushed over to him. My reward was a bone-crushing hug. "What are you doing here?" I asked when I could breathe again.

"I was just leaving the theater, and I heard the sirens. Sorry if I overreacted," he broke off. There was a hint of embarrassment in his voice. "I simply had to know that you were safe."

Our conversation was interrupted by the Dorm Director shouting, "It's all clear. No fire. Just someone, who will be getting a rules violation first thing tomorrow morning, was trying to make a grilled cheese sandwich with her iron and forgot about it. The smoke set off the smoke detectors. You can go back in. Oh, and you guys over there with the cameras—there had better not be any photos of these girls in their PJs on the internet."

It wasn't until she pointed it out that I noticed the contingent of male students with cameras and cell phones playing paparazzi. I was glad I had put on sweats, cause no amount of threats from our Dorm Director would ever keep those photos from the World Wide Web.

"Do you think anyone got pictures of us?" Al asked. I was wondering if he wanted a souvenir photo of the occasion, but he seemed worried, not nostalgic.

"I hope not. I'm just glad the light is so bad out here. I hate for you to see me looking like death warmed over."

Al smiled and looked deep in my raccoon eyes. "You're beautiful, Lottie. If you could see yourself like I see you, you'd never question how absolutely beautiful you are."

I couldn't move. Couldn't think. All I could do was look into his wonderful kind eyes and sigh. I loved fire alarms.

"Are you going in or not?" asked Stina. Where had she come from? It seemed that there had been only two people on the planet, when suddenly we were back on Asbury lawn surrounded by fire trucks, firemen and half dressed co-eds at three thirty in the morning. I gaped at her like she had just materialized from another planet.

"See you in the room," she said, giggled and left.

Al and I stood there staring at each other like two demented fools. I spoke first to break the trance. "Why were you at the theater so late?" I asked

"We were working on sets. See, paint. You caught me red handed." He held up his hand, which indeed did have red paint on it. Why did something so innocent sound like a lie? "Sometimes I get engrossed and totally lose track of time. I had no idea it was so late until I heard the fire trucks. I guess you want to get back to bed."

"I guess you need to head on home yourself." Neither of us moved.

Al reached out to smooth my ratty hair. "I should let you go back to bed," he whispered. "See you for lunch tomorrow."

How could something so benign as *see you for lunch tomorrow* sound so utterly romantic? If we weren't careful, the firemen were going to have a fire of a totally different kind to put out on the lawn of Asbury Hall.

"Tomorrow," I answered as he turned to walk away.

He stopped and turned back. "By the way, happy Valentine's Day."

186

I awoke the next morning to find the truth of Al's late night theater work. Standing outside my ground level window was a big, red, four-foot tall, plywood heart with the initials A. D. + L.L painted on it with sparkly paint. It was so silly, so middle school, so utterly the best Valentine's Day gift a girl could ever hope for.

-43-

Just You and Me
Against The Wind

"Perhaps a Valentine's Day picnic wasn't such a good idea," Al said as he returned from chasing down a paper bag with half our lunch in it that had blown across the park. "The weather man predicted it would be unseasonably warm today. He said nothing about the wind. Does this ridiculous wind never quit blowing?"

Our picnic was a perfect example of the *it's the thought that counts* concept. Al had picked me up an hour earlier with a blanket, a coffee, a Diet D.P. and a bag of tacos, all ready for a leisurely romantic picnic in the park. Reality had started to set in when we tried to get out of his Miata without the wind blowing the doors off. Maybe the thermometer said it was one of those freak days in February that are close to seventy degrees, but that was without factoring in the wind-chill. It felt like the forties, the very cold windy forties.

We tried for a good ten minutes to make the picnic idea fly. Instead our food was flying. When the wind finally conquered Al's beloved coffee, retreat to the car was conceded.

"Al, it was a great idea. Just maybe the wrong day for it." I smiled as

I tried to nonchalantly clean the coffee stains off my shirt. Yep, when the wind had blown it from Al's grasp most had sloshed my way.

Al started to put the keys in the ignition.

"We don't have to go yet, do we?" I asked. "I'm fine with a picnic in the car. Especially this tiny little car."

"It does give us an excuse to be rather close." There was that smile. With a little spark I hadn't seen before. "So tell me Lottie Lambert, what has been going on in your world the last few weeks? I've kind of been stuck on an island out in the South Pacific and feel totally cut off. I'm looking forward to a time when we can see more of each other."

"Well, I got you a little Valentine's Day gift that might help you there." With trepidation I gave him the gift I had fretted over, discussed with the council on love and basically had a mental meltdown before deciding on. The first gift exchange was such a pivotal point in a new relationship. What to get him? Something fun and whimsical that said we were in a fun and whimsical relationship? Or something meaningful and deep? But that might make him think that our relationship was getting too meaningful and deep too fast. If I gave him something too expensive he might feel stupid for giving me a plywood heart—which I totally loved. If I gave him something too cheap would he be embarrassed that I had given him a piece of junk? I held my breath and my pink eraser as I handed him his present.

"Oh, Lottie you shouldn't have," he said as I handed him my gift. Now did he really mean I shouldn't have to be nice or did he mean I shouldn't have at all? My right hand had a death grip on my magical friend while my left hand held his gift.

Al gave me an ambiguous look as he began to open the envelope. Like a gentleman he read the card first and replied, "Of course I'll be your valentine." Then he turned over the two tickets to read what they were for. "*Mary Poppins* tickets," he said neither sounding thrilled nor excited.

"It's not until next May, but I thought we could go then." Why did I say that? May was so far away. Did he feel trapped? I needed to erase that last comment. Give him the gift again. I started to wave my eraser but was stopped short by Al's response.

"I used to watch this movie as a child and totally hated it. Now..."

Of all the musicals in the world, how had I picked the one that he hated?

Before he could finish telling me how totally un-perfect my perfect gift was I flipped my eraser filled wrist and we were back to "So tell me Lottie Lambert, what has been going on in your world the last few weeks? I've kind of been stuck on an island out in the South Pacific and feel totally cut off."

"Nothing much," was all I could come up with. No gift after all. Relationship disaster averted. The tickets would stay in my purse where they belonged.

***

We spent the next two hours sitting in that itty-bitty car discussing any and every thought that we had. We talked about classes. I told him the gist of my paper on *Moby Dick*. I think I blushed when I said the title and then felt stupid for it. He told me about some of the pranks that they had played backstage during rehearsals. Seems that there is a lot of down time during practice and actors are imaginative people who come up with clever distractions. It was mystifying how comfortable I felt talking with Al (except for the final ten minutes as I really had to pee, but I didn't want the moment to end.)

Somewhere along the way, with the tacos all gone and before I had to pee, Al gave me a very penetrative look. "You're special. You do realize that don't you? Somehow I don't think you do. I hear you talk about your family, and don't get me wrong they sound wonderful and I look forward to meeting them. But, Lottie, you always talk about them like they're just short of supernatural and you're not." I had to look away. He was so sincere and I felt so inadequate. "Lottie, please look at me." I did, feeling vulnerable. "You are special." His hand gently stroked the side of my face. "I've barely gotten to know you. And I hope I'm not frightening you off by being too intense. But, Lottie, you are the most amazing, intriguing, beautiful woman I have ever met." With that he gave me the most amazing, intriguing and beautiful kiss ever. And I gave it right back to him.

"Lottie, I'm so sorry I have to say this," Al said as he took a breath. Oh great. He was going to tell me that I was a lousy kisser or that my breath stank. Which it did, but he'd had the same stinky tacos. "What's wrong?" he asked sounding panicked as he looked at my face. I was really going to have to work on not being so transparent. "Darling, I just have to get to the theater. It's getting late."

"Oh. Yeah." I was embarrassed. I truly had to quit jumping to the conclusion that every time he said sorry that the next words would be that he didn't want to see me anymore.

-44-

"All The World's A Stage"

There I sat in the darkened theater between Rachel and Olivia surrounded by the K's. It was finally opening night and there was my amazing boyfriend wowing the audience as he made hot, steamy, PRETEND romance with that Tonkinese girl. It was much easier for me to handle it since I'd been tutored by Al in Acting 101. And if I always thought of her as that Tonkinese girl, rather than long legged Taylor. Yes, handle it I could do, actually like it was still a work in progress.

The play was a huge success with a packed out audience. Even the president of the college had been there with some major bigwig donors. They must have been pretty important as they were ushered in at the last moment to the best seats in the house and then left right after the curtain call, via the stage. And yes, I did cry when Lt. Cable died. And I illogically rejoiced when Al came to take his curtain call—proof that it was just fantasy.

Al and I had barely seen each other the past two weeks. We'd been able to cram in two lunches, a run to QuikTrip for a slushy and coffee, and about one hundred and forty-seven text messages.

Tonight was going to be different. I was to wait for him after the show and we were going to do a very late dinner.

The crowd was thinning. A few parents and friends of the actors were waiting like me to congratulate their stars. I realized that I too was beaming like a proud mother as I waited for my own little thespian. It took around thirty minutes before Al appeared at my side.

"You were wonderful," I said as I gave him a big congratulatory hug. Ummm he felt good.

"Are you sure? I blew that one line really badly. And I was flat once." Al, the super confident actor on stage, seemed like a little boy needing approval.

"Trust me. You were fantastic. Give me the next five hours just to tell you how magnificent you were."

An uneasy look came across Al's face. The kind of look that always made my heart knot up and my brain race with visions that I was about to be dumped. "Lottie, well, I'm so sorry. I have to cancel. There's this really important donor here tonight. And well, the president wants me to go out to dinner with them. I'm so sorry. I didn't know he was coming. He hadn't told me—I mean the president didn't let me know in advance."

I put on my best poker face. If he had to ditch me for Mr. Mega-Donate-The-Bucks I wouldn't make him feel bad.

"Oh, Lottie. I've hurt your feelings. Believe me, I'm truly sorry. If he hadn't come so far, I'd demand another night. But he just flew in for tonight."

So much for my acting skills. "I'm fine," I lied. "We'll get together soon. You have my number. I'm sure you need to get going. You don't want to make them wait. And I really do need to be working on my Lit. paper. I shouldn't have put it off for so long. I've got to go."

Al wasn't letting me go. He held my arm and drew me close. "Can we do lunch, tomorrow? It's Saturday. I'm free 'til backstage call at five."

I didn't respond.

"Please."

I nodded my head not trusting my voice. Then Al Dansby pulled me close and kissed me like that Tonkinese girl just wished he would have kissed her.

-45-

Loose Lips Sink FriendShips

"Hey, remember us? We're those friends you used to hang out with before Mr. Dansby came riding in on his fine white steed—or should I say his little, red car," teased Stina.

"You'll have me all to yourself starting tomorrow," I reminded her. My family always planned an annual spring break ski vacation. With all our activities and crazy schedules we were never able to find a week in the summer for a family vacation, so my mother had decreed over ten years before, that spring break was family week and no excuse other than death or Jason getting drafted to the pros would be accepted. That year I was taking Stina along. With my super jock family all doing the black slopes, I usually spent most of my skiing time alone on the bunny slopes. It had actually been my mother's idea for me to bring a friend. I think she had hoped I'd bring a guy. But I'd asked Stina before I knew Al well enough to invite him along with my family. In fact I still wasn't sure I was secure enough to spend an entire week with him around the Double J's. It wouldn't be the first time a guy I was interested in had suddenly jumped ship and asked out one of my sisters. I don't even want to think about the dope who had asked them both out. Kinky weirdo.

"Sorry I haven't been around much lately. Once the play was finally over, Al and I seemed to be making up for lost time." I gave a heavy sigh. Life was good.

Stina gave a heavy sigh too. I wasn't sure if she was mocking me or simply enjoying the blissful aura that surrounded me.

"Are you all packed?" I asked. "I'll be ready to go by three tomorrow."

"Ready and willing. I've never skied before. This should be fun. But I hope I don't slow you down."

I gave a laugh. "Never worry. I'm the world's worst. After ten ski vacations, I still never venture off the green slopes—those are the easy ones. The blues are harder and don't even ask about the blacks. Major bad."

"We'll just be snow bunnies on the baby slopes and have a blast."

I sighed again. I knew I was being ridiculous. I could live a week— well actually ten days due to weekends and us leaving after class the next day. But, I could make it ten days without Al Dansby. I was a modern woman. I was independent.

I was missing him already.

"So what is Mr. Wonderful doing for the break?" Olivia asked, entering the room through the shared bathroom. She added a Post It note to the poster hanging on our bathroom door. It was a detailed chart of the LSPS's life. His schedule, his preferences, his friends. It looked stalkerish to say the least. The General was still planning our strategy. After spring break he was going down. Parts of the plan were starting to worry me. Maybe we were going too far? But then again, nothing illegal was being planned. And maybe, actually no maybe about it, telling a girl lies, and getting a girl pregnant was going too far also and deserved whatever punishment the General had devised.

Hopefully a week apart would help get things in perspective for everyone.

"Al said he was hanging out with his dad for the week. It's so strange. He's so open and sharing and we talk and talk and talk. Yet, when we're through I realize he never really tells me actual details about his life in California or his dad."

"Maybe they have issues," suggested Rachel who entered behind Olivia.

"I don't think so. He always talks with admiration of him, not like he's some evil step-father," I said and unintentionally looked straight at Olivia. Why did I keep doing that? I had undone our conversation about her step-dad just so that she wouldn't see me giving her those pitying looks, but I did it anyway.

Olivia looked at me then at Rachel. "Crap, I forgot. I have a thingy. You know a meeting thingy. I've got to go," she said a little flustered. It must have been an important meeting. Or more likely, a very cute guy.

Stina was quickly asking Rachel for more details on her break plans. Being so focused on my own self the past two months, I hadn't noticed the gradual relationship building between Rachel and Trevor. (Trevor of the Christmas dance with the asinine brother—my ill-fated date.)

"I still can't believe he invited me to spend the week at his house," Rachel was gushing. Our calm, cool, analytical Rachel was gushing about a guy. "I've liked him since freshman year. But, he always treated me like a buddy. Just one of the gang. But ever since the Christmas dance. Oooo momma."

Yes, definitely some people had much pleasanter memories of that function than I.

"You'll have a blast. I wouldn't be surprised if you didn't come back engaged," Stina bubbled.

"I don't think we're to the engagement step yet. But I sure do feel like I'm there for his mom's evaluation. Very nerve wracking."

I sighed again. I had to stop doing that. "You'll pass with flying colors. But if I don't get this essay done and turned in tomorrow I won't. Off to the library. Got to work ladies."

"Wouldn't it be easier to write here, without the distractions?" teased Stina.

"Yes," I confessed. "But I told the distraction I'd meet him there five minutes ago." And with that I was out the door.

-46-

Distractions

A table full of books and copies topped with a coffee cup. That is how I found Al Dansby in the library.

"Isn't it against the rules to have drinks in here?" I asked as I sat down by him and he leaned over to give me a sweet kiss on the cheek.

Al gave me his mischievous smile and said, "It pays to have connections." I looked over to see the barrister guy from last semester working the reference desk. Poor guy. I wondered if he had caught on yet that Al definitely was not batting for his team.

Looking over the mountain of books I asked the obvious, "Do you have a little homework?"

Al gave a heavy sigh. It seemed to be going around. "It happens every time I'm in a play. The show takes every waking second of my time and I get so behind. I've even learned to take a lighter schedule. I should have graduated this May, but instead I won't until next December." My heart gave a happy beat on that note. That would give us more time together. Then I was a little frightened. College didn't last forever. Was this just a college romance or was there a future here? I was about to have an anxiety attack over a ten-day separation. What would I do if it became permanent? I had to get a grip.

Al gestured to the stack. "Now I have two papers and an essay due on Friday before I can leave. Perhaps it's a good thing that you're leaving tomorrow. It'll cut down on my distractions." Then he looked into my face. "No, not a good thing. Then I'll simply be missing you instead."

I started to get out my laptop and get to work. Suddenly there was a present on my bag. Not a romantic little blue Tiffany's box, but a big two-foot square box, wrapped in the Sunday funny paper.

"I got you a little spring break gift," Al said.

 Since when was spring break a gift-giving holiday? Was there a Hallmark card for it? "I'm sorry, I didn't get you anything."

He chuckled. "It's nothing fabulous. Open it. I thought with you going skiing and well, and after the head/stage incident, well, um perhaps you needed this." He seemed almost afraid of offending me with the gift. His trepidation made me leery.

I opened the box relieved only to see a hot pink ski helmet. "Thanks. That's really sweet."

"Promise you'll wear it. I'm not saying you're clumsy. In fact other than the one trip to the ER I've never seen you even stumble."

There it was again. Every time I had ever done any klutzy thing in front of Al I had in fact redone it. In his eyes I should have appeared a graceful swan, yet somewhere in his subconscious he knew that I was a klutz to the point he was worried about my safety.

"It's wonderful. And pink is my favorite color." Or it would be from that moment on because it would always remind me that Al cared enough to worry about me crashing into trees.

That got me a full smile. "I know that you've skied for years and years. But they are all the fashion rage." He laughed and then turned serious. "It's just very important to me that you survive the vacation."

"Thank you. I love it. When I wear it I'll think of you." No need to point out to him that I was always thinking about him anyway. "Now let's tackle those papers."

I tried to focus on my paper, but, I kept looking at the pink helmet and what it signified. What did it signify? We were going to be separated and Al worried about my safety when we were apart. Then my brain jumped back to the earlier part of our conversation. Next December, after he graduated, would we be permanently separated? Would he still care by then? Or would he break my heart? We were able to get all of five minutes worth of work done before I was interrupting again. "What is your plan?" I asked.

"First, I'm going to get the essay done as it's the easiest. Then..."

I interrupted him. "No, not for tonight. I meant for you. After college."

"Well, it's probably pretty obvious—I plan to work in theater. Hopefully Broadway. I thought about the movie industry. But I really like the thrill of a live audience. The amazing energy of a live cast. A camera is never the same as real people. Then again a camera doesn't boo, or get up and walk out during the show." Al gave a little self-conscience laugh on that. "And you, Lottie Lambert, English major. What do you plan to do?"

What was I thinking? Why had I brought this up? I wasn't ready to share my dreams. I started to dig in my bag for my little friend. Time to redo a little. I now knew his answer and I could just do-over this conversation and I wouldn't have to answer his question.

I was stopped short by Al reaching for my hand. "Why do you do that? Whenever I ask you something important, you always seem to start searching in your purse. Do you keep all the answers to your life in there? Can I look?" he teased.

"Nervous habit I guess," I lied.

"Lottie, you don't ever need to be nervous with me."

His smile was so sincere. Maybe this truly was the person that I could trust with my fragile dreams. But, I kept my hand around the eraser in case I needed a speedy retreat.

"A writer," was all I said.

"Books or tabloids," he asked a little uncertain.

"Books of course." I had to giggle. "Does anyone really set out to write for tabloids?"

Al seemed unnecessarily relieved. "So, what have you written?"

"Nothing lately," I mumbled.

His green eyes looked very confused. "I thought writers were always working on that latest, greatest novel."

Perhaps it was finally time to have an in depth discussion concerning my total insecurities about my writing abilities that were manifested by my ex-professor's devastatingly critical analysis of my literary works.

Al shrugged his shoulders and smiled at my perplexed face. "Then again with all your school work I guess there's not much time."

Then again, maybe we could talk about it at a later date.

"I'm sorry. I'm keeping you from getting your work done," I apologized, glad to change the subject.

"True. So help me. I have to find some way to write an essay over a book I haven't read yet."

For the next hour I told Al the story of Upton Sinclair's *The Jungle* and helped him write his essay. Both of us vowed to never eat hot dogs again when we were through.

"Lottie, thanks for getting me through that book. Now, I'd like to show you one of my favorite books ever written. Follow me." Al took my hand and led me down two rows of books and then back another. My curiosity was piqued. What book could be so special that he had to personally show it to me? We ended up on the very back of the stacks.

I looked at the books on the shelf. We were in the old German literature section. I turned to look at Al. My eyes connected with his and realization slowly dawned. One really shouldn't make out in the library stacks. Just saying. But well, sometimes in life you just have to have connections.

-47-

Over the River &
Through the Woods,
& All Across Kansas &

...

Twenty hours. That's how long my family, along with Stina, was packed into my mother's Suburban. Twenty hours to do a fourteen-hour drive. A car filled with five women and lots of beverages demands many stops along the way. Nevertheless after touring every truck stop between Oklahoma and Colorado we finally had made it to our condo in the mountains.

Along the way we had had an interesting game of musical chairs. The trip had started with my dad and Jason in the front, taking turns driving. It's a guy thing and if it made them feel in control. Hey, we lowly females wouldn't fret about having to sit in the back, watch movies, eat snacks and gossip.

Somewhere around pit stop number four we had shifted to mom and dad in the front, Jason and Jennifer in the middle and Jessica, Stina and me in the back. By stop number six, Stina was next to Jason in the middle row, the Double J's and me in the back. At midnight when we finally rolled in to our condo, I was wondering if Stina would even remember that I was on the trip.

That wasn't a new predicament for me. Throughout my middle school years I had many a girl decide to become my instant best friend in order to get to know my brother better. It had taken me until high school to be able to detect this phenomenon early, but there still were times I felt I was only included in activities just in hopes my football hero brother might come along. And although I knew that Stina was truly my friend, just for me, not my brother, there still was that tiny bit of an insecure middle school girl in me that was annoyed.

The condo was dark and cold when we arrived in the middle of the night, but my dad and Jason soon used their manly prowess and had a big fire going in the fireplace. The fact that they were gas logs didn't deter from the elevated testosterone levels.

All four of us girls were sharing the biggest bedroom that held two sets of bunk beds. Once we had all our suitcases opened there wasn't much room, but it had a fun slumber party feel and Jason wasn't included. By one o'clock it was lights out and we were all finally in bed. It had been a long, exhausting day, yet we were all still wired and awake.

"I think Stina and Jason have a thing going," said Jennifer to Jessica in a very loud whisper.

"You do know that she can hear you," I reminded the twins. I never was sure if they really thought that because they were twins that they had a special voice frequency that others couldn't hear when they were talking to each other, or if they just didn't care.

Stina giggled. "You're brother is very nice. That's all. Just nice."

Yeah, right. Time for a change of subject.

"Stina, what was up with Rachel and Olivia yesterday?" I asked.

"I don't know. But they sure were going at it. I started to go in and ask, but when I heard Olivia call Rachel a liar, I was thinking I best just skedaddle myself out of there."

"I've never seen them argue like that before."

Stina sighed. "Probably just needed some space from each other. Rachel is kind of a mother hen where Olivia is concerned. Always trying to solve her problems."

"I hope they're okay by the time we get back from the break."

"I'm sure they'll be fine. They've been BFF's forever. They'll have a week apart and then come back and act like nothing ever happened." Next thing we heard was snoring in stereo. "Guess our lives are too boring for your sisters."

The snoring got louder. "Um, Lottie. Do your sisters always snore like that?"

"Sorry, but yeah, usually. But don't worry, Jason doesn't." Suddenly a pillow came flying out of nowhere and hit me in my head, followed by an evil Stina giggle.

-48-

The Slippery Slopes

It took novice skier Stina all of two hours to catch up with me on skiing ability. By lunch she had surpassed me. By the end of the first day she was beginning to be bored with the green slopes.

"Lottie, I'm so glad you invited me," Stina was bubbling. "I'm not usually very good at athletic things, but this is fun. I see now why you go skiing every year. How about tomorrow we do a blue slope."

Where was she getting the energy? It had taken every ounce of skill that I had not to kill myself on the easy green slopes all day.

"Sure, Stina," I hedged, "that sounds fun. But, well you see, green slopes are about all I can do. The rest of the family is on the blues that is except Jason. I'm sure he's on a black."

Stina tried her best not to look disappointed. "That's okay. The greens are fun. We'll just do them some more. I'm probably pushing myself too fast anyway. I'd get smeared if I tried a harder slope."

"Why don't you go on the blues with me tomorrow" suggested Jason. I hadn't noticed that he and the parents had entered the condo.

Stina looked torn. She was a loyal friend, but to be honest he was a very hot guy even though that is rather awkward to admit about one's own brother.

"Go ahead," I encouraged her. "I was wanting to sleep late tomorrow anyway. You go have fun."

And so it was decided that Jason would continue Stina's skiing instruction and I would spend my eleventh ski vacation hanging out by myself in the condo and on the baby slopes.

"That was nice of you," said my mom after everyone but she and I had eaten supper and left for a twilight run down the mountain. "I never saw this one coming. But they seem to have really hit it off right from the beginning."

First I was hurt, then I was mad, by the time my mom was talking to me I was on a guilt trip for being selfish. "You're right. They do make a cute couple. But, he better not break her heart. He's never had the same girlfriend for over three weeks—ever."

"Lottie, don't rush things. They're just skiing together." Then my mom smiled. "But they do make a really cute couple. Cute grandkids." She laughed and then went to the kitchen to brew up her special homemade hot chocolate for when the skiers came back.

I pulled out my cell phone and looked at it for the fiftieth time that evening. I had always refused to be one of those girls who sat by the phone waiting for a guy to call. But with the beauty of technology I could continue my life and still never miss a message. Sadly, no message.

"No messages from Mr. Wonderful?" my mom asked me as she handed me a cup of hot chocolate with marshmallows. Life wasn't too bad.

"No. Not that I've been checking of course."

"Of course," my mom laughed. "Do you even have any bars here? The reception is awful in these mountains."

As always my mother was right. No bars. Why hadn't I thought to consider that?

"Let's try going up the mountain a little. Maybe if we walk up to those little shops up the road, there might be reception there."

And she was right. Again. And she didn't even gloat about it.

"One missed call and four messages," I said.

"While you check them I'm going to look around that shop over there. It looks interesting."

Missed call message: static, static, Al... more static ... plans change ... more static ... Taylor... static. . . changed.

What the flying monkey was that? It must have gone straight to voicemail due to lack of reception and still it made no sense. And why was he talking about Taylor? Never one to jump to conclusions, I decided I had better read the text messages and then I could have a nuclear meltdown.

Text number one:

My plans got changed. Not going to California after all. Did you make it ok to Colorado?

No mention of Taylor. But changing plans. Had his plans changed to include Skank Woman?

Text number two:

Plans still changing. Hopefully for the good. Call me if you can.

Had the plans changed back to not include Taylor? Had they ever included her? What were the stinking changing plans anyway?

Text number three:

If you get this message please call.

Did he want me to call because he missed me? Or did he feel it was too tacky to break-up in a text? Which it is. And if nothing else Al was classy.

Text number four:

I guess you're very busy. Call when you can.

Four texts and no Taylor. I replayed the voicemail again. And again. If only I had some highly technical CIA voice dissecting device so that I could hear the static covered parts. But I didn't. All I had was an over sensitive very jealous imagination. I needed to calm down and think things through realistically. Maybe he was saying he was going to get his suit from the tailor? Or that his heart was tailor made for me? Yeah, I was stretching for any plausible, or not so plausible excuse for the mention of her name from my beloved's lips. My heart was totally schizophrenic teetering from a jealous rage at the mere mention of Taylor's name to soaring on the first two messages. He hadn't forgotten me. But by number four it looked like he thought I'd forgotten him. I had to call and fast before he changed his plans again to include Taylor.

"You have reached the cell phone of Al Dansby," his magnificent voice said. Big fat hairy bummer I'd gotten his voicemail. I wanted to talk with him so badly it almost hurt. "I am either unable to answer your call or am screening calls and you didn't make the cut. Either way please leave a message at the beep. And Lottie if that's you, please, please, please, please leave a message. I'm out of cell range."

"I'm out of range, too," I told his voicemail. "We made it here fine. Skiing is fine. Having fun, but wish you . . ." Beep. I was cut off. "were here," I finished to the nothingness.

"Did you get ahold of Al?" my mom asked walking up with two shopping bags stuffed with "bargains."

"Just his voicemail. Guess his phone is out of range too. He said his plans had changed. Maybe he's on some Caribbean island?" With some

210

long leggy black haired skank I started to add, but somewhere deep down I knew it wasn't true. Not the island part. That was very possible. But the skank part. Suddenly I had a very surreal feeling. Never with any boyfriend from first grade on had I ever felt secure enough to really believe that given the chance and a cute enough or willing enough girl he wouldn't cheat on me. But not Al. At that moment I had a mini-epiphany. There was something in him, and in our us that I knew I could trust. I trusted Al Dansby.

"Know what I've learned in life?" my mom began, startling me back to her side of the galaxy, as we trekked back to the condo. "If you can't be with the one you love,"

"Love the one you're with," I interrupted rolling my eyes.

"No, that would be stupid. No, if you can't be with the one you love, talk about him. It makes you feel better and I'm dying to know what is so special about this young man that I have yet to meet."

So we spent the next two hours with me telling my mom all the details, okay maybe not all the details—like Al's *favorite book* in the German section of the library—but all the sweet wonderful things he did and how talented he was and how every time I saw him my heart skipped a beat and I wondered how I was so lucky to have such a fabulous boyfriend. She was right. It did make me feel a little better. And it seemed to make my mom very happy too.

-49-

You Always Hurt
The Ones You Love

I sat at the cafe table by the window for a few more minutes trying to decide if I should head back to the condo and read a book or ski by myself. I'd slept late that morning and then skied down the green slope alone once. Skiing alone just wasn't much fun. However, the weather was beautiful, so sunny, with the light reflecting off the snow. The whole family plus Stina had gotten together for lunch before heading back to the slopes. I had to spend a few minutes reassuring Stina that I was perfectly fine with her skiing with my brother. I'm sure she didn't totally believe me, but she wanted to believe me and went anyway. I was about to go sit outside and read when all of a sudden a man grabbed my face and kissed me smack on the lips. Totally on instinct I slapped him into next week.

"Oh crap, Lottie! Ouch that hurt. I guess I deserved that for startling you," said my beloved Al Dansby with a big red handprint on his face.

"Al, oh sorry, oh—what—Oh, I'm so sorry," I couldn't get a coherent sentence out.

"No it's my fault. I shouldn't have just shown up here and surprised you," he kept apologizing. "Where did you learn to hit like that?" He kept rubbing his jaw.

This was not good. The love of my life had somehow miraculously appeared and I had almost broken his jaw.

Fortunately, I wasn't the average mortal. I could fix it. Out came my pink friend and in an instant I was back doing lunch with my family. Strangely, although time had restarted, no one seemed hungry.

"I was starving out there on the slopes," said my mother. "But, now I've suddenly lost my appetite. Wish that happened more and then I could lose those ten pounds I never seem to get rid of."

A chorus of *me toos* came from the rest of the group. Except Jason.

"Anybody who doesn't want their food pass it down to me," Jason requested.

Looking at the clock I figured I had less than an hour, as that was the maximum redo time, until Al would arrive and sweep me into his arm and kiss the stuffings out of me. And this time I wouldn't deck him.

When Stina asked an instant replay if I was sure it was okay for her to spend the afternoon skiing with Jason, I gave a very delighted yes that seemed to confuse her. Al was somehow, miraculously going to arrive and I was eagerly awaiting our reunion kiss.

Forty-five minutes, then fifty and then an hour passed. The waitress had come by my table at least ten times asking if I needed anything—polite waitress talk for you've finished your meal, now leave.

Something was definitely wrong. Always before in a do-over I had changed my actions, but I always assumed everyone else still did the same thing, but that time everything had changed. My family, except Jason the bottomless pit, was no longer hungry. And Al hadn't arrived. Where was

Al? What had happened in the extra hour that made him not appear? And where had he come from in the first place?

I checked my phone again. No messages. I only had one bar. Maybe that made a difference. I would have headed to higher ground to see if I could get better reception, except what if he came to the cafe and I wasn't there to meet him? Did our meeting have to take place in the same place or could location change in a redo?

After fifteen more minutes of indecision and a few more glares from the waitress, I left for more altitude and less attitude.

I went back to the shops area where I had been able to get a signal the night before. Yay, more bars. Boo, no new messages.

I tried calling him and once again got his voicemail. I almost left a message apologizing for hitting him, barely stopping myself in time. Instead, I simply said I missed him and would he call me back.

My deductive reasoning had finally kicked in and concluded that the change of plans to his vacation somehow had brought him closer to me. Sadly, my magic eraser had somehow sent him away again. Had my alteration of time ruined what could have been a wonderful reunion?

The rest of the afternoon was spent loitering around the shop area. I was afraid to go back to the condo in case Al tried to call. Finally, about five, my phone began to play the theme from *Phantom of the Opera*. That was Al's ringtone.

"Hello," I gasped. I started to cough. In my exuberance to answer the phone, I had choked on my own spit.

"Lottie, are you okay?" Yes, that was our official greeting. Some couples had "their song." Al just always seemed to be asking if I was okay.

I finally cleared my throat. "Yes. Where are you? Why is Taylor with you?" Oops, that was the wrong thing to say. I wasn't going to play the jealous harpy. Should I redo that? Or had I already messed up the day too much with my other redo?

During my indecision Al gave a nervous laugh and answered my question. "Not too far away. My dad had a sudden change of plans. So we came to Colorado, too. And no, Taylor isn't with me. He was planning to come, it's his ski lodge, but he had to work and Dad felt like skiing. Then no sooner than we got here, Dad got an urgent call to return to California for business. I thought I told you all this in my voicemail."

He. His. All that emotional stress over a He.

"How far away?"

"About an hour. I started to drive over to see you today on a whim. But then I got worried that you wouldn't want me dropping in. I know you're there with your parents and they want to spend time with you."

Little did he know that I was spending most of my time by myself.

"In fact I was in the car, ready to go and then I got this massive weird pain in my jaw. It was almost as if someone had slugged me. I must have done something skiing yesterday and it finally caught up with me. Anyway, I thought," Al became hesitant as he spoke. "Well, I just wondered if you had room for one more on your mountain?"

Always one to play it cool, I practically screamed, "Yes, we have plenty of room. You can bunk with Jason."

"Don't you need to clear it with your parents?"

He was right, but I wasn't going to chance another lack of bars and not being able to get in touch.

"They'll love having you. Come on now." Yes, I'd played that one super cool. I was so relieved to hear his voice and know that he was okay, it didn't dawn on me until later that although I had undone my slugging him, his jaw still hurt. And that my violent reception had left some inkling

215

in his mind that I wouldn't want him near.

We finally decided he would come the next morning. The mountain roads were much too treacherous at night. That would also give me time to let my mom know we were having company. Something told me she'd be delighted. My dad? That would be a different matter.

-50-

Near Death? Why not.

I was at the top of the mountain looking down on my first black slope ever. What was I thinking? I was going to die, that was exactly what I was thinking.

"You take the lead, Lottie," said the tempter who had led me to my fate. "I'm not used to this mountain, so I'll follow you." Then Al Dansby smiled and reminded me why I was in that predicament in the first place.

Al had arrived by lunch and by that point my father was resigned to having him there for the rest of the week. As predicted, my mother was elated that she would finally meet the great Al Dansby. Stina was simply relieved that she no longer had to feel guilty for spending our girl time with Jason. And the twins were miffed because they didn't get to bring a friend and my quota had risen to two. No matter the age of siblings the battle over the slightest hint of parental favoritism always hovers around the preschool age mentality. But I made a definite attempt to be gracious about it and to quit doing the happy dance when they were in the room.

After all the hellos and showing Al where to put his luggage, my parents began the grand inquisition. I sat to the side mortified, but Al seemed completely content.

My dad began with all the typical questions. How was the drive from Aspen? Where exactly in California was he from? What was his major? What did he plan to do with it? What did his father do?

Before he asked his credit score, I knew I had to intervene.

"How was that fresh powder on the mountain this morning?" I interrupted my father as he started another round of confirmation hearings. "Don't you want to get back out there before it all gets packed down?"

That was like waving a big, juicy, raw t-bone before a pack of pit-bulls. My whole family was grabbing skis and gear and muscling their way out the door. Of course my love life was important, but not in comparison to fresh powder on the mountain.

"You sure know how to clear a room," Al laughed and then drew me into his arms for the kiss I had interrupted with my right hook from the day before. "Ouch, oh sorry. Be gentle," he said pulling back and rubbing his jaw. "Strangest thing. I seem to have hurt my jaw yesterday, but I can't for the life of me remember what I did."

Before I started apologizing again, I thought I'd better change the subject. "Are you ready for some skiing?

At some point in all the time we had talked about my family's annual ski trips, I had never seen the necessity to confess that I was a horrible skier. It was part of my don't ask don't tell policy. Ironically, due to my oversight in the facts department, Al was under the impression that I was actually an expert.

Getting to the mountain he turned to the lift for the blue and black slopes.

"Don't you want to do the green slopes first?" I asked.

"It's fine, Lottie. I've skied before. You don't have to hold back on my account," he said as he proceeded toward the lift.

Now, an intelligent and liberated woman would have stopped then and there to clarify the situation. But a hormonal, lovesick girl like me just followed along and hoped I lived to see the next day.

Seventeen times. That's how many times I fell. Seventeen times Al asked if I was okay. Seventeen times I used my eraser. Seventeen times we were back on our way down the slippery slopes of death. Seventeen falls. Seventeen questions. Seventeen do-overs. Finally we were almost to the end of the black slope. Just one more turn and I would have skied a perfect run, if not counting the seventeen changes in reality.

It's always the final turn that is our downfall. Right into the tree. Fortunately, I had on my shiny pink helmet so my head was fine. Unfortunately, there are no helmets for arms.

"Lottie, are you okay?" Al asked for the eighteenth time.

"My arm," was all I could say. I wanted to cry, but I wasn't going to. That salty water that was pouring down my face did not signify that I was crying. It was a simple reaction of dry eyes encountering the cold air.

I needed to do a do-over. But I couldn't move my arm to reach my pocket. And Al's recent encounter with my right hook showed that memories might change, but injuries remained. If I did it over would I have had an unexplainable broken arm?

If I ever write a book on skiing I would advise that if you're going to get hurt, do it at the bottom of the hill. My saving grace in my ungraceful end of the ski run was that I didn't have to be hauled down the mountain in a rescue sled for all the world to see.

"Can you walk? Don't worry about your skis. I'll take care of them,"

Al said scooping up our skis in one hand and holding on to me around the waist with the other. "It's just a few feet to the first aid station. I can't believe you fell. You made it down a black slope like a pro, never falling once and then right here at the end you crash. Was it my fault? I'm sorry, was I crowding too close?" He babbled on. But, I couldn't answer. It hurt too bad. It wasn't the first time in my klutzy life that I had broken a bone. But this time was worse because I didn't want Al to see me ugly cry.

Within minutes Al had gotten me to the aid station and somehow miraculously had cell reception enough to contact my parents. Off to the hospital we went.

My mother was calm; she had raised four children and knew how to handle an emergency. My father on the other hand, was not.

"Lottie, what were you doing on a black slope? You have never been on a black slope in your life." All of this was said by my dad not while looking at me, but glaring into the rearview mirror at Al. This was not good. In my dad's point of view, Al had let his little girl get hurt.

Mom was trying to intercede. "Julius, she'll be okay. It's a broken arm. Thankfully, not something worse. It's a good thing Al bought her a helmet so it wasn't her head instead." My mom flashed a smile back at Al. The die had already been cast. In my mother's eyes Al could do no wrong, while to my father he was an irresponsible interloper preying on his precious sweet daughter. Exiting the Suburban became a clash of the testosterones. Al was trying to help me on one side while my dad was on the other.

"Ouch," I said. Maybe a little more forcefully and with some colorful expletives. But I'll remember it as simply saying, "Ouch," when my father, in his over zealous attempt to help, bumped my injured arm.

Entering the emergency room Al turned and said, "We have to stop meeting like this." He leaned over to kiss the top of my head. I think I saw actual smoke come out of my father's ears and wondered if the doctors had a cure for that too.

-51-

Little Condo In The Woods

I had been told my whole life that good things come out of bad situations. I never really agreed with that philosophy, hence my strong desire and ultimate ability to redo the bad and the slightly bad and honestly anything that had the tiniest bit of awkwardness to it. However, a broken arm on a ski trip for me actually did become a good thing. I finally had a handy excuse for not skiing, and the next three glorious days to simply lounge around in our condo in the woods by the fire with the guy who was slowly stealing my heart.

All would have been perfect if Al hadn't kept apologizing for my accident as if in some way it was his fault, and if he hadn't kept reiterating how amazing it was that I could ski all the way down a black diamond slope without a single fall and then crash into a tree at the bottom. Oh well, I guess there must always be just a little bit of deception, even in paradise.

Deception? Where had that come from? I never thought of fixing my mistakes as a deception, rather a wonderful ability. Yet, maybe, ever so slightly, it was. Did it make people think I was something I wasn't, like punctual and non-klutzy? I had to shake that feeling off. The only life that ever changed because of my do-overs was mine. It was my life. It was my right to make it the way I wanted. Still, that little word planted in the back of my mind started to fester. It was like the snake had entered the garden. Whereas before there was only perfection, slowly I started to notice how I might be manipulating others.

"Earth to Lottie." Al reached over and touched my cheek. "Are you in there?"

We were spending the day sitting by the fire playing Scrabble. We had tried cards, but with one hand—and of course I broke my right arm—I couldn't really hold on to my cards. We found Scrabble tiles easier to manipulate.

This was my kind of a game. Hey, I was an English major. Words were my stock and trade. So how come this lowly thespian was beating me like a dirty rug? I had to get my head in the game.

"Lottie Lambert, what a perfect name. You could be a movie star. Perfect moniker for a marquee. What's your middle name?"

"You're just saying that to distract me in this cut-throat game," I laughed.

"You know my evil intentions little girl," Al said with his best melodrama villain imitation, complete with a pantomimed twisting of a mustache. "No, really. I feel like I so completely know you and then I realize there are so many common knowledge facts about you that I don't even know."

"Elizabeth."

That got me a shocked look. I thought it was rather an old fashioned but common enough name. It didn't merit the look like I had said Rapunzel or Rumpelstiltskin.

"Sorry, just the name my mother liked," I apologized, not sure why.

Al smiled a melancholy smile. "It's a beautiful name. It is one of my two favorite names in the world. It was my mother's name. Only we always called her Lizzie." As always when he mentioned his mother there was that sadness in his voice. I contemplated redoing the conversation. I had had no idea that simply telling Al my middle name would result in causing him pain. I could redo it all and lie about my middle name. And then somehow convince my parents that I had to have it legally changed to Betty or Veronica or Sally or Matilda. Anything to keep from constantly dredging up sad memories for Al. I started to get up to find my eraser when Al's melancholy smile spread into a delighted grin as he said, "Like I said, it is my favorite name and now I know that it belongs to my two favorite women in the entire world."

Favorite. He had said I was one of his two favorite women in the world. I could live with that.

"What's your middle name?" I countered trying to bring back the lighthearted feeling that we had been enjoying before. "In fact, is Al all there is? Is it short for Albert?" He shook his head no. "Alfred?" Please say no, I thought and he did. "Albercombie?"

"That's not a name. No beautiful, it's Alistair. Just like my dad."

"Alistair. Alistair Dansby. Now that's a movie star name if ever I heard one." That got me a startled laugh. "It's an awesome name. So regal. Why don't you go by Alistair instead of just plan Al?"

"It's too confusing, with my dad that is. Same name thing."

"Middle name. Alistair. Give it to me now."

"Drew."

"Alistair Drew Dansby." I said it a couple of times with different accents. It sounded best with an English accent. But then, doesn't everything? "I like that. Actually I love it. I love," had I almost said you? "it." I caught myself. But I knew for sure right there on the floor by the coffee table in that little condo in the woods that I, Charlotte Elizabeth Lambert truly loved Alistair Drew Dansby.

"Are you okay?" he asked. Who knew what look had crossed my face.

I tried to regain my composure. "Um, yeah. I just. Well. I was just trying to figure out what word I could spell to kick your butt at this game."

Al laughed and smiled and the room was spinning for me. He reached in his pile of tiles and then laid a word on the board. "There it is— infatuation. How many points do I get for that?" Al asked. He already knew. He just wanted to point out to me how brilliant he was. It worked. He wasn't just handsome he was smart too. And funny. And kind. And— whoa was I drooling on myself again? I so needed to stay in the real world more.

"Plenty," I grumbled and wrote down his score. "I can't do much. I just have 'crush.'"

"You only have a crush? I thought we had much more than that," Al teased.

"You only had an infatuation," I countered.

Al studied his tiles and then put down 'adore' without a word.

I pulled more tiles from the pile. I was liking that game. 'Cherish,' I placed. It got me a smile, but no words. Instead Al began rearranging his tiles again, pulling a few off the board, but by this point I couldn't care less how much he cheated. 'Sweetheart,' came next. 'Boyfriend,' I countered. 'Passion,' he placed and I blushed. 'Desire,' I put too embarrassed to look

225

up. 'Truelove,' came the last word of the game.

"I guess I never really thought I'd have to spell it out for you," Al joked and then became completely serious. "I love you, Charlotte Lottie Elizabeth Lambert." The world was perfect. And then it got even better as he sealed his pronouncement with a kiss. And another and another. And then a clearing of his throat. Wait. What? That wasn't Al's throat clearing. That sounded just like my dad when he was miffed and wanted my attention. Oh crap!

We quickly sat up. When had we gotten on the rug on the floor? I had no memory. My first thought was my dad is going to kill us. My second was I should do this over quickly before my dad kills us. My third was I'd rather die than change any second of the most beautiful moment of my life.

"You two have missed a great day skiing. But it looks like you've been finding other ways to occupy your time," my dad chuckled as he went into the kitchen to get some coffee.

There are a lot of strange things that happen that year. Something big and unbelievable like a magic eraser I easily accepted as reality. But, my dad's calm reaction to finding me mid-makeout on the rug in our ski condo was truly a life-altering event.

-52-

Guess Who's Coming to Dinner?

Our beautiful, non-skiing ski vacation was over entirely too fast. Al confessed that he had to return to Aspen on Friday afternoon to catch his flight. We all looked on with envy at the mention of a flight as our crew knew there was another marathon twenty-hour drive in store for us on Saturday. Somehow the drive to the mountains was always exciting, the ride home—that *Twilight Zone* episode of the never-ending traffic jam.

To celebrate the impending end of our mountain adventure, Dad took the whole gang out for dinner. For most people that would be a normal occurrence. But my dad was a shrewd businessman, a master of his finances, a frugal investor—okay, he was extremely cheap.

Our table of eight dominated the cozy little Italian restaurant giving everyone there a party atmosphere. Dad sat at one end, with my mother by his side. Jason sat at the other end with Stina at his side. Was this mirror image a glimpse into the future or was I in for some major BFF consoling when two weeks later Jason would be dating someone else? I sat across from my mom with, you guessed, Al at my side. Convenient for some under the table handholding, except my hand was in a cast. Oh well, my fingers were exposed. Across from Al and Stina were the Double J's.

"Jennifer, do you see anything wrong with this picture?" Jessica asked.

"Plenty. I asked if Josh could come on the trip and got a big negative," Jennifer answered.

"Um, like me too."

"You asked if Josh could come? Excuse me, that would be my boyfriend," Jennifer was getting agitated.

"No stupid. I asked if Jeremy could come. Why would I want Josh to come?"

Al looked at me and I shook my head sadly. "Don't let them bother you."

"They don't think you can hear their conversations," added Jason from the end of the table while making the crazy sign with his finger around his ear.

"It's a twin thing," mom clarified. "So don't let them make you feel unwelcome. We are so happy to have you and Stina with our family." I think she almost said in our family, but caught herself in time.

Saved by the waitress taking our orders it quickly became total chaos. Poor waitress, especially since my dad is the stingiest tipper of all time. Her evening was not looking so good.

Once the orders were taken my mom turned to Al. The grand inquisition had taken a rest, but it had not been finished. "Al, you look so familiar. Why is that?"

Strange question. Yet, in our family strange was the new normal.

"Um, Mrs. Lambert, I don't know. I guess I just have one of those familiar faces." That was so not true. Al had one of those one-in-a-million movie star type looks.

"No, no that's not it," mom continued. "There's something there. Someone we know that you look just like. Maybe a younger version? What do you think Julius?"

My dad took off his glasses, rubbed them with his napkin, put them back on again and turned to look at Al like a specimen in a museum exhibit. "Now that you say that Julie, yeah, he does look like someone we know. Looks a lot like," then he smiled and paused for dramatic effect. "A lot like that boy that Lottie's been dating."

Strange. Al gave a big sigh of relief, like he had just escaped being outed in the witness protection agency. Had I been in the mood to contemplate, rather than salivate, I might have started to notice that Al was consistently evasive about himself. Unusual for an actor. A stereotypical actor is normally very self-focused and self-promoting, but Al always redirected questions about himself, into wanting to know more about those he was around.

"Now, Mrs. Lambert," he began but was interrupted with a "Just-call-me-Julie," from my mom.

"Julie," Al corrected and gave her a dazzling smile. My mom smiled back. Had I been a more insecure person I would have thought my mother was flirting with my man. Gross. But then, poor old cougar, who could blame her. He was very hot. Sick. There have been many times in my life that I have been thankful that no one could read my thoughts. That moment ranked as number one. I suspected it ranked in my mom's top ten also. "Do you get mistaken a lot for anybody famous?"

"Lottie does," Jennifer answered.

"Yeah, she does," chimed in Jessica too.

"Who?" Al and Stina both asked.

This brought double twin giggles, and scary unison twin speak, "The bride of Frankenstein."

"You two are ridiculous," said my father coming to my defense.

"I think she looks like the blonde girl in that movie we saw last summer," Jason added. This brought on a discussion of which movie, and that yes, when I let my hair dry wavy, I looked just like her. We then went around the table trying to decide what movie star each of us resembled. Jason got that guy on the TV show that no one could remember the name of but by using her iPhone Jennifer was able to find it. That sent my dad off on an observation that was quickly turning into a dissertation about how amazingly easy it was to access information using the World Wide Web. Jason successfully derailed him by listing five beautiful actresses that he thought couldn't come close to being as cute as Stina. This made Stina blush and everyone else at the table squirm. The twins brought us out of the awkward pause by wanting to know who they resembled and then vetoed everyone we suggested. My mom was the hardest as she and my dad kept listing actresses we had never heard of. Al decided my dad was Gregory Peck. Maybe not from looks as much as manner. Or maybe we were confusing him with the character Atticus Finch. What I never realized until somewhere in the flat boring landscape of Wyoming was that no one ever said who Al's doppelganger was.

Walking back to the condo, Al and I let the family (strange how quickly I was beginning to think of Stina as one of the family) pass. It was a beautiful starry night. The air was crisp, but unlike Oklahoma, no wind. Strolling hand-in-hand, I felt like the luckiest girl in the world. A year before I had been in a destructive, manipulative relationship that I had thought would scar me for life. But life had given me a do-over at my new school, with my new friends and my new life. It hadn't taken a magic eraser to give me that start, just my own determination to look for a better way. Perhaps I didn't need that eraser after all. Perhaps I should have gotten rid of it. Those were my thoughts right before a sudden sneeze came into my nose. A massive, snot filled sneeze that I never saw coming. And neither did Al, as he was just turning to kiss me and got snotted right in the face. Ick.

Maybe I did need that special eraser after all. Out it came. Again we were walking hand in hand. No snot on my beloved.

"Hold that thought," I said, as Al turned to kiss me. I turned my head the other way and sneezed. Yeah, I could philosophize all I wanted about the ethical and moral responsibilities of changing time, but sometimes I really did love having the means to redo the blunders in life.

-53-

On The Road Again

"I like your Al," my mom told me in hour number two of the infinite journey home. On our seat rotation the women were in the back again, the men up front driving.

"I do too," said Jessica. "Wish he had a brother."

"Does he have a brother?" Jennifer asked. "He never talks about his family."

"So mysterious," answered Jessica in her mystical voice.

Okay there was definitely some evasiveness of his California life if even the totally self-absorbed twins could notice. When we got back to campus I was going to demand some answers. If I was involved with a Mafioso, I had the right to know.

Mom was still in her own thoughts. "You know what I like best about him?"

Jennifer answered, "His hair.

Stina said, "His smile. It's so contagious."

"His butt," laughed Jessica. Then receiving a glare from my dad in the rearview mirror she amended, "Not that I was looking. No way, no how."

Then all of us girls joined in a conspiratory whisper, "Yeah, right. Nice."

"No, you silly girls," my mom continued trying to pretend like she had never noticed his butt, "I like how he likes you Lottie. In fact it appears that that poor boy is totally head over heels in love with you. And the look on your face shows that I'm right," she said. And then she smugly added, "As usual."

That got a heavy sigh from the females in the car. A throat clearing from my father and no response from Jason. He's a true guy, probably wasn't listening.

Hour four of the trip, just after the second rest stop, saw another seat rotation. Dad was driving and I was riding shotgun for the first time. Mom and the twins were in the back seat, each with some sort of headphones and electronic apparatus (or would that be apparati?) keeping them occupied. Jason and Stina had the middle. They seemed completely occupied without any electronic stimuli.

"Daddy, can I ask you a question." He gave me a wary look. Most questions that started with *Daddy* usually ended with a request for money or longer curfews. "What changed your mind about Al?"

He tried to give me a blank look, but my bad poker face was inherited and he was the person I had gotten it from.

"Come on. Something happened. When we went into the emergency room you acted like you wanted him out of my life as fast as possible. By the time I had my cast on your were bosom buddies. What happened?"

"Lottie bug, you're my little girl. Even if you are almost twenty-one, when I look at you I still see a little four year old running through the water sprinklers covered with blue popsicle juice down your face and on your swimsuit. No matter how old you get, you're still my little girl," he said with a bittersweet smile on his face. He even looked a little misty eyed. Now I was used to that behavior from my mom, but not Dad. He always seemed more comfortable helping with math homework or showing me how to balance my checkbook. He was my practical parent leaving the emotions to my mom. "I saw you hurt, badly hurt last year. I was afraid it was going to happen again. Guess I wasn't even going to give Al a chance. But having two hours stuck in the waiting room together, it was either talk it out or read a two-year-old *Good Housekeeping*. We decided to talk."

"So what did he say? What did you say? Please say you didn't say anything embarrassing."

My dad laughed. "It was a talk between the two of us. None of your business. Let's just say, I like your young man. And he likes you. And he knows that you have a huge football playing brother that will make sure that you don't ever get treated badly again."

-54-

When Non-Reality Hits The Fan

"What is going on?" Rachel shouted in her room, but we could easily hear her in ours too. Stina and I gave each other a startled look that non-verbally reiterated what Rachel had so eloquently just shouted.

"Should we go see what's going on?" Stina asked.

"Or hide until it blows over?" I asked.

We both knew what we had to do. With fear and trepidation we crossed the safety of the shared bathroom, the line of demarcation, into the war zone. And war zone it resembled. Olivia was frantically pulling down posters and throwing her belongings into two huge cardboard boxes. Her closet was already empty and the sheets and comforter gone off her bed.

"Lottie, Stina—talk some sense into her,' Rachel pleaded.

I felt like I had entered the bullring as a matador, except without my red cape. However, I was clutching my special eraser just in case I had to make a speedy exit. "Olivia, " I said very calmly, like talking to a spooked horse, "Are you okay?"

Olivia turned on us, threw down the poster she had in her hands and let us have it. "Okay? Do I look okay? Is a person okay when her supposedly best friend for life tells her most intimate secrets to someone else? Okay? When I confront her and she won't even have the *cojones* to admit it? You bet your freaking life I'm not okay. If you and Rachel want to discuss all my personal business, I'll just get out of your way and let you have at it. I'm moving out!"

And with that she picked up her last two boxes and walked out the door, throwing her room key crashing against the wall.

We all stood there stunned. What had happened? When had we betrayed a confidence?

Rachel sat down on her bed, put her head in her hands and started to cry. "How could she think such a thing? Lottie, have I ever, ever told you anything about Olivia behind her back that I haven't said to you right in front of her face? NEVER, that's the answer. How can she think I did?" Then she rounded on me. "What did you say to make her think I did?"

Fast on my feet as always, I responded, "Uh, nothing." But a slow dimming light was starting to click on. I had made a crack about not running over S.P.B. and just before spring break I mentioned a stepfather and looked straight at Olivia. All info she had once confided in me. But through the miracle of do-overs she would never remember.

"Can you two leave?" Rachel asked none too nicely. "I just need to be alone."

Stina and I slunk back into our room. We were both bewildered.

"What just happened there?" Stina asked. "Did Rachel really tell you confidential stuff?"

"No," I adamantly denied. "It's just some misunderstanding. I'll just wait until Olivia has had some time to calm down and then I'll talk to her. She has to see. It's just got to be a misunderstanding," I kept repeating like a mantra. "She has to see."

But what could she see? No one but me saw the changes the eraser made. No one knew the things that didn't happen. Again I was realizing there was detritus left from changing time. Little tiny slivers that weren't apparent at the time, but seemed to show up when not expected, in a dream that seemed too real, a jaw that hurt for no reason, or a friendship that was destroyed by my all too knowing looks.

"I have to fix this," I said out loud without realizing.

"But how can you?" asked Stina. Was the doubt in Stina's voice because the situation looks so unfixable? Or was she doubting that I was telling the truth that Rachel hadn't broken a confidence? "How do you prove that Rachel didn't tell you anything? How do you prove that something didn't happen?"

I thought and thought. I had no idea. How did you disprove a negative? With two positives was all I could guess.

-55-

Undoing Do-Over Damage

"She'll come around," Al had advised.

"She'll get over it," Butch added.

"She'll just have to get her happy panties back on sooner or later, cause this being mad and sulking just ain't a working for any of you," La—ah said, putting it all in perspective.

It had been a week since Olivia had moved to a new room on the third floor. I guessed she was trying to get as far away from us as possible while still living in the same building. It was a Wednesday lunch and we were eating in the cafeteria. It was so sad. All of us together: Al, Stina, Rachel, Trevor, Butch, La—ah, Kasha, Kaylee, Kyra, and me. All at one table. Olivia was as far away as possible, sitting with none other than the jerk soccer player. Had she totally deserted us, even Keesha? Or was she working on revenge, cutting us out of the equation? Because, Lord please, oh please, don't let her have been so depressed and insecure that she was really considering him as a friend or even possibly a date.

The K's had noticed Olivia's new dining partner also. I tuned in to their conversation.

"She had better be working on a plan and not a date, or she's going down with him," said Kyra. It was at that moment I realized two things. One that they were thinking the same thing about Olivia as I was and two, I could finally tell the K's apart.

I just played with my food. Ever since Olivia's departure I had felt like Benedict Arnold. I had caused two bosom friends to be enemies and couldn't find a way to correct the situation.

"Lottie, it's not your fault," Al consoled yet again. "You have to quit blaming yourself for Olivia's overactive imagination. If Rachel didn't tell you anything,"

Rachel interrupted, "Which I didn't!"

Al continued, "You can't fix something you never did."

Little did he know how insightful his words were. How could I fix something that I never really had done? It was my mess and my responsibility to find a solution. I had thought that time would settle the storm, but instead the battle lines between Rachel and Olivia were being dug even deeper. Not only had I ruined their friendship, but also others who had confided in Rachel, our amateur psychologist, were beginning to give her suspicious looks and avoid any confidences with her. I had to do something. The only problem with that brilliant conclusion was I had no idea what. I had already told Olivia that Rachel was telling the truth and that hadn't worked. I couldn't tell her the real truth. Come on, would anybody really believe that load of hooey?

"Darling," He said 'Darling.' Some parts of my life might have been filled with remorse and guilt, but when Al Dansby said *Darling*, it was like a ray of glorious sunshine bursting through the clouds. "You really need to eat." Then sometimes he sounded just like my mother.

-56-

Didn't See That One Coming

I was in her room. That was a step in the right direction. When I had set out to find a solution to reconcile my suitemates, I had doubted that Olivia would even let me through the door into her new room. But there I was, standing like a kid in the principal's office trying to think of a credible excuse to get me set free.

Olivia sat on her bed fiddling with her iPhone. I couldn't get her to make eye contact with me. "Lottie, it's nice of you to keep trying to patch things up with my lying ex-best friend, but be honest, it's not gonna work. Somehow you know about my horrible past and there is only one person other than my family who could have told you. So either tell me the truth or leave."

The truth. What a novel idea. Maybe it was time to tell the truth. My time-altering eraser, which I had thought was the best invention since tampons, had turned out to be the cause of unintended deception. The truth.

Right then and there I had a plan. I'd tell Olivia the truth. If nothing else she'd think I was mental, and it was my entire fault and maybe in some twisted way forgive Rachel. And if it didn't work I'd just do it over.

"Here it is Olivia. You are the person who actually told me about your stepfather and his molesting you and his sudden, accidental death."

Olivia was furious. Up until that point she had only been guessing that I knew her past. With my revelation she knew that the pitying looks had been for real. Unfortunately, my honesty sounded like another lie.

"I never told you anything like that," she said in a low, whispered hiss.

How was I ever going to explain? "It's like this, I have this magic eraser." I held it up to show her. Obviously the believing me part wasn't working, but the insanity defense was beginning to build. "My aunt gave it to me last summer. I thought she was crazy, but one day I accidentally used and it worked. When I want to change time, I just give it a wave and I go back in time. Sometimes five minutes, sometimes up to an hour. Anyway, one night you were a little tipsy. Well, if it's time to be honest, you were totally wasted. And you told me about your stepfather. Then right afterwards I could tell that you wished you hadn't. So, I thought I'd make things better for you by redoing it. That way you would never have told me. The only flaw is that when I redo things, I still remember them. You were so sad. I can't forget it. And it shows on my face no matter how hard I try for it not to."

Olivia sat there in a stunned silence. It had worked. I should have just told the truth from the very beginning.

Finally she spoke. "I expected better from you, Lottie. I might have been able to someday forgive Rachel for spilling my secrets. But for this ludicrous lie, trying to make me believe something so asinine just so you

241

two don't have to confess that you're not trustworthy. That's just absurd."

Olivia walked to the door and pushed it open. "Please leave. And please, don't try to talk to me ever again."

The truth was supposed to have been the answer. But it didn't work. At least I could do that scene over and know not to try telling Olivia the real story, but work on some better explanation. I looked at the eraser in my hand and went to wave it through the air.

"How dare you have the gall to keep playing this stupid game," Olivia shouted and grabbed my hand as I started the do-over.

Something happened that had never happened before. It was as if my life was passing before my eyes. Except it wasn't my whole life, just the parts that had been done over. There was me spilling my spaghetti, and changing seats in O.T. and oversleeping and on and on and on and there was Olivia telling me her horrible childhood and Al kissing me and me falling down seventeen times on the mountain. In an instant I had seen every single do-over I had done the past seven months.

Then I was back standing in Olivia's room. Olivia was sitting on her bed. But that time change was different than all the others. Olivia was looking at me with pure terror on her face. "What—the hell—was that?" she finally said.

"Did you see it too?"

She only nodded.

"You see. I was telling the truth. I've been doing this all year. At first it seemed like an answered prayer. Any mistake I made I could just flip out my trusty eraser and do it again. But, sometimes it didn't make things better. The hardest thing was that I still remembered the first reality. So I'd refer to things that others never thought had happened. I saw it in y'all's eyes a lot, when I talked about things then realize I hadn't kept my stories straight. No wonder it was so easy for you to think I was lying about Rachel. It seemed you had caught me in lies and half truths all year."

Then we sat there. Time passed. Olivia kept looking at me, starting to say something, stopping, shaking her head and then looking at me again.

Finally she spoke. "Seventeen times. You fell down seventeen times on that stupid mountain, just to impress a guy." Then she started to laugh. I though at first she was going to become hysterical, but no, it was just a belly busting laugh of pure relief. I joined in. Every time we would almost stop, Olivia would say, "Seventeen," and we'd start again. It felt so good to laugh. It felt better to finally have someone to share my crazy secret with. By the time we were able to regain our composure we both had mascara smeared down our faces from the tears and our sides hurt from laughing.

Olivia got up, went to her closet and started pulling out clothes throwing them on her bed. I was afraid she was cracking up from my revelation after all. "Let's get this place packed up. I'm ready to move back 'home.'"

-57-

Mission Un-Possible

When Al told me he had to be out of town the next weekend on a recruiting trip with various campus bigwigs, I should have looked more distraught. But the truth be known, the ninja force was almost ready to put the plan into action—and the less he knew, the better. It wasn't that I wanted a relationship filled with deception, it was simply that there will always be things that are only shared with the sisterhood.

Right after we moved Olivia back into Rachel's room, we started to finalize the plan. Mr. Soccer Player or LSPS as he was affectionately known on our wing of the dorm, was going down. After sharing my secret about the eraser with Olivia, she had confessed that she had had a niggling sort of half dream thought of remembering our conversation about her stepdad. Not quite an all there memory, more like seeing something out of the corner of her eye, but when she turned to look it wasn't there. Her revelation along with Al's once mentioning a half dream of having spaghetti thrown on him had helped to solidify the plan. Once we had ascertained that subliminal thought residue remained after a do-over we decided to make that work to our advantage.

Our background checks and surveillance of LSPS had shown that his Achilles heel was his place on the soccer team and his soccer scholarship. Not only was it his biggest ego boost, but without it he wouldn't be able to remain at OkMU. So ruining that for him, seemed the best retribution of all.

We had tried out many scenarios, but all either seemed too dangerous or illegal. No, it had to be something that with minor manipulations from us was truly his own fault.

"No, the Craigslist thing is too overdone," said Olivia at our council of war meeting one evening. Our room was filled with the remaining three K's, La—ah, Stina, Rachel, General Corazon, and me. The door was closed and the curtains drawn. This was to be a top-secret undertaking. In no way could the LSPS or anyone else know our plan.

"Olivia's right. Half the listings nowadays are pranks being played on others," Rachel agreed. "I thought a big scarlet **A** tattooed on his chest would be good. Kind of poetic justice."

La—ah shook her head no. "He'd just think that was cool. We have to find something that will hurt him like he did Keesha."

"But legal," I reminded them.

"But legal," they all repeated in a monotone. I guess I had stressed that a few too many times.

"So what is his major weakness?" Rachel asked for the hundredth time. "We know he thinks he's God's gift to women."

"Right," we chanted.

"But we can't set him up with someone. That could be damaging to her. And he'd just be proud if there were compromising photos of him on the web," Olivia said. We had been over and over this territory. How to do a sting operation that only hurt him and no one else?

245

"Maybe if we could convince him that there is someone after his body, when really she isn't," suggested Stina.

"But who? We already have enough people involved," said Kasha.

"She doesn't have to be involved. In fact the less the better. He only has to think she likes him." I was seeing a devious side of our sweet, lovable Stina I had never seen before. "Who on campus would it be the absolute worst for him to be caught in bed with?"

"Me," laughed La—ah. "Cause I'd kill him."

"The president's wife," laughed Kyra.

"Almost," said Stina like their answers had been at all credible. "Who is the one person who could make or break LSPS's career?"

"Coach Biggs!" we said in unison.

"But he's straight," I blurted out.

"Not him, his wife," Stina laughed.

"But he and his wife have a great marriage. She's not gonna be sleeping with some stupid college boy," argued Kasha.

"No, but LSPS has such a big head, we could easily convince him that she wants to. And admit it, of all the faculty wives around she is the hottest," Stina countered.

I had to speak up on this one. This couldn't happen. We couldn't ruin someone's marriage just to get revenge for Keesha. And I said as much.

"No, Lynette Biggs will have nothing to do with it. It will all be in LSPS's mind," Stina explained. "Here's my plan."

We spent the rest of the evening devising a plan of counter-espionage that would have made the CIA proud. Olivia and I gave each other some knowing looks. We could find a way to use the magic eraser for good.

-58-

Seed Sowing

"Doesn't he play on the soccer team?" I asked as I sat down at the table right behind the LSPS the next day in the cafeteria. It was time to start planting in the seeds of illusion. Olivia sat next to me.

"Of course he does," she answered according to our script. "I've seen him play."

"Is he the one the coach's wife has the hots for?" I asked in my best stage whisper. I could see he was listening in on our 'private' conversation.

"That's what I've heard," Olivia agreed. "I've seen her at the games watching every move he makes. Old cougar."

"She's not that old. And she's quite the hottie."

"Do you think there's really something going on?"

"If he's smart there is," I answered, trying not to gag. "Ready?" I asked and Olivia nodded. I waved the eraser.

"Now," I said as we were back in the line, "Let's sit as far away from him as possible."

"But we have to execute our plan," Olivia objected.

"We already did. You don't remember?"

She shook her head no.

"Hm, strange. I guess we have to both be actually touching the eraser to both remember. Well, we did good. Maybe we should go on the stage with Al." Since Olivia couldn't remember, I didn't have to tell her how stiff and rehearsed we had actually sounded.

Since we weren't sure how many seeds we would have sow to guarantee a good harvest, we decided it would be better to plant too many than not enough.

Right before his soccer practice came the next seed. "You're on the soccer team right?" I asked him as he was getting out of his big black truck with huge oversized tires. I always wondered what those ridiculously huge tires were compensating for.

"Yeah, why?"

"Uh, well, the coach's wife asked me to give this to you. Said you'd be the player in the black truck." With that I handed him a note.

I think you're hot. And Coach Biggs is going to be out of town this weekend. Would you like to come over and see if you score off the field as well as you do on?

My lunch was about to make a reappearance as I watched him swagger away reading the note. I wondered how long I should leave it to sink in, and also how long it might take him to read all those words, but did a redo quickly as I was afraid of accidentally not getting the note back.

A flick of the eraser and I was holding the forged note in my hand and watching the world's biggest jerk get out of the his overcompensating vehicle. I tore the evidence into little tiny pieces and threw it into the trash. Two seeds sown. More to go.

Olivia and I continued on this venue the rest of the week. The rest of the ninjas didn't know exactly what we were doing, but just that we were getting him ripe for the harvest.

"I just got back from soccer practice," Kaylee announced on Thursday. "It went smooth as butter. I sat by the coach's wife. She is so nice. We absolutely have to make sure she isn't hurt by this." I nodded in agreement. "Anyway. While they were practicing, I asked her who the guy in the grey shorts was. She pointed at the LSPS to ask me if that was the one I meant. He looked up at her while she was pointing, so she kind of looked embarrassed and waved. He waved back and I'd swear he winked. Then she turned to me and said, 'He must like you. I think he just winked at you.'"

La –ah had procured the garage door code to the coach's house.

"It was like taking candy from a baby. A big, braggy, babbling baby," she said. "That Kimberly is always a bragging how she is the Biggs' babysitter, like working her butt off for five bucks an hour is an honor. So I was just telling her how the Smiths so trusted me with their little Johnny and she had to so one-up me. And so I just told her how they had even given me a key to their house and she said how she doesn't need a key because she knows the garage door code at the Biggs', the baby's birth date. Did me a little research, found out little Biggs' birthday and voila, I got us the code. 0412."

Kasha's job was to make sure that Mrs. Biggs was going to be gone that Saturday night. "Yep, just checked her Facebook. She's off to a girls' night out in Branson—guess that's a girls' weekend out."

"And the coach has a meeting here on campus, right?" I reconfirmed.

"According to the campus faculty page, from seven 'til eight-thirty,"

Rachel agreed.

The plan was going into motion.

Our next visit with the LSPS confirmed that the subliminal thoughts were building up.

Olivia gave it her best shot as she hurried to walk next to him. "Hey, I haven't seen you around much. What you been up to?"

"Busy with soccer."

"You still dating Taylor? Haven't seen you together?"

"Nope, on to something better. Hm, strange. But, seems there's someone better who's warm for my form." Gag, I thought as I was walking a step behind. Did anyone really say that?

"That's what I thought," Olivia lowered her voice. "I've heard you have something going with the coach's wife. That can't be true."

"Stranger things have happened," and he smiled. Maybe smile is too nice of a word. He leered.

I grabbed Olivia's hand and let the eraser do its stuff.

We were back were we started. We saw him coming and turned the other way.

-59-

Reaping the Harvest

"Everybody ready?" the general asked. There we were, all eight of us in full ninja black wedged in the da godmother. Rachel made Stina and Kyra double buckle as no one was ever allowed to cruise in da godmother without a seatbelt. Rule of the land. Or the road actually. It was eight on Saturday night and hopefully our plan would work, but just in case, I had a death grip on my eraser.

Olivia and I had given him the note to meet the coach's wife at eight thirty three different times and then undone it. We were unsure if it would work or not. La--ah had left the final note in his truck that afternoon during his soccer practice. It said,

If I were to find you in my bed at 8:30 tonight, I would be very happy. No worries, he's gone tonight. The garage door code is 0412.

That note wasn't going to be retrievable, but we'd tried to make it as vague as possible just in case someone else saw it.

At eight forty LSPS's black truck pulled up. Late. And arrogant. He parked right on the street by the Biggs' house. Guess he didn't care who saw him there. Out he got and swaggered up to the garage door, looked at the paper, four numbers were too taxing for his small mind to remember, and typed in the code. Up went the door and the litterbug wadded up the note and threw it down. This was a piece of luck we hadn't planned on, but it worked for our good.

"For the first time in my life, I'm glad someone's a trash pig," I said.

"I'll go get it and then he has no evidence at all as to why he's here," Stina said crawling out of da godmother's one good backdoor.

Rachel turned the car on. "I'm moving down the block and then we can spread out and watch from the trees over there. Have to make sure we are not seen."

"But we ain't gonna miss this show," La—ah laughed.

At nine Coach Bigg's beat-up bug pulled in to the drive, hit the garage remote and went in. We waited. Lights went on in the house. First the lights by the garage, then the middle of the ranch style house and then end rooms. We waited. It was nine-O-five. Still nothing. Had the fool gone in the wrong bedroom? Nine-O-seven. The front door of the house came busting open. Out ran the LSPS in nothing but his boxers. His clothes came flying out the door behind him.

"And on top of everything else, you are off the team," Coach Biggs was shouting. "I don't ever want to see your stinking" (okay he used another word that has been edited out of my memory) "face" (actually a different body part) "again. And if I hear one word from anybody, anywhere about my wife, I'll be bringing you up on charges for breaking and entering." Then there were numerous other words that I thought an employee at a Christian university wouldn't have known. But he did and pronounced all them correctly as they came streaming out of his mouth.

There was the LSPS running around the Biggs' front yard in his pink (go figure) boxers, grabbing up his pants and shoes, forget the socks they were up in one of the trees, desperately trying to find his car keys so he could get out of there.

One of the hardest things I have ever done in my life was to keep from laughing so loudly that Coach Biggs wouldn't hear me. Then again he was shouting so loudly, he probably wouldn't have anyway.

"Ladies, our work here is done," said Rachel in a solemn whisper. "Back to da godmother."

"For Keesha," Kasha raised her hand in a fist bump.

We all bumped our knuckles together. "For Keesha," we repeated.

-60-

To IT Or Not To IT?

"Missed you this weekend," said the world's sexiest voice nuzzling my ear. I had been showing Al Dansby *my favorite books* in the library up on the third floor, the very deserted third floor. "Hope you didn't stay in your room and study the whole time."

That made me giggle. Not just his lips nipping on my ear, but remembering our ninja adventure. Seeing the LSPS running half-naked across the Biggs' yard had made me laugh all weekend. "We kept busy. All of us piled in da godmother for a fun evening out."

"Someday I would love to stowaway in da godmother and find out what you wild women are always up to."

"No, no you can't," I responded perhaps a little too forcefully. I had spent the weekend caught between the hilarity of our retribution and the fear that in some way we would be caught in our own sting operation. I also was terrified that Al might find out and in doing so I would have to take a step down off of my pedestal of perfection.

"Sorry," Al backpedaled. "It seems I have trod on the sacred ground of the sisterhood. I'll file that knowledge for further reference," he added as if writing a memo in the air, "Never question the sanctity of the sisterhood of da godmother."

"I feel awful. I didn't mean to bite your head off," I began apologizing. Where was my eraser? Oh yeah, it was back at the book table with my purse and laptop. I turned to walk back and get it, but was stopped as Al took my hand.

"It's okay. Really. You have friends. And I have friends. And there is couple time and there is friend time. And then a lot of the time there is couple with the friends time. So, since you had some quality friend time last weekend, can we have some quality couple time this one? Let's go on a date."

I smiled. "Ok. But, we kind of go out every night."

"The library and the coffee corner are not real dates. I want to do something special."

"I won't object to that. What?"

"It's a secret," Al taunted.

I laughed. "Oh, in other words you're still trying to figure it out."

Al smiled a mischievous smile. "Got me there. Still working out all the details. But I have the main event already planned."

There was something there, in the way that he said 'main event' that both filled me with anticipation and dread. We had been an item for almost three months, actually sixty-eight days, but who's counting, except me. Sixty-eight wonderful days. And in all that time IT hadn't come up. Sure there had been stolen kisses, sweet touches and be honest, substantial snogging. But not the big IT.

"What's wrong?" Al asked searching my face. "Don't you want to go out? Have a special evening?"

"Of course I do," I fudged. "How special you got in mind?"

"A lifetime memory," he chuckled.

255

A disembodied voice came over the P.A. system. I gave a startled jump. I thought it was the voice of God at first coming to chastise me for the very carnal ideas that had been materializing in my head. Then I realized it was saying the library would close in five minutes. Guess I was a little more stressed about the turn of our conversation than I wanted to admit.

***

"IT?" I whispered to Stina at two in the morning. I wasn't sure if she was awake or not.

"Huh?"

"I'm afraid the IT is about to hit the fan," I responded.

"What the front door are you talking about?" she said finally fully awake.

I told her about the conversation Al and I had earlier in the evening back in the stacks. It was always easier to talk about serious things in the dark, no eye contact, no facial expressions. "What do you think the main event is that he has on his mind?" I asked.

"Girlfriend, he's a guy. What do you think?"

"That's what I'm afraid of."

"Do you want to?"

"No—well yes, well no. Well of course I want to. I'm a red-blooded, hormonal woman. And I'm in love. I've never been in love before. I mean this one is it. So why not?" I had to think a while. "No."

"Why?" she asked. It wasn't like she was disagreeing, rather making me think it through.

"My first thought is I don't want to end up like Keesha. I know Al's different than the LSPS, but still it could happen."

"Keesha thought the LSPS was different too. That was until he dumped her," Stina reminded me.

"True. But Al Dansby is different. He's the kindest, most sensitive, most caring, most wonderful," heavy sigh, "guy ever. Did I ever tell you that I'm just a little bit in major love with him?" We both laughed. "Maybe that's not even what he meant."

"Sure," Stina snorted. "Finish your no."

"I don't like ultimatums."

"True."

"True. I still want the dream. The fairytale. Commitment. The 'happily-ever-after.'"

Stina was quiet for a while. "It's your life Lottie. Make it what you want. Remember there's no such thing as a do-over."

On that I gave a quasi-insane laugh. Little did Stina know how far from right she was. Yet how right she was. I could do things over, but I had still lived it. It was still in my memory and would always be.

-61-

1820 Minutes Or 109,200 Seconds Neither Long Enough

"You've been jumpy all week. Is something wrong?" Al asked and not for the first time. I wouldn't say I had been classified as jumpy. I had been a total basket case. There was a war going on in my head. It was less than three weeks until summer break. The only guy I had ever loved was going to drop a bomb shell on me on Saturday and I was terrified of losing him, but also terrified that I'd lose myself if I did something I wasn't ready for. Yeah, I was a little jumpy.

"I'm fine," I lied. "Just stressed about finals and summer."

He kissed my cheek. "We need to talk about summer. I've decided. . . oops there's my phone," he said as the theme from *Indiana Jones* began to play. "Excuse me, I need to take this one." He answered his phone and then stepped away leaving me sitting alone on the steps of my dorm. Summer was coming and we hadn't either one acknowledged that we were going to be apart for three months. We also hadn't acknowledged exactly what sort of item we were. I missed middle school when you could have your best friend ask if a boy wanted to be your boyfriend or not. Life was easier then, when there was an intermediary person to clarify relationships. Grown-up relationships were so much more complicated. Al Dansby returned from his call and kissed me. Then again grown-up relationships were a lot nicer, much better than kicking a boy in the shins.

"Sorry to be interrupted," he apologized again for the phone call. Another thing about Al that I loved, I came before his phone—most of the time. "That was my advisor. He wanted to move our meeting up to," he glanced at the clock on his phone, "um, now. I gotta go, so sorry. But I'll see you tomorrow evening. Six o'clock. Don't worry. I got it all planned. Are you ready for the 'main event?'" he asked with a devilish smile. My stomach dropped to my knees. "Are you okay?" he asked. "You don't look so good. Are you getting sick?"

I lied. "I'm fine. Skipped lunch." He should have known I was lying as I had a ketchup stain on my shirt. "I'll see you tomorrow." I stood and hugged him tightly as if we were going to be parted for months rather than twenty-seven hours, not that I was counting, of course.

Twenty-seven hours to make one of the biggest decisions of my life.

-62-
It Wasn't Supposed To End This Way

"You know you could be wrong," Stina counseled sitting on the end of my bed that was covered in discarded outfits. Two of my twenty-seven hours of dilemma had been spent trying to find just that right look that said both come hither and stay back at the same time.

"Stina could be right. Probably not, but she could be," Olivia added moving some clothing so she could sit on Stina's bed. Many fashion options had been analyzed for this momentous occasion.

"Either way, he loves you. Tell him how you feel. How you truly feel. If he loves you—which we all know he does, he looks at you like a sick puppy all the time—he'll understand," said Rachel in her true counselor mode. "The main thing is make sure you know what you want."

"Guys all want the same thing," Olivia said, bitterness seeping through.

Stina shook her head no. "Not always, Olivia. There are wonderful, decent guys out there." Hearts were floating over Stina's head. She'd been that way ever since the ski trip. And thankfully, Jason had followed through. He had called. He had texted. He had even driven over on the weekends to see her. It was a first for him. Maybe a last, as things seemed to be getting serious. I wondered how soon we would be having this same conversation again about the two of them. The ultimate awkward would be a discussion about my brother, his girlfriend, and their sex life. It would be just one step down from walking in on your own parents doing it.

My phone buzzed. "Well, he's here. Wish me luck, or is it break a leg?" I asked. I received hugs and last minute advice. I felt as if I was going off for battle rather than a date.

"Be sure to take your eraser. Just in case you need a speedy exit," Olivia whispered in my ear as it came her turn to hug me. "Just in case."

There he stood in the foyer, his back to me as I came up the stairs. As he turned his face lit up. All the worrying I had done seemed so silly. This guy loved me. He really did. And loving me as he did, he would want me to be happy.

"You look magnificent," he said as he walked over to me and kissed me on the cheek. "Are you ready for a life changing evening?"

I nodded yes with no confidence at all.

He loved me. Right?

We walked to his car. Al was in a euphoric mood. I was terrified. I had every thing I wanted in him except for commitment. Could I stand to risk losing him? Could I live with myself if I did something I wasn't ready for?

He opened the door to his little red car and helped me in. It was a top-down kind of night. The car I mean, not me. Or maybe for me to? That decision still had to be made. "You forgot your seatbelt, again," I said, as he started the car, hoping to sound normal. I reached across his chest, lingering there for a moment, then pulled the strap and buckled it. And we were off.

"So where are you taking me? You've driven me crazy all week. Are we off to the city?"

"Nope," was all he said.

"Here in town?"

"Yep."

"Please tell me."

He turned the corner and then turned to me. "Someplace I've never taken a date, with a chef that has never cooked before."

I felt like I was talking to the sphinx. What kind of answer was that?

He turned into a residential section. I shouldn't have known where we were going, but due to our former ninja stalking skills it all started to become clear. We were off to his condo.

"Your house," I guessed.

"Right," he said delighted. "I'm making you dinner. Impressed?"

"I didn't know that you cooked."

"I don't. But I got a little help here and there. Then I called my dad. He walked me through it. Viola, I figured out how to make spaghetti. You do like spaghetti, don't you? I never thought of it until just now. I've never seen you eat it, but for some reason when I thought of cooking for you, it was what I thought of first." He was so proud of his accomplishment he seemed to be babbling. That was good, as I couldn't think of two words to put together.

"So is that the main event?" Maybe I had been worried for nothing.

Al just smiled. "That's for after dinner. You have to wait."

We pulled in to a lovely duplex. At any other time, I would have oohed and aahed over the magazine perfect landscaping and architecture. It wasn't your typical college student housing. I hadn't really ever consciously thought about it, but nothing about Al Dansby was typical college student.

"My dad thought that investing was wiser than renting since I was going to be here for four years. So we bought this duplex. I use one side and rent the other to a really nice couple." Yes, he was babbling.

We entered through the garage. It wasn't the bachelor pad I expected. Everything was new, top of the line and clean. Except the kitchen. There were pots and pans everywhere, spaghetti sauce on the stovetop, the counter and the backsplash. "Sorry about the mess. I didn't know spaghetti sauce could be so violent. I had to call my dad again and he said to use a lid," he confessed. "Never thought about a lid." He laughed at himself.

We moved through the war zone into the open living room/dining area. The table was set with matching plates and flowers. As Al lit the candelabra on the table, I could see that his hand was shaking. Whatever the main event turned out to be, it seemed to be making him almost as nervous as it was making me.

Suddenly he blew out the match and pulled me to him. "Lottie, I had this all so planned out. I tried so many different ways to say it, rehearsed just like a play. I even worked on my blocking, trying different entrances and speeches. Life is so much easier in a play. The author has given you all the perfect lines at just the right timing to say things so eloquently. But, I can't endure all of Act I tonight waiting for Act II. I can't wait. I can't sit here and try to eat when all the while you're right there and . . ." He stopped talking for a second. It was like he had lost his place in the script and was trying to remember. He took a deep breath and started again.

"Lottie Lambert, I know we haven't actually known each other that long. But, I've just felt, known, was sure from the first moment I talked to you, that you were special. I'd heard of love at first sight, but thought it was a fantasy, that was until I saw you. So, we've been dating three months,"

"Seventy-Five days," I interrupted.

"Seventy-five days," he corrected himself. "And they've all been wonderful. But, Lottie, I can't wait any longer. This relationship has to move to the next level."

There it was. How could it possibly be, but it was. Did guys have a phrase book that they studied in how to pressure a girl? 'This relationship has to move to the next level!' was word for word the same as the ex at OU. I was crushed. I was devastated. I needed time to process. I was crying. I was leaving. Out came my eraser. My salvation. And with a sob, and a wave of my hand, I was back in my room listening to my phone buzz.

"I can't go." Two sets of stunned eyes looked at me. Olivia's eyes were wiser.

"Can't go or already been?" she asked obviously making no sense to the others.

I gave her a simple nod as the tears came.

"I'll go make an excuse for you," came her reply. Stina and Rachel started to object, but Olivia took charge. "Let her be. She knows what she's doing. We'll work through this. But right now, just let her be." With that Olivia left the room to go tell Al Dansby, the man of my dreams, that the main event was off.

-63-

Death Doesn't Give A Do-Over

Someone was pounding on my door. I had locked my dorm room door, something I had never done in all my time at Asbury Hall. I just wanted to be left completely alone for a few minutes or days. My heart was broken. I needed time to work things out. My logical mind knew that Al and I would find a way to sort things out. I loved Al and he loved me. But it had hurt so badly to be given the same tired line again, just by a different man. I needed time to absorb it. I probably was making too much out of some simple words. By morning I'd feel better. Olivia had told him I had a stomach virus. That had bought me some time to think. But not enough time. Al had called, but I refused to answer the phone. I didn't know what to say or do, so avoidance seemed my best bet.

Still someone was pounding on the door. And on the adjoining bathroom door.

"Lottie, open up."

"I don't have my key. We never lock the door," I could hear Stina say to someone else behind the door.

"Lottie, open up now!" shouted Olivia. "It's an emergency!"

I jumped up and ran to the door. There was hysteria in Olivia's voice and I knew something was wrong, as she wasn't that good of an actor.

"A wreck. He had a wreck!" Information was coming at me from all sides. But nothing was making sense.

Rachel took charge. "Sit down. I need you to listen closely. Al has been in a bad wreck. We don't know any details yet."

I didn't sit. Instead, I grabbed my purse and keys and ran for the door. "Where? When?"

"I'll drive," Rachel said.

We piled into da Godmother with none of the joy of previous trips. All our other problems had become trivial as we faced the reality of life and death. Olivia was shouting directions and Rachel was driving like a possessed woman. I sat in the middle row waving that horrid eraser for all I was worth. Nothing changed. I was in the middle of a do-over so nothing could change.

The accident scene was impossible to miss. The beauty of an Oklahoma sunset was being decimated by the flashing of the emergency lights on multiple police cars and fire trucks that lined the road. An unused ambulance sat idle as the paramedics watched uselessly.

Rounding the corner, I jumped from the van before it was completely stopped. Police and official people of all types were loading a body on to the Lifeflight helicopter. That wasn't a good sign. I ran for him, but a police officer held me back. I tried to explain, but she wouldn't let me get closer.

"Hon, they won't let you go on the flight. They're taking him to the hospital in Oklahoma City where they have a better trauma unit. He's bad off. Didn't have his seatbelt on, so he was thrown from the car."

By then my suitemates had caught up with me.

"Can't I please, please just talk to him," I was begging.

"Hon," she said in her mother voice, not her cop one, "he can't hear you. He's in real bad shape. Are these your friends?" I just stared. "Girls, you can drive over and meet him at the hospital in the City." She gave Rachel all the details. I couldn't focus on what she was saying. The helicopter was leaving. And it was all my fault. He'd been upset because I stood him up. He'd been thrown from the car, because I wasn't there to remind him to put on his seatbelt. Al Dansby was in a helicopter being rushed to the hospital all because I couldn't face life's decision and work things out instead of always wanting to run away and look for the easy solution in a do-over.

Death didn't give do-overs. I prayed with everything in me that Al would make it. I bargained with God. Just let him make it and I would get rid of that abhorrent eraser. Just let him live and I'd grow-up and face life instead of looking for the easy out. Just let him live.

-64-

Waiting

Wait. That's what we did. Wait. Pray. Cry. Wait some more.

We couldn't go back to see him. First there were tests. Then no word. Rachel, the mother of our group, had taken over. The nurse at the desk was probably tired of dealing with her, but Rachel was going to get answers.

Slowly the waiting room was filling. First the K's arrived. Then Butch. Then the theater group. Within an hour the waiting room was full. When the president of the university arrived we finally were able to get some answers.

President Newman came running in. I knew that they were close, but I was surprised at the look of concern on his face. "I'm here about Al Dansberough," he said at the desk. Maybe they weren't as close as I thought. He got the name wrong.

"Dansby," I corrected as I walked up to him.

"Lottie, right?" I didn't know that he knew I existed. "How is Al? Any word at all?"

"They won't tell us much. Just that they're doing tests." I was trying so hard not to cry. I had to keep it together. But talking made it harder.

"They haven't let you back?" He turned to the nurse again telling her who he was. "Can we see him?"

"You can go on back, but not the friends."

"She needs to come," he said looking at me. "She's his fiancée."

Suddenly the waters parted and we were allowed to enter. Walking behind the nurse down the long sterile corridor I whispered to the president, "Thanks for lying for me."

He looked back confused.

"We aren't engaged," I clarified.

"Oh," was all he said. Then changing the subject. "Al's dad is on his jet here. Should take another hour or two. We'll need to make sure the press doesn't hear. It will be chaos around here if the paparazzi gets wind of this."

There had been many times over the past year when I had felt like Alice down the rabbit hole. When I first used my eraser on that fateful spaghetti day. When my dad hadn't erupted when he caught me making out with my boyfriend on the rug at the condo. But worrying about the press and paparazzi for a car wreck when the guy I loved more than life itself was fighting for his own life, seemed too surreal to even register.

All those thoughts left my mind as we turned the corner. It took me a second to even recognize him. His face was battered. His beautiful hair was matted with blood. He was so pale. There were tubes and machines everywhere. Only because I heard his heart monitor beeping was I sure that he was even alive.

I moved over to his side. I tried to find a place on his hand to touch that wasn't connected to some monitoring device.

269

"Al, I'm here." He didn't move or acknowledge me in any way.

"We're not sure if he can hear you," the E.R. nurse said. "But talk to him anyway. I think it helps. Makes them remember that they're still needed and wanted here."

"Al, please don't," I started. "I love you. I always will. Please don't. . ." The word die stuck in my mouth. Saying it aloud would make it all seem too possible. "I won't ever do-over a second of our lives together, if you'll just stick around and spend that life with me. Just don't go." It was all I could say.

Time became a blur. I don't know if I stood there for ten minutes or two hours. All I knew was that I was terrified to take my eyes off of Al's battered face. Somewhere down deep I felt that if I could will it strong enough he would wake up and be well. Afraid that if I looked away, when I looked back he'd be gone.

There was a flurry of activity behind me, but I didn't look back. A hand touched my shoulder. It was the president. "Al's dad is here."

"Hello, Lottie," he said. He sounded so much like his son that I couldn't speak or I knew I would cry. "I had hoped to meet you in a different way. I'm Al's dad." I glanced over at him. He looked vaguely familiar. An older version of his son. But my eyes went right back to Al, willing him with everything in me to live.

Later people would ask me what it was like to meet my all time favorite movie star, Alistair Dansberough. At the time all I cared about was his son.

-65-

Time To Grow-Up

"Lottie Bug, Stina brought you some clean clothes. The nurse says you can use a shower down the hall," my mom said. My family had arrived right after Al's dad. My mom had rapidly taken over. She was a rock for which both Alistair and I were thankful.

"Do I smell that bad?" I asked sitting staring at Al's face. We had made it through the crucial twenty-four hours. Other than a few potty breaks, I hadn't left his side. We'd had some great one-sided conversations. Al was in a drug-induced coma. Alistair had tried to explain it all to me. Al had a broken leg, broken arm, broken ribs. All down his right side he was broken. But that was fixable the doctors said. It was his brain they were worried about.

"I'll sit with him while you're gone," Alistair said. He was just coming back from getting a cup of coffee. "Maybe if he smells this it will help revive him." He tried to joke, but it was obvious his heart was breaking.

"When you're changed, your friends want to see you. They're in the family waiting room," my mom added.

Clean and slightly refreshed after my shower, I entered the packed waiting room. I hoped that Al would live to know how much he was loved. There were hugs all around and questions over and over that I had no answers for. The one they all wanted to ask, but thankfully, never did was, "Is he going to live?"

Olivia pulled me aside. "It's not your fault. I know you think it is. But it's not."

"He was upset. He called me and I didn't pick up. Then when I finally did, I wouldn't talk to him. He knew you were lying about the stomach virus. He was upset because I wouldn't tell him why I was upset. I wasn't there to tell him to put his seatbelt on. I did the first time. But I wasn't there the second time. They said it wouldn't have been that bad of a wreck if he hadn't been thrown from the car. If he had had his seatbelt on. But I wasn't there. I didn't tell him." I knew I was being redundant, but that's what had been cycling through my head ever since I heard the cop say he wasn't wearing his seatbelt. "It was my fault."

"No it wasn't," she insisted. "Things just happen."

"You're right," I answered. "Things do just happen. Sometimes bad things. Sometimes good. Sometimes just silly things like spilled spaghetti. Things just happen. And we should just live through them, work them out, find a solution, not go back in time to try to change them." I took the eraser, the once wonderful ability to relive and change all of life's little mistakes, from my pocket. "Take this and get rid of it. I never want to see it again. Life gives you one chance. That's all that's guaranteed. That's all that's fair. From now on, no more deceit, no more conveniently fixing blunders, no more trying to look perfect, no more do-overs. It's time for me to face life and deal with it head on, no matter how bad the outcome."

-66-

A Different Perspective

The hours morphed into days. Everyone kept on their hopeful faces when they were in the room with Al and me. They came. They checked his vitals. They adjusted his machines. They smiled at me. They left. My battered and bruised Al Dansby slept on.

"Here," my mother said, handing me my laptop. "Write about it."

"I'm not really a writer. I'm just a wannabe."

My mother shook her head. "No, you just lost your confidence. If ever there was a time you needed to regain it, it's now. Write what you're feeling. Get it all out. They say it is therapeutic." Then my mother gave me her most sad, but hopeful smile. "You and Al will have fun reading it together someday—with my grandkids."

With that she left the room.

I stared at my laptop for a while before opening it. My mom had been right so many times before, I'd take her advice again. I opened a file and wrote.

I wrote about the first time I saw his beautiful face walking across the campus as my mom chased my granny-panties. I snickered. Large underwear blowing in the Oklahoma wind were not the tragic occurrence I had thought back then. I wrote about spilling my spaghetti and his surprised face. It wasn't until I wrote it that I realized, he hadn't been upset at all. He had seen the humor in it and had seemed only concerned about me. At the time, all I had seen was the humiliation. I wrote about the first time I heard his voice while ordering coffee. As I wrote I could almost hear him speak. I wrote about how sweet he was to pick up my books when I plowed into him on the sidewalk that day. So what if my pants had been unzipped? It was hilarious looking back on it. All of it was fun and beautiful. I hadn't ever needed a do-over, just a different perspective.

It was a few hours later when Alistair came back to relieve me. I had written pages and pages of our time together in both realities. Through all the writing I had seen a recurring theme, that all the silly embarrassing things I had so desperately wanted to do over at the time, were some of the best memories I had of falling in love with the broken boy who slept wired to life-sustaining machines next to me.

"You doing okay?" Alistair asked.

I nodded.

"Thought I'd give you a break. Stretch your legs. Go get some food. Somehow or another a feast has been brought in to the waiting room from the ladies in your church back home."

That would be my mother's Methodist Women's Circle. Those women were amazing. Always there with a casserole when needed.

"But, before you go, I just wanted to make sure you were good with everything."

I gave him a confused look. How was I good with the man that I so desperately loved lying there on the brink of death? I guess my face spoke volumes.

Alistair shook his head. "That didn't sound right, did it? I don't always do so well without a script. Life's not like the movies where you get a retake anytime you flub a line." He tried to laugh, but it didn't come. "I meant about me. I know Al didn't tell you who his parents are. I just wanted you to understand why."

"Why?" I asked because to be honest I didn't have a clue why.

Alistair took a sip of his coffee. "It's hard growing up like Al did. I mean he had a great childhood. No doubt about that. Lizzie was the best mother ever. It's just that when both of your parents are famous actors, well. . . How do I explain this? We tried to shield him from the paparazzi and the tabloids. But no matter what, in Hollywood, there are. . . well people use others a lot. Al would make friends in school only to find out their parents had arranged it so they could meet me or Lizzie. They always had a script or project they wanted us to look at. He had girls who wanted to date him just to meet me."

"I can relate." He looked at me like I couldn't. "No, really, I can, on the small scale. I had many a friend who only wanted to hang out with me because of my brother the football hero. It hurts. Makes you feel used."

Alistair smiled. "I guess you can understand. Anyway, when Al was ready to go to college he wanted to get away from it all. President Newman was an old friend of mine from my college days. We worked it out for him to come here. No one was to know who his parents were. Taylor was the only one who knew. She and Al have been friends since childhood. I thought she'd be his undoing, but she's been a trouper. Never a slip. When I came to town, I had to come incognito. The mysterious donor. I still feel bad for causing Al to stand you up for your date after the play."

I snickered. "That was you. I thought that donor, for all his money, had the worst toupee and silliest mustache I had ever seen."

"Sorry, for all the charades. It was simply so vital to Al that he make it on his own abilities. And that someone love him, for him."

"There's just one problem." I saw concern flash across Alistair's face. "Dansby. It's such a beautiful name. But it's not real. Al Dansby isn't Al Dansby, he's Al Dansberough."

Alistair laughed. "Of all the things to worry about. Rest your mind. Dansby is our real name. Dansberough is the stage name. Back in the 80s my agent had me change my name. He didn't think Dansby was macho enough for an action hero."

-67-
Finally

"Hey, you look awful."

Those were the most beautiful, poetic, wonderful words I had ever heard. Al woke-up. And I guess I did look pretty rugged. Three full days and nights of sitting in a hospital thinking my entire future was gone had that effect on me.

"You don't look so great yourself," I replied with tears streaming down my face. "I'm glad you're back."

"I never left."

"Don't ever."

"Okay."

"Promise?"

"Promise."

"Lottie, where am I? And why do we now have matching casts?" He tried to sound lighthearted, but I could hear the fear in his voice.

I told him about the accident and the helicopter ride and tried to explain all the medical issues although I didn't understand them myself. And I told him over and over how happy I was that he was awake and talking, and most importantly alive.

I sat there looking into his beautiful green eyes. The world was right again. Then it dawned on me that others might want to know he was alive also.

"Your dad's here. I better go get him. Oh, and then you have some explaining to do—Alistair Dansberough?" Al tried to smile, but I could tell that it hurt.

"Can you do something else first? Do you know where my jacket is?"

"You can't leave! You're not well."

"No," he softly chuckled. His voice was scratchy and horse. It was the most glorious sound. One that I had thought I might never hear again. "I need something from the pocket."

I went over to the closet and dug through a bag of dirty, blood stained clothes. I found the jacket and held it up.

"Look in the inside pocket. I hope it's still there."

There was a little black velvet box. I walked back over to the bed.

"This isn't at all the way I had planned. I had dad FedEx that out here so I'd have it in time. It was my mom's. I made you dinner. Set the table with china and everything. I wanted everything to be perfect, so you could have a special memory forever. But, I can't wait any longer. I can't take the chance of something keeping us apart. I'm sorry. I can't really get down on one knee right now. Can you open the box?"

My hands were shaking so badly that it too a couple of tries before I got it open. Inside was an exquisite princess cut diamond ring.

Al smiled. "Um, can you put it on your finger? My hands all seem to be attached to different machines."

I did as I was told.

"Lottie, I know that we're both still young and I'm fine with a long engagement. But, please say yes. Please, will you marry me?"

No need to guess what the answer to that question was. I tried to gently kiss his swollen lips. Even in ICU, Al Dansby was a great kisser. And a throat clearer? No that was *his* father the tough-guy, action hero, standing in the doorway with tears running down his face.

"Hey dad," Al said like it was a normal day in May. "I'd like you to meet Lottie, your soon to be daughter-in-law.

-68-

Violins

I always knew that Al was a special person, but it wasn't until the fear of losing him was over, that in sank in how many people had been pulling for him.

A constant prayer vigil had been going on back on campus while he was still unconscious. Once news spread that he was going to be okay the hospital waiting room became a revolving door of concerned students, faculty and staff just stopping by to give their well wishes. The nurses had their hands full keeping a full-blown rave from taking place in the waiting room there was such a festive air of gratitude going about. Butch made sure to keep Al supplied with coffee and La-ah smuggled in some tacos. President ?? was good to his word and the paparazzi was kept out so that Alistair could worry about his son and not the press. Of course Taylor of the long legs made a few visits and it was apparent that Alistair thought of her as just a good friend of Al's. Men are pretty oblivious at times, but I could see she wasn't too happy about the big rock that had taken up residence on my left ring finger.

Enjoying a break from the constant stream of visitors, Al and I were alone, when there was a gentle knock on the door.

"Is it okay if we stop in?" asked Coach Biggs. I almost didn't recognize him in a suit rather than his regular sweatshirt and those double knit pants that only coaches wear. Next to him stood his wife looking a amazing in a cocktail dress.

"We don't want to bother you," she said. "But we were in the city anyway to see a show and wanted to say how happy we are that you're better."

"Yeah, just wanted to let you know that we've been praying for you," Coach added.

Once again Al was touched that so many people cared and said as much, but the actor in him was also curious when he heard the word show. "What show are you seeing?"

"Mary Poppins," Mrs. Biggs replied the excitement coming through her voice. "Someone anonymously gave us tickets. People can be so nice. Wish I knew who it was so I could thank them. It has always been my favorite story and I can't wait to see it as a live play."

It made me feel good to know that the tickets Al hadn't wanted for Valentine's were going to a good use. That was until Al responded, "I used to hate that movie, that was until I saw the play in London. It was amazing. One of my favorite musicals ever. I'd love to play Bert the Chimney Sweep someday. You all will love it."

And once again I was reminded that when I was so afraid of my gift being less than perfect, I'd missed out on giving Al the perfect gift.

Al and I had had substantial amounts of time to talk during his invalid status. I had contemplated telling him the truth about the magic eraser, but decided his poor head had had enough trauma with the wreck without finding out his fiancée was mental. On the final evening of his hospital stay I did get up the courage to confess my misunderstanding of the main event.

"I forgot to ask, but I guess you did. Did you survive your stomach virus?" Al asked out of the blue.

I gave him a confused look at first. I didn't have a clue what he was talking about. Then remembered. That was the excuse Olivia had given for my canceling our date.

"I wasn't sick."

He gave me a searching look. "I know. I knew then. So why?"

"I was an idiot."

"No you're not," he chuckled. "No secrets. Did I do something wrong? Did I hurt your feelings? You have to tell me. I never want to hurt you."

So I began my confession. "I thought you were arranging the evening to have . . . well, you know. . . to do it," I whispered at the end.

"It?" he whispered back like it was a major conspiracy.

"You know exactly what I mean. I was afraid. I wasn't ready. But I didn't want you to—well." There I stopped. When I said it out loud it seemed so preposterous. Would a guy who loved me so overwhelmingly as he obviously did really dump me because I wasn't ready? Why had I been such a fool?

"Lottie," he asked, "have I ever told you that I love you?"

I nodded my head.

"Then don't you understand that I would never coerce you into doing something you weren't ready for?"

I shook my head no.

He looked at me with so much love, I wondered how I could ever have been worried.

"I have a confession to make," he began. "Of course I want to be with you. You're gorgeous and sexy and alluring and hot. Sometimes I have to watch myself that I don't drool all down my shirt when you come into the room," he gave a self-conscious laugh. "But I've grown up watching people in shallow relationships jump from bed to bed. I've seen how hurt they are. I don't ever want to be hurt like that, and I couldn't live with myself if I ever hurt you. Call me old fashioned, or just call me weird. But if it's okay with you, if you want to wait, I'll wait with you."

With a look down and then back up, Al looked intently into my eyes and stated matter-of-factly, "And by the way we will never do *it*."

I gave him a startled look. Had there been damage in the downstairs department from the accident that I didn't know about. Or was he gay after all?

"No," he said with the most mischievous smile I'd ever seen him make, "We will make beautiful, wonderful, earth shaking, passionate love with violins playing and our hearts soaring that could never be label with such an insignificant word as *it*. But only when we've both decided we're ready."

-69-

Once Is Definitely Enough

It was another family event at the Lambert house. Time to celebrate my engagement to Al Dansby. So many things had changed over the year. And some hadn't. All the usual relatives had arrived and happily our numbers had increased. Stina had become a reoccurring fixture in Jason's life and my mother was very hopeful that she would soon become permanent.

After a week and a half in the hospital, there had been some discussion as to whether to send Al home to California with his father or let him return to his condo—which was quickly vetoed as he wasn't even able to shower on his own. My mother quickly took over and my parents had brought Al home and moved him into the downstairs guest room. My mother was totally in her element—mothering.

I had my souvenir from skiing cast removed, but poor Al still had one on his arm and one on his leg. At least, he finally had a walking cast and was a little more mobile.

"So is life better when you can do it over?" asked Aunt Charlotte materializing next to me as I was closing the refrigerator door. I jumped and almost spilled the Diet Dr. Pepper I was getting out of the fridge. Where she came from, I had no idea. Didn't even know she had arrived.

"Yes, no and then no," I answered. She gave me a questioning look, so I continued. "At first it seemed an answered prayer. So wonderful to get out of awkward situations and fix problems. But the more I redid the more I realized that I was missing out on not just the bad but the good consequences of my mistakes."

Aunt Charlotte gave a knowing look. "Instead of resolving your problems you just kept redoing them."

I nodded. "I almost lost the one person I love the most from being afraid of difficult situations. From running from confrontations. That little eraser came close to ruining my life. But it also made me see that most of the things I thought were horrible were just the silly things that happen to everyone. Okay, maybe they do happen to me a little more than others, but spilling your food in the cafeteria isn't a catastrophic, life changing experience. Not spilling it can be."

Aunt Charlotte nodded her head in agreement as if she actually understood what I was talking about. "Are you ready to give it back?"

It wasn't until she asked that I remembered I didn't have it anymore. I had given it to Olivia. "I got rid of it. I don't know where it is now. I wanted it out of my life as fast as possible."

A look of worry passed across Aunt Charlotte's face, then she shrugged. "I hope it didn't fall into unwise hands." Before she could finish my mother distracted her.

"Aunt Charlotte, I didn't see you come in," my mother said and hugged her. "Did you meet Lottie's Al? Come look at the choices we've begun collecting for the wedding. It's going to be fabulous."

"Mom, the wedding date hasn't even been set. We have plenty of time," I said looking across the kitchen table at numerous *Brides* magazines and fabric swatches. Even as I was giving my mother a hard time, I was more excited about planning a wedding than she.

"Lottie, this isn't just any wedding. It's your wedding. My precious baby girl's wedding. I want it to be perfect." My mother was beginning to tear up and I heard my dad sniffle.

"And the bridesmaids have to look smashing," bubble Stina.

"You always do," Jason quietly commented and then I swear he blushed. Looked like my mom would be getting to plan more than one wedding.

"Let your mother have her fun," my dad added. "You only get married once," he said giving Al and me a look that reaffirmed that it had better be permanent.

Al smiled his magical smile and kissed my hand right above my engagement ring. "Once is all I need. Then you'll be Charlotte Lottie Elizabeth Lambert-Dansby forever."

"No do-overs on that," was all I said, with none of them, except for me and not so crazy Aunt Charlotte, realizing how significant those words had been.

Other Books by Christine Jarmola

Murder Goes to Church

Kill The Cat: An Anthology of Award Winning Feline Fiction

A Weekend With Effie: A Collaborative Novel by Marilyn Boone, Heather Davis, Christine Jarmola and Jennifer McMurrain

Contributor to:

Chicken Soup for the Soul: Angels Among Us

Seasons Remembered: A WordWeavers Anthology

Christine Jarmola

Take a small-town Oklahoma girl, mix in two academic degrees, summer mission work in Spain, marrying a European, living in Switzerland, time spent in Kentucky and Georgia, books written, plays directed, students taught and two children birthed and that will only tell you a small portion of the adventures Christine Jarmola has experienced so far in life. As the past president of the Oklahoma Writers Federation Christine takes her writing and the writing profession seriously, but not too seriously that you won't find yourself snort-laughing often when reading her work. She can usually be found either working on her next book or backstage at Oklahoma Wesleyan University. And she can always be heard screaming at her ornery cat, Toulouse, who is always remodeling her house into his version of shabby chic with his ten front claws. Keep up with Christine and some times Toulouse's current adventures at www.cdjarmola.com.

16285104R00181

Made in the USA
San Bernardino, CA
28 October 2014